D1623967

STUCK

Other books by Elisabeth Rose

Coming Home
The Right Chord

STUCK

•

Elisabeth Rose

AVALON BOOKS
NEW YORK

Published by Thomas Bouregy & Co., Inc.
160 Madison Avenue, New York, NY 10016

Library of Congress Cataloging-in-Publication Data

Rose, Elisabeth, 1951-
    Stuck / Elisabeth Rose.
        p. cm.
    ISBN 978-0-8034-9944-7 (hardcover : acid-free paper)
    I. Title.

PR9619.4.R64S78 2009
823'.92—dc22

                                        2008048213

PRINTED IN THE UNITED STATES OF AMERICA
ON ACID-FREE PAPER
BY HADDON CRAFTSMEN, BLOOMSBURG, PENNSYLVANIA

To Colin, Carla and Nick

I gained Brad's knowledge of wood and woodturning from my father, an expert craftsman. Thanks Dad.

Thank you to Carla for reading the manuscript and offering suggestions for Gina's city-based sections, and thank you to Kathleen for the inside information on teenage girls and for naming the kitten.

Chapter One

"Hold that elevator!"

Brad's finger hovered over CLOSE DOORS. Tempting, very tempting, to jab the button, but then he'd be guilty of behavior equally as obnoxious as this bossy, flinty-eyed woman's. Her voice resonated around the marble foyer, bouncing off the smooth, polished surfaces like a steel ball bearing, ensuring everyone in the vicinity heard the demand. No. The order. There was no please attached. No attempt at garnering sympathy from those already ensconced for imminent liftoff.

She in the bright red suit clip-clopping on dangerous-looking black stilettos toward the elevator with her briefcase and her I'm-so-important attitude. A slim-fitting skirt hampered her stride, but she couldn't walk any faster in those heels without doing herself a mischief.

What the heck. He wasn't in a hurry, had no need, or innate urge, to be spiteful. He jammed his index finger on OPEN DOORS. The other occupants waited with blank faces.

They had their own briefcases, business suits, and auras of importance. Two of them murmured behind him. Something about the Shanghai market and whether Li Cao Lin would come through as promised. Brad was the one out of place. Standing there in his jeans and navy jacket with his important papers stuffed into the inside pocket, and his favorite loafers that were comfortable for city-pavement pounding but not very smart. If he could be bothered about such things. Which he couldn't.

Ms. Red Suit arrived in a haze of perfume. Brad offered a smile, which she ignored. No "thank you" either. Even Fifi automatically practiced the basic courtesies, and she was only five.

He pressed seventeen. She glanced at the panel but her floor must have been already illuminated because she stepped back beside him and began drumming her fingers on the smooth leather surface of the briefcase, which she held clasped before her. Maybe she had the crown jewels inside, or state secrets. The doors closed.

Brad's mind wandered back to his workshop—the sideboard, old-fashioned and heavy. The largest object he'd ever designed, with ornate paneling, an inset mirror, two big drawers and cupboards for glassware. Puzzling over an ancient Chinese method of construction using perfectly fitting joints—no glue, no nails. Very difficult to pull off. His plans were still in their infancy, but he knew the timber he'd use and the overall shape was there in his head.

The doors sighed open. The Shanghai-market worriers got off. The elevator hissed and continued upward. Ms. Red Suit exhaled heavily each time the doors opened, which they did at almost every floor. She glanced at her watch. Switched the briefcase to her left hand. Then to her right. Adjusted the strap of the purse hanging from her shoulder. Fidget, fidget. People got on and off and on, and finally the last man got off at fourteen, leaving Brad alone with tense-as-piano-wire Red.

Brad shoved his hands in his pockets and whistled softly through his teeth. The girls had been singing that tune this morning—catchy melody. Great hit with the under tens. He grinned at the memory of two clear voices singing as they all left the house for primary school, high school, and train station, respectively. For once Claire had deigned to join in with her little sister.

Pain in the neck having to come in here to Sydney. Much rather be working. The Australian red cedar was a lovely, rare timber. He had to do it justice. But his girls were rare and lovely, too, and far more important than any piece of wood. Everyone's children were. So was their health and education. Well worth fighting for, and if meant a trip into the wilds of the concrete jungle, then so be it.

He caught Ms. Red Suit's eye and tried another smile. Nothing. She looked straight through him. The woman must have ice running through her veins instead of blood. Or oil. Maybe she was half machine. What were those things called? Cyborgs? Bionics? A layer of flesh covering a metal framework with the innards of an emotionless computer. Did the people who constructed those machines have the same sense of artistic achievement as he did when he produced a sculpture out of wood? Or a beautiful but functional object, like the rocking chair he'd recently made? Wood had a beauty all its own, a natural beauty of texture, grain, and color formed by time and chance, forged by the earth, the sun, the wind, and the rain.

He must have been staring, because she turned her head abruptly and looked at the progress indicator. Elaine always used to nudge him when he daydreamed in public. She'd giggle and tell him to stop staring. Elaine . . .

He'd been staring again, lost in the past. He shifted his feet and looked down at his shoes, black and solidly planted; her shoes—narrow feet, pretty, graceful ankles, nicely rounded calves accentuated by those stupid heels—back up to her face. She'd been staring at him but looked away quickly when their eyes locked.

Her hair couldn't be naturally that color—jet-black. It was beautiful. Thick and lustrous and swung gently when she turned her head even though it had been clipped into a short, helmet-style bob. Like ebony. If it was natural she may have Asian or Mediterranean ancestry, though her features didn't betray anything in particular and her skin was creamy pale. Irish? Her features would be softened if she changed her hairstyle. As it was the cut line was quite harsh—maybe that's what she wanted. Tough career woman. Any sign of softness and it's out. What a life.

Fifteen lit up briefly as they passed, then sixteen. Seventeen. He allowed her to precede him but she didn't acknowledge the courtesy beyond a brief glance. She turned right, so did he, following her along the gray carpeted corridor to the large glass door with the *NETWORKS* logo on it.

Was she one of the faceless decision makers he was coming to see? Late to work if she was—it was nearly eleven. She pulled the door open and he held it. Then she noticed him.

"Thanks," she murmured. A tiny smile flashed on and off before she turned and strode to the reception desk where a sleek young woman sat staring at a computer screen.

"Georgina Tait to see Simon French."

"Good morning, Miss Tait. Mr. French is expecting you. Go right through. First on the left." The receptionist pressed a button and warned Simon French of his visitor. Georgina Tait headed for his office.

The girl looked at Brad with a bland, professional smile on her pink-toned lips. "Can I help you?"

"I'm here to deliver a petition to protest the installation of a mobile phone tower in Birrigai."

She frowned. Her mouth opened and closed, her eyes widened. "Uh. You can leave it with me."

"I don't think so. I want to speak to someone in charge and give it to them personally. Who's the boss?"

All traces of professional friendliness disappeared from her face. How dare this upstart come barging in and disrupt the civilized order of things? "Mr. Munro is the managing director but he's in Melbourne today, and you need an appointment. I'll see if anyone else is available." She all but glared at him. "Would you like to take a seat?"

She bent her head and consulted a list.

Brad ensconced himself in one of two squashy black leather armchairs in the corner by the door. A small glass-topped table held copies of some financial magazine and today's *Herald,* which he'd read on the train coming in. The receptionist was muttering into the phone. She replaced the receiver and looked across at him with an I-told-you-and-it-serves-you-right expression.

"I'm sorry, you may have to wait awhile. No one is free at the moment."

"I'll wait." He'd translate that "free" as "no one wanted to deal with him."

"You could make an appointment," she suggested hopefully. Brad stood up. "But it would have to be the day after tomorrow. Everyone is so busy . . ."

Brad sat down again. "I only need a couple of minutes," he said. "Surely someone has a couple of minutes."

"Mr. French would be the best person, but as you can see he has an *appointment*." She emphasized that magic word.

"I'll wait until he's free." At least Mr. French was real. He'd seen him, and he and Red couldn't be in there all day. He'd give them an hour. He wasn't coming back if he could avoid it.

"Suit yourself." She returned to her fascinating screen.

Brad opened the paper and pulled a pencil from his pocket. Half an hour later—during which time he'd done the Sudoku, most of the Quick crossword and solved four clues of the Cryptic—a door opened and Georgina Tait reappeared, followed by a man who had to be Simon French.

Brad leaped to his feet as they approached.

"Thanks for coming down, Gina," French was saying. "If you leave those details with Sally we can do the rest by fax."

"Fine. Thanks, Simon." They shook hands and he turned away for his office.

Brad said quickly, "Excuse me, Mr. French."

The receptionist interjected hastily, "I'm sorry, Mr. French, this gentleman wants a word but he doesn't have an appointment."

The smile left Simon French's face as he looked at Brad. "Could you see Sally and make a time, please," he said. "I'm very busy at the moment."

The visiting woman handed a piece of paper to the receptionist and headed for the door, clearly uninterested in becoming embroiled in the uncomfortable little scene.

"This won't take a minute," said Brad firmly. He pulled the wad of paper from his inside pocket. "This is a petition against the position of your telecommunications tower in Birrigai. It's signed by eight hundred and fourteen residents and we'd like some sort of investigation done in regard to finding another site."

"In Birrigai?"

"Yes. The site you've chosen is right next to a primary school and across the oval from an aged-care home and the shops. You may not care about the health of children and the elderly but I can assure you we do. Just because we're in the country doesn't mean our voice can't be heard or that you can ignore us."

"I appreciate that, Mr. . . ."

"Harding. Brad Harding."

French's face assumed an even blanker expression. "Mr. Harding. You have the right to object but you need to write to the address on the sign at the site. I think you'll find the closing date has passed."

"We've already done that and had no response whatsoever. Please take this. A copy has gone to our local member and to the state and federal ministers for communications." He shoved the solid wedge of paper into the unwilling hand. "I won't take up any more of your valuable time. Thank you."

Brad left Simon French gaping in the foyer and strode from the Networks offices. Jerks! They probably wouldn't even read it.

Miss Whatsit in her bright red suit was standing at the

elevators. She glared at her watch and stabbed at the DOWN button again even though the light was illuminated.

Brad stood next to her, lips jammed in a straight line. What a waste of time. He wasn't any good at this protest stuff. None of them were, really. They were casual country folk who trusted other people to do the right thing. They were no match for a corporation with nationwide tentacles and government plus big business backing.

The elevator arrived. Miss Red stepped in and pressed *G*. Brad followed.

He'd have time for a sandwich and coffee before the one o'clock train. Maybe a quick trip to Birdland to check out the jazz CDs. The trip wouldn't be a total write-off. And he'd delivered the petition, for what it was worth. The committee seemed to think the effort was justified.

He glanced up at the floor indicator. The elevator passed fourteen.

And stopped.

The lights flickered, went out for an instant, then emergency lighting must have kicked in because a different, yellower light took over.

"What's happened?" Deep blue eyes glared at Brad as though he'd secretly activated a brake.

"We've stopped," he said, because that was all he could think of to say. The deep, deep blue of the Pacific far from shore. He hadn't noticed before. He would have if she'd looked at him properly.

"Obviously." Venom would be sweeter.

She snatched up the emergency phone. "Hello? Hello. What's going on? I'm in the Bellevue Building on Park Street, and the elevator just stopped. I don't know. Wait." She rounded on Brad. "Which one is it? There are four."

"The number's right there," he said and pointed to an identification plate with all sorts of codes on it. "*I'm* in the Bellevue"? Was he invisible? Irrelevant?

"Oh. Right." She read out the numbers, listened for a moment, said, "Two," then to Brad, "Do you have any medical problems?"

What sort of question was that? He shook his head. Did she mean mental? He could ask her the same thing.

"None. When can you get us out?" she said into the phone and then screeched, "You're kidding!" Listened again. Slammed down the receiver.

"What did they say?"

"The power's out. They don't know when they can rescue us." She pulled a mobile phone from her handbag, glared at it, and tossed it back into the depths. "No signal."

Gina cursed under her breath. Just her wretched bad luck to be stuck in an elevator when Fred was back at the office expecting her at the Carlton Wright meeting. What a feeble excuse. "Sorry, sir, I was stuck in the elevator." She wouldn't buy it from one of her team and didn't expect he would either.

And that man was one of the scruffiest individuals she'd seen since university. The types that shuffled about in old jeans, worn-out sneakers, and protested about things. Waste of space the lot of them. Who wore that style loafer any more? And had hair that long? Some nutter. He was in there at Networks protesting about something. Progress, probably.

She sniffed experimentally. At least he didn't smell bad.

That would be the absolute pits. Stuck in an elevator with someone who stank, like those bike couriers. Spent their days peddling like maniacs around the CBD wearing lycra and nylon—wouldn't recognize a deodorant if the can hit them in the face. She always avoided riding in an elevator with one of them if she could possibly manage.

"My name's Brad."

His hand was extended toward her. She grudgingly gave it a quick shake after a cursory inspection for grime.

"Georgina." His fingers were clean, firm, and warm, although slightly rough-skinned, and the index finger had a scar on the joint. His dark eyes twinkled in the dim light. He didn't seem perturbed in the slightest.

"Pleased to meet you," he said. That had to be a joke. Where did he think they were? A cocktail party? She made her lips stretch sideways for an instant.

"This better not take long," she muttered.

"Was the power off everywhere or just in this building?"

She snapped her attention away from her watch, which informed her four precious minutes had passed already. "I don't know. Does it make any difference? I'm stuck here and I should be back at work. There's an important meeting. That's all that matters to me."

He said in a mild voice, "It could be the whole CBD. In which case you won't be able to get to the meeting and neither will anyone else. I take it your office is an upstairs one."

Gina stared. Whether he was pulling her leg or not he was right. She put her briefcase down against the wall.

"Yes. We're on the eighth floor."

"Unless," he continued, "you're all fitness freaks and sprint up the stairs."

Fred and Craig were out of the office this morning too. They'd arranged the meet for twelve fifteen. Was Fred a fitness nut? She had no idea. Personal lives were kept out of the office. He looked fit. But eight floors . . . the man was well over fifty. And Craig couldn't manage two flights without collapsing. She could do it easily, of course. Going to the gym regularly saw to that.

The guy was grinning. *That* had been a joke. She managed a proper smile. He wasn't panicking, which was reassuring. One level up from the stinky bike courier would be a panic merchant. "I wish *I'd* taken the stairs. I'm not keen on elevators," she said.

"Claustrophobic?" An eyebrow raised slightly. Was that alarm hovering beneath the interested expression?

"Not really. I just prefer to be in a bigger space." She glanced around, licked her lips. It was a very small area. About three good paces by two. "Usually the ride doesn't last very long, and I don't have time to think about it." Her thoughts were usually several steps ahead of where she actually, physically, was. Anticipating—that was the clue to success in business. Getting in first.

"I'm sure we won't be here much longer."

The patronizing note made her snap, "Don't worry, I won't collapse in a screaming heap."

"Sorry." Still not perturbed. "I'm used to talking to my daughters. They're five and twelve going on thirty. It's funny how being around children changes the way you think and speak. The whole world looks different. All new and exciting."

As if that was an excuse for treating her like an imbecile. Couldn't he distinguish between an adult and children? This "new and exciting" she could do without. But he hadn't finished.

"The littlest one, Fifi, doesn't much like enclosed places either. She wants her bedroom door left open at night." He frowned, thinking. "I don't think she's been in an elevator yet. I doubt she'd like it much."

"I know how she feels." As if she cared about his kid. Had they really named the poor child Fifi? Sounded like a poodle or a cancan dancer. Gina looked at her watch again.

"Not much point checking the time," he said. "Won't get us out any faster."

"Doesn't this bother you?" she demanded. There was a difference between not panicking and downright annoying calm.

He shrugged. "It's happened. How we react to it determines how stressful we find it."

"What are you, some kind of guru?" Just as she'd thought. A crystal-gazing hippy type with crazy new age ideas about life. Probably unemployed and unrealistic in the extreme, a social bludger and bringing those poor girls up the same way. "I suppose you think this is karma," she added.

He laughed. His teeth were in good shape—white and straight. "Are you expecting something bad to happen? What have you been up to?"

"Why me?" she shot back. Outrageous—such a personal remark from this total stranger. This calm, scruffy stranger. With good teeth and warm brown eyes.

That made him laugh even more. "If it was me we'd have plummeted to the basement straight away."

Despite his infuriatingly good humor she had to smile. "Maybe it's both of us and my karma stopped the plunge."

Her supercilious smirk went right over his head. He nodded, looked her disconcertingly straight in the eye. "That's right. We're yin and yang. A balance."

The philosophy of the East now, was it, or that crazy astrology? All total garbage. Gina folded her arms. This guy was hardly evil personified—the worst he'd have done was have an overdue library book. "So what's in your deep, dark past?" she asked flippantly.

To her surprise the smile left his face as though a light went off somewhere inside. "Oh, I'm sorry. I didn't mean . . ." She floundered, found her feet. "I was joking—trying to."

"No, I'm sorry. I started it." He smiled again but it wasn't the same carefree grin. Gina dropped her gaze to the floor, the walls, the control panel. "Who do you work for?" he asked after a moment or two of uncomfortable silence.

"Bright and Caulfield."

"What do they do?"

"We do asset valuations for companies and various independent clients. For example, if a company is wanting to expand or buy property we advise them on whether where they've chosen is a good spot to use and what they should pay for it. That's what we're doing at the moment." She paused and corrected herself with a grimace. "What I should be doing at the moment. Presenting a report."

"So you're an accountant."

"Of sorts. I'm more a business advisor. Economics and so on."

"Interesting." The doubtful way he said it implied he thought the exact opposite. He would. He'd regard her as part of the evil capitalist takeover of the world. Money made the world function—without it he'd be the first to complain about the lack of services and amenities. His type always were. Thought society owed them a living.

"Very. Pays well too." May as well rub it in while he was busy being snide and holier than thou.

"No doubt." He stared at his feet, then his head shot up and he stared straight into her eyes. "Is that what you were doing at Networks? Advising them on whether they're pay-ing the right amount for land in Birrigai?"

"Birrigai? Never heard of it," she said, anger and frustra-tion rising like lava. "What's your problem?"

The vehemence surprised her as much as him. His startled gaze shocked her. She had no reason to attack this man. His opinion meant nothing to her. But something about his bland dismissal of her work, which meant her life, really made her furious.

"I just wonder whether people like you ever think of the consequences of your economic decision making. Networks certainly doesn't."

"Just where do you get off casting aspersions on my profes-sion? Which, by the way, I'm very good at and which you've already admitted you know nothing about. And I'm certainly not discussing my dealings with Networks with you."

She gave him one of her brain-shriveling glares. That's what she'd overheard Adrian telling Sophie once in the tea-room: "Gina hit me with that brain-shriveling glare." Handy to know she owned one. Useful skill when keeping the un-derlings in line. This person, however, this Brad, appeared to be immune.

He shrugged. "You're free to do whatever you like."

There it was again, that mild dismissal. Treating her like an annoying, precocious child. He had a very masculine aura, a self-confidence that could only be male. He was just totally uninterested in her and her profession. What did *he* care about? Apart from his children and some place called Birrigai.

"And what I like is my job," she said, despite the fact that he'd begun that annoying, blank-faced humming again. "I work hard at it, and how dare you turn your nose up at what I do? Do you have a job? What exactly do you do that makes you so morally superior?"

He grinned, displaying those nice white teeth again. "Where did that come from? Morally superior? What on earth are you talking about?" Were they naturally that good? Hers had cost a fortune in orthodontistry plus regular whitening, cleaning, scraping, and all the other unpleasantnesses her dentist could come up with.

Gina drew a deep breath. This was a stranger. She didn't need to get into any sort of discussion with him, certainly not a debate on moral questions concerning making money, and she didn't need to be ashamed of her large salary. She'd slaved for every cent. Ignore him. Her watch said they'd been there fifteen minutes. She tapped her foot and exhaled.

What if he was an aid worker? One of those extraordinary people who devoted their lives to caring for sick children or starving people in Africa. That would explain his casual dress, need of a haircut, outdoorsy fitness, and it would easily make him morally superior. All she did was make money for herself and other equally well-off people.

He was humming softly *again*! That irritating little tune he'd been whistling before, staring at the wall with a blank expression. Ignoring her. Easily, it seemed.

"What do you do? *Do* you have a job?" she asked again.

He blinked and looked at her. He'd forgotten she was even there! "Of sorts."

"What does that mean?" She frowned in exasperation. Did he do this deliberately?

"It means I pay taxes like everyone else but I don't classify my work as a job because it's something I love to do. It's the only thing I can do, the only thing I'm good at. I suppose it's a vocation."

"But—what—is—it?" Gina enunciated each syllable slowly and precisely.

"I'm a woodturner."

"A carpenter? You mean you make furniture?" A tradesman. The last thing she'd expected. Nothing wrong with that, of course. It was a job, and skilled tradesmen were becoming highly priced and in great demand as apprenticeship opportunities shrank.

"I can be a carpenter if necessary, and I do make furniture. Among other things."

"What other things?"

He screwed up his face in thought. "I make whatever is there in the timber. Sometimes I see something in the color or the grain or the shape of the wood. Other times I have an idea and find the right piece of wood to express it. Maybe a bowl, maybe a nonfunctional sculpture or a walking stick. Anything."

"You're an artist," she said. Not much potential for wealth there.

"Is that a dirty word?" His eyebrows lifted. She must have pulled a face.

Gina hastily rearranged her features to bland politeness. "No, no. Not at all. I love music and art. And reading."

Brad nodded. "The world would be a sad, gray old place without artists."

"True. It's not really a job though, is it? It's not work. Not really."

That got his attention. "It's my profession. It's not a hobby."

Gina smiled and raised her own eyebrows slightly. Here was a weak spot in his casual demeanor. Perhaps a little poking and probing was in order. To pay him back.

"But you can basically do what you like each day, can't you? Not like a proper job."

"Have you ever done anything even remotely creative?" he asked with a tiny edge to his voice. He added with a smile, "Apart from applying your makeup and deciding what to wear." Hah! The first little offensive jab despite the grin. Now they were getting somewhere. He had feelings in there. He cared about this.

"I played the piano when I was a child."

The brown eyes had suddenly become more intense, darker in the narrow face. Uncomfortably so. And a lock of hair flopped forward over his brow. "No, I mean have you ever created something from nothing? Did you ever compose tunes yourself, write poetry, paint, or draw? Anything?"

"I wouldn't know where to start," she admitted, fascinated by the way that lock of hair made him look passionate and romantic all of a sudden. Like Liszt or Byron or one of those equally driven artists of the nineteenth century. Maybe it was the dim glow from the emergency bulb throwing his features into shadowy hollows and plains. Making his eyes deeper and darker . . . sexy. "I'm a numbers girl."

"It's hard work coming up with new ideas and working out how to express them. Somebody designed that suit you're wearing. And those shoes." He gestured at her clothes with a wave of his hand. "They sat and thought and sketched and spent hours working out the style and the line. Don't tell me that's not work. Then someone else made them—although early on in his or her career your designer probably cut and sewed as well. I do the first part and the second. So does every other artist."

"You get paid for it." This reaction was way beyond her expectations and her knowledge of the subject. He ran his hand through the errant flop of hair with an irritable gesture. Back to the ordinary man. Gina swallowed. Get a grip, she was starting to hallucinate, have romantic fantasies about the guy.

"Some of us do, most don't, or at least nowhere near the true cost of the time involved. We do it because we have to, something inside of us forces us to express our ideas. None of us are in it for the money."

There it was again—that dirty word, *money.* Gina smiled a knowing little smile. "I bet you charge as much as you can, though, and I'd also bet you wouldn't do your artworks for nothing."

"I have donated pieces to charity auctions and of course I want to earn as much as I can. But unless I hit the jackpot and become flavor of the month, the best I can hope for is to make enough to support myself and my girls."

The brown eyes bored directly into hers, daring her to keep up this ridiculous and petty little game of one-sided one-upmanship. He was a good, decent man. The thought popped into her head. Lucky, lucky girls—both of them.

"Fair enough," she said weakly. Girls? Not family? Where was the wife? Would she be connected to the earlier sudden switch from cheer to gloom? Were they divorced? Had she run off and left him with the two girls? Big age gap between them, twelve and five.

"How do you sell your pieces?" She was interested now, not just to needle him but because she wanted to know. About the wife too.

"I have a gallery owner who likes my work. It's quite well-known. I do all right. I get commissions. More so now than early in the game." Was that modesty, that "I do all right"? Hard to tell.

"What are you working on at the moment?"

"A sideboard."

"Gosh." She'd imagined him diddling about with footstools and doorstops.

He smiled and his eyes lit up. "From Australian red cedar. It's beautiful wood. Do you know it?"

Gina shook her head. There was light-colored wood and dark-colored wood, rough surface or smooth. Beyond that . . .

"There's hardly any around anymore. They cut it all down years ago. I was lucky and came across an old chap who had a stack of it stored away in his shed. He sold it to me, said he'd never get around to using it before he died."

She returned his enthusiastic smile politely. "You *were* lucky."

"Sorry. Wood's probably not very interesting to anyone else."

He was right. She looked at her watch again, more for something to do than any need to know the time. She slipped off her jacket and folded it carefully onto her briefcase.

"Warm," he said. "Bit stuffy too."

"We've been here nearly twenty-five minutes."

"Good thing there were only the two of us. Imagine if it had happened earlier when we were all jammed in."

"I'd hate to be here by myself." Gina glanced around the confined space and shuddered. Had it shrunk?

Brad sat down on the floor resting his back on the wall with his hands draped casually over his bent knees. "Are you okay?"

"Yes." But she wasn't completely sure, and she mustn't have convinced him either.

"Sit down, Georgina," he said. "It looks bigger from here."

She smiled and inspected the floor. Bit dirty with scuff marks but no real filth. Her skirt would have a dusty bottom. He straightened and removed his jacket, folded it and held it out. "Sit on this."

"Thanks. It's Gina. My friends call me Gina." Gina removed her shoes and sank gratefully onto the coat, folding her legs carefully in the tight skirt. Not meant for sitting on the floor. Uncomfortable. She placed the shoes neatly by her briefcase. Mints. There were mints in her purse. She rummaged, then found and held out the roll.

"Thank you." He took one and popped it into his mouth. "That's a relief. I thought you might have been looking for cigarettes."

"I don't smoke." She grimaced. "Wouldn't that be horrible? Stuck in here with a smoker."

"Hideous. I didn't come prepared for a siege situation."

"Me neither. We've no water."

"Probably just as well. We've no toilet either."

"Oh!" Gina gasped as the import of his remark sank in. "What will we do?"

"Do you need to go?"

"No, but I might later."

"Don't think about it. We'll be out before it's a problem."

How long would that be?

Brad rested his head on the wall and closed his eyes. Gina wasn't so bad after all. Bit prickly and very tense. Lovely smile when she used it properly. Not that bitchy little smirk, but the wide, genuine one that made her eyes flash. Smelled nice, fresh. Thank goodness she wasn't one of those women who smothered themselves in industrial strength perfume. How claustrophobic was she? So far, so good but she looked a bit edgy when she took his coat. Twenty-five minutes? That made it nearly twelve. He'd have to be on the one o'clock train or he'd miss the school pick-up at three. Didn't leave much time.

Mel would take the girls—standing arrangement—Clairey would go there when she found no one home, but Fifi would be worried. He smiled at the thought of the sweet face surrounded by fluffy dark curls. Just like Elaine's at the same age. She would spend hours poring over photos of her mother if he let her. Natural, though, to want to absorb as much as she could of the mother she'd never know.

"Are you all right?" The soft voice broke in on his thoughts. Brad opened his eyes abruptly. He wiped his hand quickly across his face, managed a kind of smile at the concerned face of his companion.

"Sorry. I'm fine." His laugh sounded terribly stiff and self-conscious. "How are you doing?" He mustn't let himself wallow like that. Hardly ever did these days, but this was an exceptional circumstance.

She smiled but her lips wobbled. She pressed a palm flat

against one cheek then the other. "Is it me, or is this space getting smaller?"

"It's not getting smaller. Close your eyes and it will be whatever size you want it to be. You can be wherever you want to be."

"I want to be out of here," she said dryly, but she shut her eyes.

"We will be soon enough."

"Is that what you'd tell your girls?"

"We tell each other stories if we're waiting somewhere," he said. "Fifi usually tells us about Winnie the Pooh."

"Winnie the Pooh's good. What's your other daughter's name?" Her voice sounded strained, like someone trying hard not to think about throwing up. Or not to panic.

"Claire with an *i*. She's learned to say that straight off." He kept his own voice calm and even, laughed. "Clairey doesn't like to waste time."

Gina smiled. "No time-wasting—a girl after my own heart." She opened her eyes and looked straight at him. "Tell me a story." Desperation. She was on the edge. Her hand strayed to the top button on her blouse and unfastened it, flattened the collar wider. Not teasing or sexy, but wanting more air, cooling overheated, flushed skin.

"If you tell me one afterward."

"Done."

"Take some deep breaths," he said. "Slowly."

She closed her eyes again and breathed deeply. A thin sheen of perspiration wet her upper lip. The heat of her body enhanced the perfume. The fragrance twined into his nostrils. Her chest rose and fell as she drew in air. She lifted her hand and undid another button, still with her eyes fast shut.

Brad swallowed and averted his gaze. But the urge was there. Come from nowhere. Sudden, in a rush. The urge to bury his face in the sweet-scented skin, run his lips over the smooth line of her jaw. Over her mouth. Release the tension that made her body brittle and her manner hard. Uncover the soft, sexy center of her.

"Go on," she said.

"This is a true story." Lust was forced aside. He slipped into bedtime-storyteller mode. "It happened two weeks ago. I was in bed and I was woken up at about three o'clock in the morning by a scratching noise in the wardrobe. I got up and had a look but there was nothing there and the noise stopped. I went back to bed and about ten minutes later it started again. This time I turned the bedside light on and snuck up really quietly. It was coming from a bottom drawer where I keep old photos and a few winter beanies, scarves, and odds and ends. I pulled it open and moved a few things and a mouse jumped out. He'd made a nest in the photo box and used wool from the beanies and opened up a lavender bag, plus chewed into one of those wheat-filled bags you heat up and put against your back."

Gina laughed, eyes still firmly shut. "He'd made himself a nice little luxury home complete with food. What did you do?"

"Took the whole thing outside and dumped it right away from the house. Mice scattered in all directions. Four of them, I think."

"Meanie. Nights have been cold lately." But she was smiling.

"Tough. Anyway that's not the end. I went back to bed. It was about four. I was just drifting off to sleep when I heard more scuffling. I got up and opened the wardrobe door because the drawer was empty now. On the bottom of the cupboard were some little bits of paper. They hadn't been there when I looked before."

"What . . ." Gina's eyes popped open, but he held up his hand.

"I went back to bed and a few minutes later I heard this." He rapped his knuckles once on the floor. "And then a minute later this." He rapped his knuckles again and paused, watching her expectant, absorbed face, the eyes alight with curiosity and laughter. "I got up and opened the wardrobe door again and there were two toffees at the bottom. The ones wrapped in paper."

"What on earth!" Wide blue eyes stared in amazement. "Toffees?"

"That's exactly what I thought until I remembered I'd had some in the pocket of my old trenchcoat, for the girls. Another mouse was in the pocket of the coat trying to get the toffees out. I bundled all the coats up and took them out and hung them on the washing line. He dropped out and scarpered into the geraniums."

Gina relaxed back against the wall laughing. "That's extraordinary. I can't top that. Is it really true?"

Brad nodded solemnly. "Every word. We'll have to get a cat. Our other one disappeared a year ago. I've been resisting but the girls have a perfect case now."

"I have a cat but I think he might have a stroke if he was confronted with a real mouse. He's a gorgeous, fluffy, white Persian—Aladdin. I call him Big Al."

"Where do you live?"

"In an apartment a couple of blocks past the park. Darlinghurst. What about you?"

"Southwest of the city in a little place called Birrigai. It's about a ninety-minute drive. Same by train."

She grimaced, guilty. "I don't know it."

He smiled. "So you said. It's southern highlands area, east of Mittagong and Bowral, close to Sunderland."

"It must be lovely."

Gina's shriek drowned Brad's reply as they plunged abruptly into pitch darkness. With a rattling screech the elevator plummeted but stopped almost immediately, then shuddered.

"It's falling!" Gina screamed. "We'll die."

Something creaked deep in the bowels of the shaft. Brad's eyes strained open, seeking light. Nothing. Not so much as a glimmer.

Chapter Two

Her body crashed against his. Fingers clawed at his shoulders.

Brad gripped her firmly, easing her across his legs to sit on his lap so he could cuddle her as he did the girls. She flung her arms around his neck, pressing her head into his shoulder. Her cheek was wet against his chin when he turned his head. Her body heaved with great, gasping sobs. He could feel the outline of her ribs under his hands through the flimsy cotton blouse.

"No," he murmured into her ear. "We're all right. It won't fall. It has big, strong cables holding it, plus they have extra emergency cables." He had no idea if that was true, but she relaxed marginally, and the death grip she had on his neck eased slightly.

He rested his cheek against her hair. Her heart was hammering so hard it beat against his chest and reverberated through his body. His was pumping overtime too. He wrapped

both arms around her, rocking gently and murmuring meaningless, soothing noises even though every nerve ending stood
erect—waiting—waiting for the next slip, the sudden plunge.
Better to go locked together if they were to go at all, comforting and hugging each other as they fell fifteen floors.

Gradually his pulse slowed, and the pounding of blood
faded in his ears. Her heart resumed a more normal pace,
thudding against his chest. The silence was deafening. After
a time she raised her face slightly. He couldn't see a thing,
but her breath feathered against his cheek, calmer now. Her
hand slid from his neck and landed lightly on his cheek,
traced its way to his mouth.

"Thank you," she murmured. Then her lips brushed ever
so gently across his, salty tasting from her tears, soft and pliable. She paused, waiting for his reaction. Nibbled again,
more purposefully this time. Demanding a response.

Awareness returned. Awareness of a warm body with
curves and soft, delicious-smelling skin. This was a woman
in his arms, not one of his children. The realization hit home
as Gina pressed against his chest, twining her fingers in his
hair, settling herself, pulling him closer.

"Gina," he murmured, unsure of what he was about to say.
Whether he was going to stop her right there or . . . not. But
her mouth was on his again, desire leaped and the same adrenalin racing through his veins met hers in a wild explosion of
passion as he crushed her to him.

Her kiss was delicious; her mouth generous, eager. Mint.
She tasted of the mints they'd eaten. He groaned with pleas-
ure. She giggled throatily into the kiss but didn't release him.
Not that he wanted to be free.

She held his face between both her hands, crushed his

mouth beneath hers. Brad went with her—urgent, hard, craving. Lost. Another time, another woman, passionate and loving. So long since she'd been in his arms. Elaine. His love.

"Oh El . . . ," he murmured into the perfumed chaos of hot breath, sweat-slick skin and desire.

Gina froze. Reality smashed down on her, swamping her brain, locking her limbs and her voice box. Thoughts filtered through the dense fog. She was kissing a total stranger in an elevator. Her body responded instantly. Her legs propelled her backward and off his lap so fast she fell awkwardly on her side, but she managed to scramble away until her head bumped the wall and she felt his coat under her fingers. She shoved it aside with a cry of disgust. Her fingers shook so much she couldn't button her blouse but she managed to re-arrange her skirt and tuck it in.

"Gina." His voice came softly, tenderly through the darkness. "I'm sorry."

She opened her mouth but no sound emerged, just the harsh gasping of her breath.

"Gina?"

"So am I," she muttered. "Sorry."

"Are you all right?"

She dragged air in through tight lungs and a choking throat. "Apart from being totally humiliated, you mean?"

"Don't be humiliated. Sex can be a natural reaction to fear and danger." He was that calm stranger again. If she hadn't just been on the receiving end of such passion she'd think he was a cold-blooded zombie. He wasn't, he loved someone named Elle . . . his wife.

"Something to do with ensuring the survival of the species," he added.

"Oh." A shaky laugh erupted. One she couldn't control. The laughter escalated. Hysterical, she was hysterical now. In the pitch black, in an elevator with a stranger she'd just hurled herself at. It was a nightmare. "That's one way of looking at it," she gasped between bursts. "Another way would be I'm a cheap . . ." But the gulps of laughter turned into great gulping sobs before she could finish.

"No," he said. And he was beside her now, his arms feeling their way around her and pulling her against his chest. Not for sex, just comforting. "You're not cheap. You're frightened, but you're also beautiful and completely desirable. I liked that you wanted to kiss me. I liked kissing you. I'm frightened too."

"No, you're not," she muttered, but the panic receded. He'd felt the same way. The shame was shared. It was theirs. A secret.

His hand stroked her hair. The sobs subsided slowly but that name screamed in her head. She pulled reluctantly from his grasp and stood up, swaying slightly in the dark. She stretched a hand to the wall to steady herself. This time her fingers managed the buttons. She smoothed the blouse, adjusted the waistband of the skirt. Her makeup would be a total train wreck but apart from that, no evidence. Anyway, nothing had happened beyond a pretty torrid kissing session.

He was the one with the guilt problem. She was single and unattached, he was a father and, presumably, a husband.

"Elle," she said coolly. "Is she your wife?"

Brad's gut clenched as the words came at him from somewhere in the blackness. Little pellets of shrapnel stinging and cutting at the most tender places. Gina had redonned her armor, her façade. To be expected after such a display of vulnerability, such a total loss of control. From both of them. He was shaking from the passion she'd released. Thank goodness for the darkness. Thank goodness she'd pulled away when she did.

"Elaine. She was," he said.

"Divorced?" she asked after a moment. The tone had modified from attack to hard curiosity. He shook his head, but she couldn't see that gesture, of course. "She died. She died in childbirth having Fiona. Fifi—we call her Fifi."

He waited for the inevitable gush of remorse. Death did that—made people regret words, attitudes, and actions that otherwise they'd never apologize for—but Gina simply said, "I'm sorry."

She sounded unutterably sad. He heard the rustle and swish of her stockings and the muffled thud as her bottom landed on the floor and she stretched her legs out. "I didn't think that happened nowadays. It seems so . . . so medieval. Or third world."

"It does happen. Hemorrhaging."

"How horrible."

Brad nodded again. Remembered she couldn't see. "Yes."

"So you brought up your daughters on your own. A newborn baby must have been tough."

"Yes. With help, of course. People—women—don't think a man is capable of that."

"But you are?"

"If she'd been our first I'm not sure I would've attempted it but we already had Claire and she was almost seven. Quite grown up."

"Six and three quarters." Gina laughed softly. "Those extra months seemed so important. I used to insist on being five and a half and then when I learned about eighths, seven and seven eighths. Now I'm thirty and desperately trying to chop hours off, let alone months."

"You don't look thirty." She didn't. He would have put her at twenty-eight tops. Twenty when she relaxed and smiled.

"Don't I?" He could tell she was pleased.

"No. You look forty." A foot kicked him on the leg. "Owww."

"You deserved that. Where did I hit you?"

"On the thigh." He rubbed the spot, grinning in the dark.

"It was a random shot. I can't see a thing."

"Me neither. You'd think some light would seep in around the door but I guess if the power's off there is no light."

He felt about on the floor and found his jacket.

"Do you want to sit on my coat again? This floor's getting hard."

"You have it, thanks. I bet I look more like eighty at the moment. Better cover your eyes when the light comes back on."

He refolded the coat and sat on it. "You don't need make-up, Gina. You have lovely skin."

"Because I pamper it."

"Maybe, but you were born with it. And your gorgeous eyes. Do you have Irish blood? That black hair . . ."

"Irish and Scottish."

"Thought so. Celtic ancestry."

Something groaned and creaked beneath them.

"What was that?!" Her words sprang out, harsh and demanding.

"Don't know. Things settling?"

"We should try the phone again. If we can find it."

"I'm against a wall." Brad stood up and felt his way along the wall until he came to the corner. His outstretched left hand met her right.

"Whoops, wrong way," she said. But she clung to his hand when he lowered it.

"If we turn around we'll face the door," he said. Her free hand groped for his as they turned and stepped forward, arms outstretched. "It was on the right, your side."

"Got it." She released his hand.

"Perhaps they've forgotten we're here," he said and laughed. "Gone to lunch."

"I doubt it." Gina replaced the phone with a sharp click. "This useless thing isn't working either." At least the claustrophobia had been superseded. He'd rather have her angry than panicking.

"Have you read *The Day of the Triffids*?"

"Stop it," she snapped. "It's a power outage not an alien invasion."

It was on the tip of his tongue to ask how she knew aliens didn't cause the power cut but the sudden surge of anger in her voice made him switch to a less-flippant utterance.

"Wonder if we can climb out ourselves. Trouble is I can't see a thing and the ceiling's too high for us to reach. I'd have to hoist you up and you'd have to try to push open the maintenance hatch. If there is one. Did you notice?"

"No." The tone of her voice indicated she wasn't up for acrobatic routines in the pitch-dark any more than jokes. "This is ridiculous. What are they doing?" She stamped her stockinged foot and the elevator shuddered.

"Don't do that," he said sharply. "Just control yourself."

"Control myself? Perhaps you should consider controlling *your*self."

"Me? You were the one who threw herself on me. You started it."

"I was frightened. I was seeking comfort, and you took advantage."

"I did not!" What an outrageous statement. How could she stand there and say that? "You offered. And don't you even think of launching some kind of case against me for sexual harassment or assault. I'd be well within my rights to do the same."

All he could hear was the sound of her furious breathing coupled with his own. What if she did accuse him of sexual assault? She was the type who would. Her word against his. He pressed a sweaty palm to his forehead and dragged it back through his hair.

"I won't. Of course, I won't," she said eventually in a much-subdued voice. "I don't want anyone to know about . . . that. Do you?"

"Not particularly. No."

"You don't have to make it sound so unpleasant."

"It wasn't unpleasant." What was going on now, for heaven's sake? Surely she wasn't angry because he didn't want to broadcast their mutual loss of control.

"You said you liked kissing me."

"I did." And given half a chance he'd do it again. Under different circumstances, of course. When they were both thinking rationally.

"But you said it as though it was a bad experience."

"It wasn't but you don't want anyone to know either." Was she serious?

"No."

"We agree then." Had he got this straight at last? How did women manage to twist things around so much?

"Yes." She sounded quite decided.

"Good." Pity though. Just talking about kissing her made his lips tingle.

"But it won't happen again."

"Definitely not."

"Just so you understand."

"I do, so you can stop talking about it now. It's finished, over, forgotten. Done with." He paused. Couldn't resist. "Unless the elevator drops again."

And she laughed. A deep, gurgling chuckle that made him grip his hands together to prevent himself from reaching for her and demonstrating what she was going to be missing.

"Shut up," she said in a voice alive with laughter.

"Can you see your watch?" he asked. "Mine doesn't have a luminous face."

"My phone does," she said. "If I can find my bag. Hang on."

She scrabbled about on the floor at their feet for a few moments. A tiny square of light glowed, wavering about as she moved to his side.

"Wow, it's so bright," she exclaimed.

"What does it say?"

"Twelve thirty-three. But knowing the time won't get us out of here any faster."

"I can see that smirk, Miss Guru," he said, even though he couldn't see anything other than the tiny screen. "I'm never going to catch the one o'clock home."

"Doesn't look like it. Do you have to?" The light clicked off as she closed the phone.

"It's a ninety-minute trip and the next one is an hour later. I pick Fifi up at three and Claire gets home about four fifteen. It's not really a problem. Melinda from up the road will take Fifi if I'm not there."

"But they'll be worried."

Fifi definitely would. He could count on one hand the times he'd missed the pickup and most of those she knew in advance to go with Mel. "Yes. They'll think I missed the train. But I always phone if something happens. What about you?"

"No one will worry about me. Big Al would be annoyed if he doesn't get his dinner, but I'd hardly call that worrying about me."

"What about work?"

"They'll work around me. Networks will tell them about the elevators when they ring looking for me. It'll be a nuisance because I've got the reports in my briefcase, and they'll have to reschedule the meeting. They'll be angry but they won't worry about me."

"Friends?" Surely she had someone who cared for her rather than for her position in the company.

"They won't know until I tell them. No one depends on me the way they do you."

"Free as a bird."

"Yes. I like it that way."

Brad laughed. "I can't remember being that way."

"What about before you had children?"

"Elaine and I were together for years before Claire was born."

"You must have met young."

"We were at school together."

"Cripes. I can't imagine being with anyone I went to school

with." Her horrified reaction was a common one and he expected it, but she laughed and added, "My school was all girls, though."

"Very funny." He paused. "We were just lucky."

"Lucky?"

"Sounds odd, I suppose. But I consider we were lucky to have had so much time together. Imagine if we'd met and married and had Claire in the space of a year or two?"

"You'd only have had about eight or nine years instead of . . . how many?"

"About fourteen."

"Not long," she murmured.

"No. But they were good years."

Brad reached back until he found the wall, leaned against it, and folded his arms. He licked his lips. The darkness made words come more easily. There was something he'd left unsaid, that he needed to tell her, now, while she was accepting and gentle.

"Gina, I knew I was kissing you." He heard a sharp intake of breath beside him. "I don't know why I said . . . what I did. I'm sorry."

"You said we wouldn't talk about that." Her voice faltered.

"I know . . . I just . . . wanted you to know. I haven't had . . . you made me feel the way she did and it's been a long time. But I knew it was you."

"You still love her." It was a statement. Noncommittal.

"Yes. But she's gone, and I know that. I'm not holding on to a memory. I mean, of course I remember her, but I'm not deliberately cutting myself off from loving someone else."

"But you haven't had any women since? Any girlfriends?" A definite change of tone. Lighter, almost teasing. "No sex?"

"I didn't say that."

She pounced, taking advantage of his defensive indignation. "You implied it."

"It's difficult when there are small children around."

Now he was on the back foot and she knew it. He heard the teasing clearly when she said, "So, no sex for five years."

"I said difficult, not impossible." Good thing she couldn't see the flush on his face.

"S-o-o-o. Who? Melinda?"

"She's married and it's none of your business! What if I ask you about your sex life?"

"What do you want to know?"

"Aagh." Brad snorted. "Nothing. It's none of my business. Look, this is a dangerous topic. We said we wouldn't talk about sex."

"All right. You're right." She sighed. He heard the rustle of fabric as she sat down. "We didn't exactly say that but I take your point."

He ignored that remark. They remained in complete silence for some time. Brad had no way of judging how long. He took two unsteady paces away from where he thought she was sitting, arms stretched blindly before him. Odd how even though he knew there was solid floor beneath his feet, his mind conjured a gaping chasm. Her voice startled him.

"Was Elaine a healthy woman?"

"Yes. Why?" He touched the wall and turned, leaning against it facing her voice.

"I just . . . the thought of a healthy young woman dying in childbirth . . . it's wrong. It's so sad. Tragic. She must have been about my age."

"She was. It's not common," he said gently. "We knew there

was a risk if Elaine fell pregnant again. After Claire there was a miscarriage and we thought that was it for our family. They told us she wouldn't conceive naturally."

"But she did."

"She did. Two years later. She was ecstatic. I was petrified. They gave us the choice of an abortion but Elaine wouldn't even consider it. She said flat-out no even though the doctor told her it could most likely prove fatal for her and possibly for the baby."

"But you?"

"I wanted them both. I couldn't make that choice. But I should have convinced her. We should have used . . . something . . . birth control. I could have had a vasectomy. She wouldn't let me."

Her heard her shift her legs. After a pause she said softly, "Your bad karma."

"Yes."

"That's crazy thinking."

"Probably." He sighed. "I don't dwell on it. Not anymore."

"I think I'd do the same as Elaine," said Gina slowly. "Not that I have any children but I think I'd put my baby before myself if it had a good chance of survival."

"The mothering instinct is very strong."

"I doubt I'll have a chance to find out."

"You're only thirty," Brad protested. "You'll marry someone sooner or later."

"I earn megabucks and I'm smart. Women like me generally terrify men. The ones I don't terrify are old, married sleazes looking for a fling on the side. Or just plain sleazes who won't commit. The rest are married, and I'm not stealing someone else's husband."

"There must be some good single blokes out there in corporate land," he said helplessly.

"Maybe." She paused. "I've never told anyone that before. Not a man. About how I feel. Desperate and dateless."

"Not dateless, surely."

"No, but I may as well be for all the good it does me."

"I've told you things too," Brad said. He slid his back down the wall until his bottom hit the floor. "It's the strangers on a train thing. People tell strangers things they wouldn't tell their husband or wife because they know they'll never see them again. Their secrets are safe. Also, I suppose, there's the fact that a stranger doesn't care—the information means nothing to them."

"I guess that's right. What a relief."

Brad sighed. He stretched his arms over his head, flexing his shoulders and back as he lowered them. This had to end soon. Surely something was going on out there. Gina sat silently across from him. He could hear her breathing and the rustle of her clothes when she moved. She was an interesting girl. Nothing like he'd first thought when she yelled across the foyer. If he hadn't held the doors the timing would have been different. He'd have gone in to see French before Gina and would never have gotten to know her. Or kiss her. The desire that had raged through his body was extraordinary; he'd felt nothing like it since Elaine and if the truth be told not often even with her. They knew each other too well. But Gina . . . she was all surprises and contradictions. Her body was slender and strong and soft. Exciting.

"You don't terrify *me*," he said.

"Hah." After that one snort of cynical laughter she lapsed

into silence. He heard her scuffling about in her purse. "Like another mint?"

"Yes, please, except I can't see you to get it."

Her foot touched his. "If we both lean forward and touch our toes we can do it. Which foot is that?"

"Left." Brad scooted his bottom forward so his fingers could reach his foot and then hers. Groping hands found his. The roll of mints was shoved into his palm.

He extracted two mints then folded the silver paper over the roll. Slid back to lean against the wall. "Like to try catchings?"

"Okay. Go."

"One, two, three." He tossed the mints in a gentle arc in the direction of her voice.

"Aaah," she yelped. "Whoops. I missed but it landed in my lap."

"One point for me."

"Ready?" She counted. The roll clunked against the wall by his head.

"Way too high."

"Your turn."

Brad patted his hand about hopefully. "I can't find them."

"Bummer. I don't fancy crawling about on this floor."

"They can't be far away."

"Don't bother."

"They might be our only food source."

"Oh, please."

More silence. Brad sucked on the mint, glad he'd taken two when he had the chance.

"What did your wife do? Did she work?" The question came from nowhere. Why was Gina so interested in Elaine?

Not that he minded talking about her but he didn't dwell on
the subject. Preferred to go forward rather than back.

"She was a painter. Elaine Ellis. She did landscapes. Her
works sold quite well."

Gina, slumped against the wall, sat up straighter. "Wow."
What a woman she must have been: successful artist, mother,
adored wife.

"Having a family slowed her down a bit but she loved it—
being a mother. Painting's the sort of career you can manage
around children. With both of us home it worked pretty well."

"Sounds ideal." For them. If you wanted that sort of life,
stuck out in the country somewhere with an erratic income,
knee-deep in children.

"Like I said, we were lucky."

"Are your children artistic too?"

"Claire draws very well; Fifi loves to sing. I don't know
where that comes from. Neither of us are musical."

"My mother sings. Amateur choirs. She used to sing
around the house, practicing her parts. It was so embarrassing
when we were teenagers—I have an older brother, Oliver—
when we had friends over."

Brad laughed. "I think I'm becoming an embarrassment.
Not because I sing but because I just *am*."

"Teenagers are so conservative. A mother belting out the alto
line to 'Oh Fortuna' from *Carmina Burana* while she peeled
potatoes wasn't exactly cool. More like weird to a visiting
fifteen-year-old." Gina smiled. Dear Mum, still singing on un-
daunted after all those years. "Now, I think 'go for it, Mum.' "

"Claire started high school this year. She's . . . it's hard
now that she's older. Hitting puberty and all that. Boys, makeup, fashion. Stuff I know nothing about. Except the teenage

boy bit; I dread the day she brings some spotty, randy youth home. I know exactly what they're like."

Gina chuckled. "Oh yeah. I remember. But school seems endless when you're a kid-kindergarten at five, six years of primary, six years of high school. All designed by adults to torture children. It won't get any easier, believe me."

"Thanks a lot. She's changed completely in about eight months. She's cheeky and so touchy. I worry that I'm not capable, that I'm losing her. She needs her mother now."

"She can talk to that woman-friend, can't she?" Gina sighed. What did she know about raising children?

"Yes, but she doesn't. Mel's not exactly up on the latest fads and she has three boys."

"She'll be fine. You love her, that's the main thing." Not much use but it sounded right.

"I don't know her new friends. She has to bus to Moss Vale to go to high school."

"Maybe you should invite them home. We always had friends round when I was a teen. Despite the singing mother."

"Maybe." Brad sucked on the second mint. "I seem to have lost about a hundred IQ points since she started there."

Gina laughed. "Same with my parents. Weren't yours like that? Suddenly got heaps smarter when we turned twenty-one."

The light came on.

"Thank goodness!" Brad blinked and rubbed his eyes against the harshness of a light that had previously seemed dim. Gina was already rummaging frantically in her purse, hair awry, lipstick smeared, eye makeup smudged. One knee poked through the nylon.

"Don't look at me," she muttered, pulling out a small compact and studying herself in the tiny mirror. "Aagh, what a shocker."

"I think you're gorgeous," he said.

She flicked him a disbelieving glance. "You've got lipstick on your face."

Brad pulled out his hanky and scrubbed at his mouth and cheeks. True enough, red smears adorned the white cotton.

She busied herself with a comb, tugging and patting shiny locks into order. Out came a towelette to remove the messy makeup. She paused mid-scrub. "Like one?"

"Thanks." She tossed him the packet. He removed a tissue and slid it back. Refreshingly moist and cool across his brow. His cleanup was easy. Hers wasn't.

Lipstick and eyeshadow next. Studied herself again, twisting and turning to capture all the angles. Good as new. Apart from one detail.

"Your blouse is buttoned wrong," he said.

"Cripes." Another frowning grimace as she stood up, re-buttoned, and retucked. Smoothed her skirt. Armor all in place. No more vulnerable, soft Gina. She wouldn't meet his eye. Her gaze skated everywhere except to his face. Embarrassed. One thing to share confidences in the dark, another to look him in the eye afterward. Someone she barely knew. Someone she'd kissed and groped. Shared intimate passionate embraces. A complete stranger.

What was she seeing, or trying to avoid seeing? A man she wouldn't normally touch with a barge pole? A man she found unattractive in the extreme? Everyone looks attractive in the dark.

Bzzzz. The alien sound startled them both. Gina gasped, but Brad stretched out and grabbed the phone from its hook. A laconic voice said, "Hello, mate."

"Yeah, what's happening?" he said.

"Get us out of here!" yelled Gina over his shoulder into the receiver.

"Sorry, mate, we've just about got it sorted. Major system failure. Everyone okay in there?"

"Just," said Brad tersely.

"Well, hang in. Give us ten minutes."

"No choice, is there? Thanks." Brad hung up. "Ten minutes," he said to Gina.

"Well, you were very polite!"

"What's the point of abusing them? They're doing their best."

"Are they? It's not good enough. We've been in here for hours."

"No, we haven't. It just seems like it."

She glared at her watch. "One hour and eleven minutes and we're not out yet."

"What are you going to do? Sue someone?"

"If I thought it would do any good, you bet I would."

Brad shook his head. "Can't you just accept that sometimes things happen and the best thing to do is deal with it. Let it go. I don't want to relive this experience over and over. Why would you want to draw it out any longer by suing someone?" He flung his arms in the air and let them fall to his sides. "City people! Everyone else's fault. First thing you do is look for someone to blame. Pathetic."

He stopped, conscious of Gina's expression—a mixture

of fury, shock, and dismay. Her eyes bored into him now like steel spikes. Blue steel.

"You completely smug, self righteous . . ." She clamped her lips together momentarily then started again. "*My* time is important! My time is worth money. I know you won't think that matters at all—not to an *artist*. You'll be above such mundane considerations. You've got your creativity to keep you warm and people like what's-her-face . . ."—an arm waved wildly—". . . Melissa."

"Melinda," he murmured.

"Whatever . . . to help you through life's crises. I don't have anybody. Just me. I rely on me. Things like this really mess up my day and a whole lot of other people's day as well. There was a huge amount riding on the report I was presenting. A huge amount. Millions of dollars. Contracts were to be signed. All . . ." She stopped, shrugged. Her newly reddened mouth twisted in disdain. "What do you care? Like you said before, strangers on a train. Our personal problems mean zip to the other person. I don't care about your kids, you don't care about my work. That's the deal. Right?"

Brad stared at her flushed, angry face. Was that right? What was the urge he had to reach out and hug her? Tell her she did have someone—him. But she didn't really. He wasn't part of her world and never would be. She wasn't part of his and never would be.

The deal? They were still stuck in the elevator so the strangers-on-a-train condition still applied. He'd never see her again. She obviously couldn't get away fast enough. And did he care about the millions supposedly in jeopardy? Not a fig. Any emotions she aroused in here would fizzle and die when exposed to reality outside their prison. Like hothouse plants, they needed special conditions to survive. Artificial conditions.

"Yes, that's right," he said.

"You won't ever say anything to anyone about . . . what happened?" Her cheeks were taut, the lips compressed into two straight lines as she waited for his response.

"No."

"Can I trust you?"

"Can I trust you?" he countered, matching her tone.

She held out her hand. "Our secret. Shake on it."

He gripped her hand, small and fragile in his roughened palm, but her fingers clung tightly. "Our secret," he said.

She let go and turned her back to pick up her jacket, unfolding it and smoothing out the fabric. She slipped it on and fixed the collar of her blouse to sit flat against the lapels. She tut-tutted over the hole in her nylons but put one foot into a shiny black shoe, then the other. Ms. Red Suit was back. A businesswoman with a businesslike expression on her businesslike face and a businesslike manner to go with the lot. Don't mess with Ms. Red Suit.

Except he had.

"Their ten minutes are up," she said in a voice that boded ill for whoever might be in the firing line when the doors opened.

Chapter Three

The elevator shuddered. Something whirred, something else clanked.

"We're moving," Gina cried.

"Hallelujah." Brad's arms whipped around her and squeezed so hard she could barely breathe. He started laughing and spun her around as the elevator descended rapidly. Her eyes were moist, but whether from laughing or relieved tears she wasn't sure.

"Put me down," she said, but not fiercely, as she clung to his shoulders.

He set her down gently, releasing his grip, smiling into her eyes. Intimate, warm. "If I had to be stuck I'm glad it was with you," he said.

Gina's neck prickled as unfamiliar heat flooded upward to her cheeks. Blushing! She hadn't done that since she was about thirteen. Her face would be clashing attractively with her suit. She stepped away, dropping her gaze. "There are the mints." She bent swiftly and scooped the little blue roll into her bag. Brad picked up his jacket.

The elevator stopped with a jerk. The doors hissed open. Bright, reflected sunlight from the glass and marble foyer hit her in the eyes. Two men in uniform and a group of curious onlookers crowded around the door as she and Brad stepped out, blinking and breathing deeply of the fresh air.

"You people all right?" one of the men asked. "Sorry for the inconvenience."

"We're all right," Brad said. He turned to Gina. Brown eyes gazed down at her for a moment, held her captive while he considered. Came to a decision. Released her. "I have to run. The girls."

"I have to run too," she said. "To the ladies." Was that disappointment? What had she expected? What had she wanted?

"Told you we'd be out before it was a problem." He grinned, stuck out his hand. "Nice meeting you, Gina."

She gripped his hand, smiled. "Likewise, Brad." Cool. Distant.

And he was gone. Just like that. Darting through the gawping crowd. She caught a last glimpse of his back exiting through the revolving door.

One of the men was saying something apologetic to her. Gina stared at him blankly. "Excuse me, I have to go to the ladies."

"Sorry, yes, of course. Just over there." He pointed to the far right, away from the main door.

She pushed through the crowd. Brad had left without a backward glance. Hadn't wanted her number. Hadn't wanted anything except to go. His daughters were his priority, not the woman he'd been incarcerated with. Her phone shrilled harshly and she reached for it automatically as she walked. The screen read FRED CALLING as in Fred Cartwright, her boss.

"Hello, Fred."

"Thank goodness, Gina. I've been trying for hours. Are you all right?"

"I was stuck in the elevator at Networks."

"The power was out over the whole area—three blocks, us too. It's been a disaster. Had to can the meeting."

"So, have we rescheduled?"

"Had to. We're on for five o'clock this evening."

"Where?"

"Our office. Where are you?"

"I just this minute got out. I'm heading for the ladies'."

"Right. Get yourself cleaned up, then head back here."

"I'll have to go home and change."

"Do whatever you have to but be quick."

"All right."

He disconnected. Gina pushed open the door to the ladies' room. Why did she feel like bursting into tears? She never cried just like she never blushed. She locked herself in a stall. By the time she emerged, the urge to howl had diminished. Her equilibrium must be returning. The face that stared back at her in the mirror over the washbasins looked normal enough. None of the other women using the facility gave her a second glance. Why did she feel different, as though something had shifted inside? Must be residual shock from being in the confined space.

Gina left the building and turned right to the next intersection, waiting impatiently to cross the street. So noisy, air smelly with exhaust fumes. The man next to her was smoking, his cigarette leaving a trail of pungent blue smoke that made her nose wrinkle in disgust. Foul, filthy habit. She edged away. She'd walk to her apartment rather than take a taxi. Walk across the park. All that lovely open space.

The lights changed. The crowd surged forward separating at the far side to stream away left and right. Gina continued straight on into the cool, green oasis. Her pace slowed. She looked up at the sky through the overhanging branches of the gigantic fig trees lining the path. Blue patches and ragged puffs of cloud danced lazily overhead. Warm air patted her cheeks and lifted the hair from her forehead. Bright sunlight dappled the grass in splodges of emerald on dark green, pigeons strutted about looking for scraps of lunch. Cheeky sparrows hopped from bin to path to bench.

What did an Australian red cedar tree look like? Were there any in the park? In the Botanic Gardens?

People sat or lay in the sun and the shade, eating lunch, snoozing, reading, relaxing. Some wandered aimlessly; others strode with purpose as she normally did—well, as she always did. Striding into the future, two steps ahead of everyone else.

Her stomach gurgled. She was thirsty too. Nearly home. Across the road at the lights, one block up, turn right, two blocks down. Not so good in these heels but better than being enclosed again. Even a car would be unpleasant at the moment. A shudder rippled through her body.

No more elevators today. She swiped her card to enter the building and headed for the stairs. Only four flights. Easy in stockinged feet with her shoes suspended from the fingers of her right hand.

Big Al, curled in the armchair by the window, raised his head sleepily and stared when she walked in.

"Hiya, Al, guess what happened to me!" she called, but he tucked his head back under his paws and ignored her.

"I got stuck in an elevator," she said softly. "For over an hour." She placed her briefcase and shoes by the front door and her bag on the kitchen bench, then went to her bedroom. "With a man," she called. She stripped off her jacket and skirt, folded them for cleaning, dragged off the ruined stockings—into the wastebasket—unbuttoned her blouse. "A nice man."

She dropped the blouse in the laundry hamper and stared at herself in the full-length mirror. Slim . . . skinny no matter what she ate. Matching cream-colored, lace-edged bra and panties. Flat stomach, bony collarbones and hips. He said she was gorgeous. He said he enjoyed kissing her. So gentle and tender. She'd made him feel that way. A strange man.

"Brad," she said. A tear rolled down her cheek. She watched, fascinated as it hovered on her jaw, then fell to her throat. Cool, wet, completely alien. Brad what?

Enough.

Gina went to the bathroom and stood under the shower for a couple of minutes, then dried herself swiftly and dressed. Clean underwear, clean powder-blue blouse, light gray suit. New tights, fresh makeup, same shoes.

A cup of instant noodles for lunch, eaten on the balcony to take advantage of the fresh air and the view. Odd to be home at this time on a weekday. Big Al resented her unscheduled appearance. His fluffy tail flicked with annoyance when she woke him by running her hand down his back.

"I don't know his name," she told him. He wasn't interested. He stretched each leg with elaborate care and stalked off.

Briefcase in hand she stood at the bus stop. Brad who? He'd be on the train by now, anxious to see his daughters. He adored them, that was obvious. They'd welcome him home with hugs and kisses, and he'd scoop them up in his arms the way he'd done her. Effortlessly. Spontaneously.

He'd tell them how he'd been stuck and how they'd been scared when the lights went out and the elevator fell. They'd listen and be concerned. Even the twelve-year-old troublesome one. They'd ask who he was with and he'd say a lady named Gina. And no more. Not to them. To Melinda?

No. He'd promised.

The bus lumbered to the stop. She sat staring out the window at the city street, crawling with traffic, noisy and dirty in the bright sunlight. She pulled out her phone. The urge to tell someone of her ordeal swelled within her. Someone who'd make sympathetic noises, listen to her tale and understand the ordeal. Mum? No answer at her unit. Cathy. She'd call Cathy, at home with her two-month-old baby. The first of her friends to embrace domesticity. Someone with time to chat.

"Gina. Hi." Something bubbled in the background.

"Hi. How are you? How's the bub?"

"Gorgeous. You must come to visit; you haven't seen her for ages." That hadn't been by chance. Shelley had puked up milky mess on her hot pink cashmere sweater last visit. Not something she wanted to repeat. "She smiles properly now."

"I should, I'm sorry. It's been frantic lately."

"I can imagine. I'm not in a hurry to go back to work." With a city law firm. "How are you?"

"Fine. I was stuck in an elevator this morning. For an hour and a half."

"Really! Where? How high up?"

"The Bellevue Building, about the fifteenth floor. The power was out over the whole area."

"Scary. What about your claustrophobia? Were you by yourself?"

"No. There was someone with me, luckily. I would've freaked completely by myself." Someone called Brad, with the calm, kind face and the explosive kisses. Her cheeks were hot suddenly.

"I'll say. Hang on. Shell's whining. Hang on." The baby yelled in the distance. The bubbling noise stopped, and the yells came closer. "Sorry I'll have to go and change her pants. Pooh-ee. Good thing you're not within smelling distance."

"Okay. I'm nearly at my stop anyway."

"Call me later."

"Bye."

Gina stepped down from the bus and began walking toward the towering office block housing Bright and Caulfield on the eighth floor. She took the stairs.

Brad who? She could do a Google search for wood turners from Birrigai, if she really wanted to know. Out of idle curiosity. To see if he was any good.

Mel passed him a mug of tea. Brad took it gratefully. She pushed the plate of jam and cream-covered pikelets closer, taking one for herself. The way she cooked displayed a flagrant disregard for impending health problems caused by clogged arteries and obesity. Joey and Will were cases in point, taking relentlessly after their very curvaceous mother. Funny how Stan and fifteen-year-old Mick managed to stay so skinny. Tapped into a different gene pool, obviously. Gina too. So slim. Light and fragile in his arms but with such amazing passion in her.

"Thanks for everything," he said.

"No problem. Fifi was in a bit of a state but she was over it by the time we got home and started making these." She gestured at the pikelets. "As soon as I told her you'd called she forgot all about you." Her eyes twinkled. Brad grinned.

"It wasn't much fun," he said. "Especially when the lights went out."

"I can imagine." She shuddered. "Good thing the woman was nice. Gina, was it?"

He nodded and drank deeply of the hot tea. He smacked his lips appreciatively. "She started out all tense and aggro. Typical city type, but after a while she calmed down." He paused, remembering: moisture beading her upper lip, struggling to control her fear, her perfume enveloping his senses. "She was a bit claustrophobic."

"Poor thing."

"Yeah." He took a pikelet and ate the whole lot in one bite. Homemade strawberry jam with fresh whipped cream. Delicious.

"Were you on your way up or down?"

Brad swallowed hastily. "Down."

She eyed him speculatively over her fourth pikelet. "Lucky."

"Doubt whether they'll even read it. I should have made an appointment to see the managing director and taken a reporter with me."

"They'd still fob you off with meaningless mumbo jumbo."

"It makes it more difficult." Another pikelet disappeared into his mouth. "They have to stand there and tell you straight out they don't believe their mobile phone towers are health hazards. Even one within spitting distance of a school."

"They don't care," she said viciously. "Just because we're in the country they think they can do what they like to the brainless hicks."

"Yeah, well. We'll make them see they can't." He stood up. "I'd better take the tribe home. How's your dad?"

"Still the same, poor old chap. Cheerful enough but doesn't remember much. He's having a nap at the moment." She smiled and heaved her bulk off the chair. "He loves having the kids around even though he doesn't know which are his grandkids and which aren't."

"Fifi and Claire are here so much they may as well be. They call him Pop the way your boys do."

"Sweet, isn't it?"

Mel patted him on the shoulder. Brad stuck his head out the kitchen door and called down the hallway, "Come on, girls!"

Claire appeared first, sulky faced, dragging her school backpack along behind her. Brad took it and swung it over his shoulder. "Crikey, that's heavy."

Brown eyes rolled with utter contempt. "I know, Dad! I keep telling you. They load us up with so much homework. It's child labor."

"Where's Fifi? Fifi!" He called again. "We're going."

Joey burst from the bedroom at the end of the hall. Fifi followed, laughing hysterically, her pink school bag swinging from one arm.

"You should have seen what Joey did!" she screeched.

"We don't want to know," said Claire.

"Don't start," said Brad, catching her eye.

"Thanks, Mel," said Claire, turning her back on her little sister.

"Thanks, Mel," echoed Fifi. She flung her small arms as far as they'd go around Mel's middle.

"You're welcome, sweethearts. Any time."

"See you later." Brad chivvied his brood out the door and down the path between the straggling rosemary and lavender bushes to the front gate.

Two houses along they turned in through the wooden gate with HARDING carved into the top bar and cheery yellow daffodils spreading wildly along the fence in thick profusion. Brad ducked his head as he followed the girls. The flowering plum was pretty with pink blossoms in full bloom but it needed a pruning. One branch drooped low enough to take someone's eye out. And old Ralph's gum tree from next door had dropped another load of twigs and small branches on the driveway. It really should be cut back before something larger dropped off it. Lawn needed mowing too. Again.

"We *need* a kitten, Dad," said Fifi, emphasizing the *need* dramatically.

He unlocked the door. "Maybe we do."

"Really?" Claire's aloof, twelve-year-old disdain dissolved momentarily. "You said you didn't want another one." She charged in first, hurling her jacket in the general direction of the hallstand on the way past. It missed and landed on the floor.

"Hang that up, please."

She paused, scowled, but hooked it up. "You said 'no more cats.'"

He shrugged. "I'm allowed to change my mind. Here, take your bag."

"Huh." She stomped away to her bedroom, dragging the offending bag along the floor but releasing it in the middle of the hallway.

Fifi dumped her bag by her bedroom door and scampered to the living room to switch on the TV. Cartoon voices began arguing.

Brad picked up Fifi's bag and removed the lunch box and school newsletter. He glanced through the single page as he went to the kitchen. Kieran had written another notice outlining the health dangers, trying to motivate more parental support in the fight against the telecommunications giant Networks. They already had a vigorous committee but it was always the same dedicated group of four or five people in a parent body of over a hundred. Everyone in town needed to become involved, whether they had children or not.

The trouble was that radio waves and microwaves were invisible pollutants and the long-term effects were difficult to pinpoint conclusively as to the source. They were a relatively recent health threat. If the river or surrounding bushland was covered in some sort of toxic chemical waste there'd be an incredible outcry. That radio waves affected the structure and function of the brain, caused cancers, tumors and other illnesses was much harder to prove convincingly, and given the convenience and popularity of mobile phones and other cordless communication systems, was a seemingly impossible task.

The proposed tower site was close to the small shopping center as well as the school. The staff at the aged-care home across the other side of the playing fields had voiced concern, but it was church run and the governing body was in the city, removed from the immediate vicinity. Children and the elderly were considered not important enough in the eyes of the power brokers. And by the time the effects became widespread in, say, thirty, forty, or even fifty years time those responsible for the decision making would have retired or died. The children would pay the cost.

Claire walked in and picked up the cordless phone.

"Who are you calling?" he asked.

"Don't I get any privacy in this house?"

"Pay your own bills and you will."

"If you let me have a mobile you wouldn't have to worry, would you?" She added nastily, "Although if you had your way no one would have one and we'd all be back in the Stone Age."

"Claire, you don't need a mobile phone. You're twelve years old. You see your friends every day. And mobile phones do fry your brain. You should read some of the stuff Kieran's dug up about it. It's horrendous."

"Yeah, yeah, whatever. I need to ask Tamsin about science homework."

"That shouldn't take more than five minutes. Last time you called her you were on the phone for an hour."

"So? I don't check how long you talk on the phone."

"My calls are work related."

"Well, I can't help it if you don't have a social life." She snatched up the phone and walked out.

"Don't be long. I need you to make the salad for dinner." Brad stared after the bristling figure. Her jeans were too tight and too low-slung, leaving a gap of bare skin between belt and T-shirt. "Everyone wears them that way," that's what he was informed when he protested. Her nails were painted a variety of different colors from day to day, and she and her friend Amber had experimented with hair dye last weekend. Amber's mother, Joan, had laughed. "Can't do any harm," she said when she saw his shocked face. "It'll wash out in a few weeks, and they could be doing far worse, believe me."

That's what terrified him. How would he know? Claire regarded him as her jailer at best and her bitter foe at worst. Fifi was barely tolerated and only occasionally, like this morning, did the old affection shine through. She used to adore her little sister. She used to adore her father.

He opened the fridge and took out a packet of mince. Italian meatballs with yesterday's leftover homemade tomato sauce and spaghetti. Salad. Quick, tasty, and easy. Fifi's favorite.

He scrubbed his hands, put two ripped-up slices of bread in a bowl and poured milk over them to soak. The mince went into a mixing bowl with an egg, garlic, spices, parmesan, and parsley. Mixing was mindless work, leaving him free to think about other things. What a day. A complete waste of time. Except he'd met Gina.

How was she doing? Gina and her lost million-dollar deal. He smiled. An exaggeration, surely. Perhaps he should call and ask how she was. She lived alone apart from the cat. Lonely. He got that distinct impression despite her avowal of liking her free-as-a-bird existence. Desperate and dateless was a real giveaway.

What was her name? Had she said? No. Yes. At Networks. Something short. Watt? Thorpe? Hunt? He shook his head. Hopeless with names, always had been and he hadn't been interested at that stage. Quite the opposite. What was the firm she worked for? Two names. One was like cauliflower. Something and cauliflower—unlikely. He hadn't paid attention. Before their intimacy. Before she'd kissed him.

Brad frowned. He poured the milk off the bread and squeezed the soggy remainder into a pulpy mass.

If she came on as flinty to her dates on first meeting as she had him no wonder she was still single. But she wasn't like that at all, not deep down. Inside, under the fierce attitude, the makeup, and the expensive clothes she was a frightened woman struggling to hold her own in the world—just like everyone else, himself included.

Maybe it was the fear that made her so harsh. Fear of failing.

Making meatballs was a hands-on experience. Brad plunged the bread and his fingers into the mixture and began kneading.

Maybe he was wrong about the fear, maybe she was just very, very ambitious and very, very determined. She'd certainly recovered quickly enough from that lapse of control. And it had been a terrifying few seconds. They'd faced the reality of a horrible, crashing, smashing death in the pitch-dark. No one could blame them for what happened.

How long had it been since he'd kissed a woman with such passion? Or vice versa? Or felt his blood rise so hard and fast? What was it about Gina?

"What do I have to do?" asked a sullen voice beside him.

Brad blinked. "Fill the spaghetti saucepan with water and put it on the gas, please. Then you can make the salad."

He began rolling the mince into balls and placing them on a plate.

"Do we have to have spaghetti again?" Claire bent down and started crashing pots about in the cupboard under the bench.

"We had it a week ago and this is meatballs not bolognese. Find the big frying pan while you're down there. And a saucepan for the sauce."

She banged the frying pan on the stovetop. "Why can't we have more interesting food?"

"Such as?"

"I dunno. Something. Anything except boring spaghetti."

"You suggest it, I'll cook it if I can."

Water gushed into the saucepan. Claire lit the gas and sat the pan on top. "Curry," she said. "I had curry at Tamsin's house. Her mum is a fantastic cook."

"Fifi wouldn't like curry."

Brown eyes rolled in contempt. "Why do we have to only have what *she* likes? She hardly likes anything. She's such a baby."

"You were the same when you were five. You only ate peanut butter sandwiches, apples, and macaroni cheese for about six months."

She stared at him, her lip curling. "And you *let* me?"

"Not much we could do apart from force-feeding you and there are laws about that sort of thing." He grinned at her but received no answering smile, not even a glimmer of amusement.

Brad rinsed his hands. He lit the gas under the frying pan, waited for it to heat and tossed in the first meatballs. The remaining tomato sauce went into the saucepan on a low heat. Claire's water was just beginning to simmer.

"Salad, please," he said.

"Why can't Fifi do something?"

"It's your turn." He added pasta to the now-bubbling water.

"It's always my turn."

Brad gripped the spatula and gritted his teeth. "For heaven's sake, Claire. Do you have to be so difficult? All the time?"

"Don't shout at me!" she yelled.

"I'm not shouting."

She grabbed the wooden salad bowl off the shelf in both hands and hurled it to the floor. "You are. You always shout at me. You're always so . . . so . . . It's so unfair. I have to do everything. She does nothing. Just because she's the favorite."

"Claire—" But it was too late, she'd gone in a whirl of outrage, slamming down the hall to her bedroom and enclosing herself with an almighty crash that reverberated through the elderly house.

Brad stooped and retrieved the salad bowl, one of his, turned from a branch of the old walnut tree in the backyard, several years ago. A crack wriggled through the grain from the edge to the center. He held it in his hands sadly. He could make another but that wasn't the point. That fine crack line forcing the wood apart from itself seemed to symbolize the ever-widening division between himself and his daughter. A rift he was powerless to prevent. Everything he did was wrong. It didn't matter what he said or what he did, it was wrong.

How could he halt the progress of that crack? How could he reinstate himself in Claire's eyes as someone she could rely on, someone she could trust and confide in, someone who loved her with no strings attached, unconditionally. Gina's words popped into his head. "You love her, that's the main thing." But *was* it enough or was that a simplistic response from someone who really had no idea what it was like to be a parent?

"I'm hungry, Dad."

Brad smiled down at the heart-shaped face topped by a mop of dark curls. "Won't be long, poppet. Meatballs."

"Yummeee. What happened to the salad bowl?"

"It fell on the floor and got cracked." He put the bowl down and tested the spaghetti bubbling in the water.

"Did Claire do that?"

Brad sighed. "Yes."

Fifi sighed with an exaggerated heave of the shoulders. "She's such a cranky girl these days. It's poverty."

Brad snorted as a surprised burst of suppressed laughter fought for release. "Poverty? Is it?"

"Yes. Mel said."

"Oh." He nodded with a wise expression.

She shook her head. "Men don't understand. It's women's business."

"No, poppet. Mel's absolutely right, men don't." He bent and dropped a kiss on the soft cheek.

"Was it scary when the elevator stopped?"

"A bit. Not at first. Mainly when the lights went off." Brad flipped the meatballs carefully. A delicious smell wafted around the kitchen.

"Ooooh. I was worried when you didn't come."

"I thought you would be but I was still on the train when you finished school. I told Mel what had happened."

"We made pikelets."

"I know. I had four. They were excellent."

"Claire said I'm a baby but I'm not a baby, I'm five." She studied the fridge door, covered in notes and an array of colored magnets shaped like animals and the alphabet.

"You're not a baby anymore, that's for sure. You're growing so fast you need new clothes all the time."

Fifi rearranged the letter magnets to read Fifi and Dad. "I hate Claire and I hate her boyfriend too."

Brad stared. "Her boyfriend? Who's her boyfriend?"

"I'm not allowed to tell." She slapped both hands over her mouth.

"Too late," he said. "Now it's our secret."

Fifi pulled a dramatically fearful face. "She made me promise or she'll cut all my hair off. Will she cut my hair off, Dad? Because I told you?"

"No. She won't. Who's her boyfriend? Is it Mick?"

"No. He's from high school and he's called Scott."

"How do you know him?"

"I don't know him. I've never seen him." The subject was losing her interest, fast. "Can we have garlic bread?"

Brad frowned. He needed more information if he was to broach this topic. "Not tonight. How come you don't like Scott if you've never met him?"

"When she talks to him on the phone she tells me to go away. She's horrible to me."

"I see. Set the table please, Fifi. We need spoons, forks, and glasses. We're ready to eat."

Brad drained and rinsed the spaghetti while his mind worked overtime. Claire had a boyfriend he knew nothing about. Who was this kid? How old was he? How long had this been going on? She was twelve, for goodness' sake! Twelve. A baby. Was she on the phone with him right now? Had she begun telling blatant lies and terrifying her little sister into the bargain?

He set the spaghetti to drain over the saucepan with a lid to keep it hot and marched to Claire's room, giving a perfunctory knock on the closed door before barging in.

She was lying on her bed, the phone glued to her ear. "Da-ad!" she screeched, covering the receiver with her hand. Two brown eyes glared furiously. She said into the phone, "I've gotta go. See you."

Brad stretched out his hand. She threw the phone to the end of the bed and folded her arms across her chest.

"Who were you talking to?"

"Tamsin. I told you."

He picked up the phone and pressed REDIAL.

"What are you doing?" she demanded, bouncing off the bed.

Brad fixed her with a steely gaze and put the receiver to his ear. A woman's voice answered. "Hello."

"Hello, it's Brad Harding speaking. I'm Claire Harding's father. I'm . . . um . . . I'm checking the number. Who have I rung, please?"

"Oh hello, Brad. I'm Susan James, Tamsin's mother. The girls were talking just now." She paused. He could almost hear her thinking *What's this guy's problem?* She asked delicately, "Can I help with something?"

"No, no problem. I'm just . . ." He glanced at Claire's smirking face. "Being an idiot."

"Oh."

"I'm sorry to have bothered you. Good-bye, Susan."

"No problem, Brad. Nice to speak to you finally. I have one of your salad bowls. From the Sunderland Gallery—it's a favorite. I love the color and the pattern in the grain. Claire told me you were her father when she was here for the sleep-over. I was so impressed! She recognized it as your work. She said you also make furniture."

"Yes, that's right. I've just finished a rocking chair." He

stopped, awkward and very conscious of Claire's baleful eyes upon him. "Thanks, Susan. Sorry to trouble you. Good-bye."

"Bye."

"See! You don't even trust me." Claire stomped out the door. "I told you I was calling Tamsin."

"I'm sorry, Claire." He followed, shamefaced. "Dinner's ready."

Red-faced with rage, she rounded on him in the doorway to the kitchen where Fifi was carefully setting forks and spoons on the table. "Who did you think it was?"

"Scott," said Fifi brightly.

Chapter Four

"**D**id you tell?!"

Fifi's face crumpled, and she darted past Claire to cower behind Brad.

"Clairey, it doesn't matter," he said. "You didn't need to keep him secret."

"Don't call me Clairey," she shrieked. "I'm not a baby."

"Yes, you are," cried Fifi. "You're crying."

"Shut up, shut up, shut up! I hate you." Claire's voice rose to a hysterical squeal. "I hate living here. I hate being in this family."

Fifi burst into loud sobs and clung to Brad's leg.

Brad, hampered by the limpetlike grip, raised his hands palms facing out. "Okay," he cried. "That's enough. Claire, I'm sorry I doubted you. It was stupid and I was wrong, but you mustn't threaten Fifi like that. You know she can't keep secrets."

"She's a baby," she shot back viciously. "Baby, baby, baby."

Fifi stamped her foot and redoubled her howls. "Am not!" she screamed.

Brad gritted his teeth. He held Fifi's arm firmly to prevent her charging in to attack her sister. "Fifi, stop crying. Go and sit on the couch with teddy and calm down while I talk to Claire. It's not your fault."

Fifi sniffed and hiccupped, but did as she was told.

He turned to Claire. Tears streamed down her distorted face, but she didn't cut and run to her bedroom, or slam out of the house the way he'd expected.

"Darling, I'm sorry," he said. "Truly I am."

She sniffed and yanked a tissue from her pocket. "You don't trust me," she muttered into the tissue between snuffles.

"I do. But I don't understand why you didn't tell me about Scott."

"Because you'd do what you just did." Defiant red-rimmed eyes glared at him ferociously.

He shook his head. He couldn't deny that. "Tell me about Scott."

Claire studied him through her reddened, soggy eyes. He smiled encouragingly. "He's in year nine," she said.

Crikey! Two years older. "Tell me while we fix dinner." He went through to the kitchen, removed the lid from the spaghetti, and ran the colander under the hot tap.

Claire followed. She picked up the cracked salad bowl and put it down again.

"Use another one," he said. "Plenty more where that came from."

"Sorry," she muttered.

"It's all right. Don't do it again."

She opened the fridge and took out the lettuce.

Brad doled pasta into three bowls and topped it with meatballs and sauce.

"Fifi, come on," he called. To Claire he said, "Don't you dare go on at Fifi about this. Five-year-olds don't understand." And they weren't the only ones. "Juice and the parmesan, please."

He placed the bowls on the table where Fifi sat waiting with her teddy bear perched on her lap. She gazed up at him with wide, fearful eyes. "Am I in trouble?"

"No."

"Is Claire still angry with me?" she whispered.

"Probably, and with me, too, but don't you worry. It's not a secret anymore."

"Pheewwee." She smiled a wide, relieved smile and began poking at a meatball with her fork.

Claire turned with the salad. She plonked it on the table, went back for the other things, and pulled out her chair.

"Yummee, yummee meatballs," chanted Fifi in a singsong voice.

Claire scowled at her, but said nothing.

Brad poured juice for Fifi. "Would you like to invite Scott over?"

Claire's fork clunked against her bowl. Her jaw dropped. "Dad!"

"What? Don't you want to?"

"No-o." She stared at him as if he had two heads.

"Why not? I'd like to meet him."

She rolled her eyes and shoved in a mouthful of salad, shaking her head at his idiocy. Brad caught Fifi's eye and grimaced. She giggled.

"When are we getting our new pussycat?" she asked.

"Maybe next Saturday. I'll be too busy this weekend."

"What sort of cat will it be?"

"We'll see what's there at the animal shelter." He twirled spaghetti on to his fork. "The lady I was stuck in the elevator with has a white, fluffy Persian cat called Aladdin. She calls him Big Al."

"What's her name?" asked Claire.

"Georgina. Gina for short."

"Gina what?" asked Fifi.

"I don't know. I can't remember"

"Why not?"

"Dad's hopeless with names, you know that," said Claire.

"Was she nice?"

"Yes, very. Eat your dinner." Nice didn't apply to Gina. Many other adjectives did but not nice. Too bland, too dull. Too not Gina at all. Gina was . . . Gina.

"I am. Does she have kids?" Fifi crammed in half a meatball.

"You're disgusting, Fifi," put in Claire as Fifi struggled to chew her overflowing mouthful with bulging cheeks and sauce running down her chin.

"No. She's not married."

Fifi swallowed. "Maybe she wants kids. Maybe she'd like us. And Dad."

"What? Us?" cried Claire. "She wouldn't want you, no one in their right mind would want you, and anyway Dad doesn't want a wife, do you Dad?"

Brad struggled to sort out the vast array of issues contained in those few sentences. That Fifi hankered after a mother was understandable and not a new concept. That she should latch onto Gina as an available single, childless woman was a leap of unimaginable proportions. She hadn't even met her and probably never would. He looked at Fifi's crestfallen, sweet little tomato-sauce-stained face.

"Anyone in their right mind would love to have Fifi and you, too, Claire," he stated firmly. "They'd be honored. But you're right, I'm not looking for a wife. But if it ever happens, and I meet someone I'd like to marry, she will have to pass your test."

"Our test," cried Fifi, her face alight with laughter. She grinned at Claire.

"Our test!" Claire laughed. "Right!"

Brad smiled at his two gorgeous, beautiful, perfect daughters. His and Elaine's. If only she could have been here with them to share the laughter and the joy. If only. But they wouldn't be having this conversation if she were here. He jabbed his fork into his pasta.

"That must have been freaky," said Claire. The crisis seemed to have passed, thank heavens. Until the next explosion. Trouble was he could never see them coming. "Being stuck in an elevator, I mean. I'd panic if that happened to me."

"I wasn't too freaked but Gina didn't like it much. 'Specially when the elevator dropped."

"It dropped?!" exclaimed Claire. Her eyes widened in alarm, her pasta-laden fork stopped midway to her mouth. "You didn't tell us that."

"It only dropped about this much." He indicated with his hands.

"But you might've died," she cried, and he realized belatedly how that fear must affect her deep down, even though she never referred to her mother's abrupt death. Not that they avoided the subject. He assumed they'd both dealt with it.

Plus he'd forgotten, in the aftermath of the boyfriend and telephone turmoil, that he hadn't mentioned that part of it to the girls and hadn't intended to. But not for this reason, more because of the questions that would naturally follow. Questions about Gina. Questions that lead to memories that would lead to other memories. Exciting, sensual memories that stirred his blood and left a deep, unresolved hankering in his soul. Something long dormant had been woken.

"No. We wouldn't have died. It wasn't that dangerous. Just scary for a few minutes."

"Gina was lucky you were there," said Claire.

"Why?" His eyebrows rose in astonishment.

"Because you don't panic." She gave him a rare smile and for the time being, at least, he was back in the sun.

Gina stared at the results of her search. No Brad anything. No Birrigai woodturners. The ones whose photos she had discovered in connection with shows or display days were all elderly or middle aged, and looked nothing like him. If he was a professional and an expert, he should have a Web site. Although . . . She wrinkled her nose. He didn't look very up on the latest technology and he'd probably have some ideological aversion to the Internet anyway.

Big Al rubbed against her ankles, purring. Gina yawned. It was after eleven thirty. Should go to bed. She stretched her arms over her head with clasped fingers. What a day.

If only they'd exchanged last names. He'd mentioned his wife's! The artist. What was it? Elaine. Elaine what?

Gina lowered her arms, frowning. Elaine. Hopeless to enter

that and expect a meaningful result. A yawn stretched her mouth and cheeks so wide her eyes watered. Must go to bed. Fred expected her there at the usual time despite the postponed meeting this evening that had stretched on until nearly seven thirty. Then they'd had a wrap-up session after the clients had left, discussing the next stage of the program. Fred had ordered in Thai food so as not to interrupt the thought processes. Normally she wouldn't have minded— quite the opposite. She enjoyed the brainstorming sessions and the late-night camaraderie of working. No one except the cat waited for her at home.

Tonight, though, was different. She positively itched to rush home and search the Internet for her woodturning companion.

A total and utter failure.

She shut down the computer and stood up, eyes stinging from tiredness. Big Al skipped ahead of her like a big, fluffy, cottonwool ball as she headed for the bedroom. He leaped gracefully and took up his position on the end of her bed. In the bathroom Gina washed, brushed her teeth, and slipped on her nightgown, filled a glass with water and took it to the bedroom. Her bed welcomed her weary body, enclosing her in fresh-smelling sheets and feather quilt.

Elaine who? Brad who? Why did she care? If she wasn't careful this could turn into an obsession.

But she'd always been this way. As a small child, when something caught her attention or snagged her curiosity she researched and read and poked and probed until she knew all there was to know about it. Her father had been the same, but whether he'd simply recognized and encouraged it in her, or imposed his own strictures she couldn't tell.

"Look it up," he'd say when she asked about Gallipoli or what the capital of Ethiopia was. No Internet for him. He'd pull out the giant, blue-covered atlas, the encyclopedia, or the fat, dark blue dictionary with the fraying spine, and together they'd pore over the information. When she reached high school this deeply ingrained quest for knowledge was the driving force behind her education. That, plus her father's natural assumption she would top her classes. And for the most part, she did.

Dear Dad. She missed him terribly, but his death had been a release from agonizing pain and suffering. Too much to bear, for all of them, him and those watching the slow, relentless decline.

No reading tonight, too tired. Gina clicked off the bed light, yawned, and settled. Eyes closed. Breathing slowed. Another yawn.

"Ellis!" Her eyes popped open in the dark. "Elaine Ellis." Big Al stirred at her feet. She reached for the glass of water on the bedside table, drank half in one thirsty gulp, and lay back against her pillows turning the name over in her mind. It had come to her in that drifting, mindless state before sleep. She hadn't been thinking of anything in particular, not consciously. Funny how that happens—try like crazy to remember a name and it's impossible. Stop trying and up it pops. The brain working quietly away in the background.

She rolled over and dragged the quilt up to her chin, snuggling into the cozy warmth. That new sheepskin mattress protector was heaven—so soft and comfortable under the sheet. Expensive but worth every cent, and why not spend what she earned on things she enjoyed?

She had no one else to please.

Elaine Ellis. What had she been like? Tragic way to go—so young. So unfair the way nature worked. The cliché was that the good die young . . . seemed so in this case and there were plenty of evil elderly people around—all those mad old dictators and warmongers causing untold misery in the world. Why hadn't they died young? Maybe some had, before they got going on their evil way. Who could tell?

He'd said Elaine with such longing. What was it like to be loved that way? To love that way? They'd known right from the start they were meant to be together. Known as children, or at least teenagers.

What were the chances of finding your soul mate at school? She snorted aloud at the thought. Big Al got up and resettled onto her foot, a heavy warm lump. She pushed him away. Not much chance at her all girls high school.

How was Brad doing? It'd be nice to phone and ask—a neighborly thing to do even though they weren't neighbors. They'd had a common, disturbing experience and that had created a bond. It could have been a disaster. Almost had been in more ways than one.

He had a nice voice, very soothing. He'd been kind. He'd kept her from panicking, stopped the claustrophobia taking hold. No. Even though she knew his name now she wouldn't call. No need. No.

Brad Ellis.

He'd be in the phone book.

Craig stared pointedly at the clock when Gina arrived at work late the next morning. Twenty past nine. Oversleeping was something she very rarely did. Deaf to the alarm, she'd only woken when Big Al meowed for breakfast, standing with his four little feet pressing heavy on her chest. Getting stuck in that elevator must have shaken her more than she'd thought.

"Sleep well?" Craig asked with a smirk. Thick lenses magnified his gray eyes to an alarming proportion in a round face that was habitually the pasty pale of uncooked bread dough. Thank goodness she hadn't been stuck in the elevator with him. A new ex-smoker with a wheezing pair of lungs to go with the tetchiness of abstinence. He had a sharp financial brain, though. Very sharp and very ambitious, with a wife equally so. They had mortgages and children to maintain. Craig kept her on her toes. Technically their positions were equal. In practice, Craig thought himself her senior by age, sex, and length of time with the firm.

"Very, thank you." Accompanied by a blank-faced look. How dare he criticize? She worked as hard as anyone. Harder.

"Meeting at ten," he said and marched away to his cubicle.

"I know," she muttered. The meeting had to do with the government contract they'd landed—assessing the value of the state primary schools in various country areas where population shifts had changed the demographic. Buildings and land. It was a massive task involving almost all of the staff, and Fred was in charge.

Everyone else was already hard at it. Cherie murmured "Good morning" as Gina passed by. Lincoln, the newest, youngest member of the staff smiled with his "Morning, Gina," then reimmersed himself. He was shaping up well. His first performance review was in a couple of weeks, but there'd be no problem. The work he'd done on her team for the newly completed Networks project had been excellent. Everyone had worked hard—Lincoln, Cherie, and Sophie. Simon French had been very pleased yesterday.

Gina reached her cubicle in the corner with the window and the view. Craig's smug grin still rankled. No doubt he'd make sure Fred knew how slack she was. She slammed her briefcase on the desk and opened it for the files she'd taken home to study and hadn't. Didn't matter, she'd already read them. Taking work home before a meeting was habit. A sort of doubling up, a safety routine in case she missed something vital and made a fool of herself the next day. Hadn't ever happened, but still she did it, reading papers through in bed, or during her solitary, microwaved dinner for one.

She booted up the computer. Coffee first before she tackled the e-mail. Lincoln joined her in the kitchenette. He took his red and white I Love NY mug from the shelf.

"How did it go with French?" he asked. Gina, coffeepot in hand, indicated his mug with a nod of her head. "Yes, please," he said.

She poured his, then her own. Her mug featured a smiling cat that vaguely resembled Big Al. Present from a work mate who'd moved to the Bright and Caulfield office in London, something Gina would love to do. Either there or New York.

"They seemed happy."

"They don't understand some people don't like having Networks company antennas on their roof."

"If people want mobile phones and TV reception and all the rest of it, then they have to put up with the antennas." She stirred sugar into her coffee.

"True. But we were the ones fronting up trying to assess the costs and getting the abuse."

He and Cherie had been, Gina hadn't. "Progress has a price."

He sighed. "I guess."

"You did a good job, Lincoln." Gina smiled.

He grinned back at her. "Thanks. We should celebrate."

"We don't usually do anything like that here," she said. "There's always another project looming so we get straight on with it."

"Oh. Okay." Lincoln pulled a face.

"Nothing stopping you though."

"And you?"

"Don't think so, thanks. Ask Cherie and Sophie."

She turned to go back to her desk. This wasn't a sociable office. They didn't do Friday drinks like some workplaces, they didn't do much. Not that it bothered her, but she hadn't been out socially for ages. Not since . . . she frowned. Ollie's birthday. That was in early August. Over six weeks. What a workaholic bore she was. And as for dates . . .

She'd boasted to Brad that she had a private life. Hah! *Had* being the operative word. Daniel had been the last and he'd moved on last June. Brad was probably doing better than she was in that department. A handsome, single father, fit and, well, ripe for some nice, homely, grasping woman to slip into his bed. He wasn't averse to the idea either. Elaine was a beloved memory but she wasn't an obstacle to another Mrs. Ellis.

Brad with some woman. Any woman. Any other woman. That whole thought was repugnant. This was ridiculous. She barely knew the man. And kissing him was the result of blind panic, just as he'd said. A primitive biological urge.

She drained her coffee. Work. Nine forty and she'd done nothing except chat to Lincoln.

Gina stared at the in-box crammed with messages. Spam

galore. She scanned through, deleting the most obvious rubbish. Her mother, newly retired and loving it, had e-mailed.

Hi G,

I'm heading up to Coffs for two weeks with Aunty Joyce then we're going on to Brisbane together for the party. Don't forget!!! Grandma's eightieth on the seventeenth. Find yourself a date and bring him along for a fun weekend.

Love and kisses, Mum

She typed an appropriate reply, avoiding a response to the crack about dates and fun weekends, saying she'd already booked her flights. Mum knew perfectly well there was no man on the horizon. That was her little joke, knowing how concerned Grandma was about her single state. It would be worth dragging someone, anyone, along just to cheer her up and stop the comments. Wonder how she'd react to Lincoln—six years younger. What would he say to an invitation to a party in Brisbane? For an eighty-year-old.

Fifteen minutes before the meeting. Not much time to start on anything else.

Gina quickly typed "Brad Ellis" into Google, and glanced about for any curious observers. All quiet, all her coworkers engrossed, as they should be. As should she. Only Cherie was in a position to see her properly, but she couldn't see the screen.

She returned her guilt-ridden gaze to the computer. No Bradley Ellis woodturner. Try Elaine Ellis. Gold! A review of an exhibition and a small newspaper article about her untimely death. Gina read it slowly. The words conveyed little of the woman herself but spoke of her talent and her unique approach to a classic form. The last sentence read, "Elaine Ellis leaves behind husband, talented woodturner Bradley Harding, and daughters Claire, seven, and the surviving new-born baby, Fiona Elaine."

Gina's hands clenched in triumph. How stupid could she have been? Of course Elaine used her own name! Most professional women did nowadays.

A search on Bradley Harding produced much more information. A place called the Sunderland Gallery in Sunderland handled his work. Gina studied the photos of his pieces. They were marvelous. Staggeringly beautiful sculptured shapes drawing on the natural line of the wood, emphasizing the color and grain. Elegantly curved bowls, a lovely rocking chair in glowing dark timber, tables, chairs. He was more than a master craftsman, he was an artist. A well-known and very well-respected artist. And she'd sneered and scoffed and made fun of him, looked down her nose at his attire, inspected his hand for dirt before she shook it. What an unutterable snob. Had he realized?

And then she'd thrown herself at him. Taken advantage of the darkness and the proximity and kissed him like an impetuous teenager. He probably thought all his Christmases had come at once.

For the first time in many, many years Gina experienced the disabling effects of unutterable shame. It began as heat deep in her torso and rose inexorably to her chest and neck where it became uncomfortable and prickly, as well as hot. She ran a finger under the collar of her blouse, but it did nothing to relieve the flow of heated blood to her face. How could she face the man again?

She exited the site and leaped to her feet, shoving her chair back so fast it hit the wall behind her with a jarring thud. What on earth was she doing? She had work to do and no time to waste Googling the past. And that's what Brad Harding was. Yesterday's news. She'd never have to face him again.

"Anything wrong?" Cherie's startled voice cut through the writhing mess in her head.

"Meeting. I'm late." She grabbed the folder on her desk with a pained smile at Cherie across the way. Her face must look like boiled beef. Certainly felt like it. Throbbing with blood. This was what her mother used to complain about—menopausal hot flashes. Something to look forward to.

"No, you're not. You've got two minutes," Cherie said and returned her attention to her screen.

"What on earth was that?" came Adrian's voice from the next cubicle.

"My chair slipped and hit the wall," said Gina. The red-hot flush settled to warm. The prickling of her skin subsided to calm.

"Sounded like it went *through* the wall," he called.

Gina pulled her chair away from the white painted surface and looked. There was a dent in the plaster, and small white flakes dotted the carpet. Cripes. What was happening to her? She was going out of her mind. Losing her grip.

Her phone rang and she snatched it up.

"Gina, Brad Harding's on the line for you," said Sophie.

Gina's breath stalled. It couldn't be him. There must be two. Hot blood returned to her face with a vengeance. Crippling. Her free hand was shaking and she stared at it in amazement. The one holding the phone was suddenly clammy and wet.

"Gina? Shall I put him through?"

No, no, no, no, no! But . . . what did he want? She couldn't be rude to him again. Not after what she'd done and thought and said yesterday. And she wasn't a coward either. Her father had taught her that. Own up, take the consequences.

"Um. Yes, please." The line clicked. She breathed deeply, sat down, gripped the edge of the desk. "Gina Tait," she said. Miss Iceberg.

Then he was there in her ear with that warm, laidback voice. "Hello, Gina. It's Brad. From the elevator."

"Oh, hello."

"Am I calling at a bad time?"

Miss Iceberg began to melt. "No. Yes. I have a meeting in a minute." The words tumbled out in a messy sprawl. Great cracks appeared in the ice. "Can I call you back?" She didn't meant to say that? Why had she said that?

"Sure." He recited his number. "I'm home all day. Working."

"How did you find me?" she blurted, still in partial shock at his manifesting himself so soon. Had she conjured him up from his cyber existence with some sort of subliminal brain waves?

"I remembered the company name after a bit. And yours. I heard you say it at Networks."

"I didn't know your last name," she said. No way would she admit to a Googling addiction.

"No. You'd better go to your meeting. Don't want to get into trouble from the boss."

"Right." Meeting? What meeting? Miss Iceberg was now a puddle. "Yes. I'll call you."

"Gina?" He spoke quickly before she disconnected. "Are you all right? Today, I mean. After yesterday." The word *yes-*

terday was redolent with meaning. The slight hesitation between *after* and *yesterday* told her everything. He was embarrassed, too, but not angry, not ashamed and above all, not put off.

"Yes, fine. Thanks. I'm marvelous."

And she was. Now. Craig stared at her suspiciously when she joined the meeting, and she presumed it was because she was wearing a very wide smile.

Brad waited in the foyer of Gina's building the following Friday at twelve thirty. Low, wide, studded, black leather covered benches resembling single beds provided supremely uncomfortable seating in the enormous granite-floored space. On one vast wall a large, metal mobile sculpture revolved slowly and hypnotically. The elevators were tucked away at one end behind a timbered wall. A coffee shop operated at the other.

Brad sat close to the elevators so as not to miss her. All the women who strode past looked alarmingly similar. Businesslike, determined expressions, hair drawn back, dark conservative clothing, muttering to colleagues, clutching briefcases, forging ahead in their careers. Would he recognize Gina? If she wore her red suit again, he would.

The lunchtime traffic increased. Brad stood up clutching his food-laden green bag and wandered across to the glass wall facing Macquarie Street. How he hated the city. All those cars clogging the roads, buses and taxis shoving their way through the crush, people racing to get wherever, talking nonstop on mobiles, plugged into headphones. Fumes, rush, noise, noise, noise. More and more isolating for the individual. Society was on a downward spiral into chaos. What sort of future did his girls have?

This afternoon he'd make sure he got answers from Networks. Surprisingly, they'd phoned him, and he had an appointment with someone called Thelma Riley. Thank goodness there was no need to live here. Thank goodness the girls were breathing clean country air and learning solid social and community values. He may not have much spare cash but they didn't want for the really important things in life. Love, family and . . .

"Hello, Brad."

Chapter Five

She was in pale gray today with a yellow shirt under an open jacket. She'd tucked her hair sleek and smooth behind her ears, revealing small silver hoop earrings. A silver chain encircled her throat, a shiny black belt emphasized her neat figure. Pants suited her. Without the stilettos she was shorter. Her head came to his chin. The light, fresh fragrance she wore teased his memory, tantalized his senses.

"Hello, Gina." He almost leaned forward to kiss her cheek, but she held out her hand briskly so he shook that instead. Her fingers lay cool in his for the briefest of polite moments. "How are you?"

"Well. And you?"

"Fine, thanks."

She seemed nervous, kept glancing around the foyer and fidgeting with the handbag slung over her shoulder. The same one she'd had in the elevator. Maybe she thought someone she knew would catch her slumming, meeting a man who wasn't wearing a suit.

"Shall we go?" he asked, swallowing any disappointment that thought engendered. That's why he'd come after all, to find out these things. "It's such a lovely day I thought we could have lunch in the park." He lifted the green bag to show her he'd come prepared.

"Oh." Surprise followed by what? Dismay? Disappointment? Distaste?

"We can go to a restaurant if you'd prefer." Idiot! He could have given himself half a chance, should have realized a woman like Gina would want to eat inside at a table with proper service and a menu.

"No." She smiled, seemed to decide after a rapid assessment. "No. The park would be lovely. I don't see much of the day when I'm at work. The weather becomes irrelevant."

They headed for the doors. Relief lightened his voice. "That's a shame. Unnatural too."

"Not much choice for office workers." She rummaged in her bag and came up with sunglasses.

"I couldn't live like that."

"As I said, not much choice if you do the work I do." An edge in her tone to emphasize her point for the slower-witted. The glasses hid her eyes, masking her thoughts. They were brittle, he'd bet. She was brittle, just as she'd been when she entered the elevator. Still in overdrive. Work mode. Did she ever relax? Did she know what it even felt like?

The sun fell warm on his face, welcome after the manufactured chill of air-conditioning. He pulled his own glasses from his shirt pocket. She walked by his side down the wide steps to the footpath, and swung left to pause at the corner, waiting for the lights.

"We're closer to the Botanic Gardens," Gina said suddenly. "Let's go left."

Brad followed as she strode away. He had no idea if she was annoyed or eager. That impatient tread could mean either. The picnic lunch that had seemed so appropriate given her claustrophobia, may prove to be a complete miscalculation. Plus the food he'd brought might be totally wrong. She could have a million allergies or be a vegan. She might hate flavored spring water and fruit.

If that were the case, so be it. This was a debriefing after the elevator episode, to discover if there was anything to the chronic, lingering image in his head. A laying to rest of troublesome memories—that kiss and the feel of her body. Proving it was circumstance alone that had created such passion. Circumstance, opportunity, and enforced abstinence.

So far it was pretty obvious he wasn't rekindling any comparable emotion in Gina. Her whole demeanor screamed, "What am I doing with this guy? Let's get this over with as fast as possible." But she could have turned down his invitation.

She stopped at the next light. He stood beside her, and she looked up into his face suddenly and smiled. That wide, natural, lovely smile.

"I had no idea you were so famous," she said. Her hair shone in the sunlight. The mouth beneath the shades curved cheekily.

"I'm not." He laughed.

"You are. I Googled you."

"That sounds nasty."

This time she laughed. "On the Internet. I looked you up and found out you're a very well-respected artist in wood."

"Does that make me more acceptable?" He grinned as he spoke, but to his amazement the smile faded, and she looked away quickly. The crowd surged forward taking her with them. Brad hurried after her.

He caught her arm lightly as they stepped onto the pavement. "Sorry," he said as she said, "I'm sorry."

Her cheeks were pink. His fingers slid down the silky fabric of her sleeve. She began walking toward the entrance to the gardens, her stride less purposeful. Surely she wasn't such a snob. She'd been interested that day to discover he was an artist.

"That was a joke," he said.

Gina licked her lips. "I'm sorry. I was very rude to you in the elevator."

"Were you?" Had she been? If she had, whatever she'd said had been negated by what followed.

"I think so. Yes." She stopped walking and looked directly up at him.

"You're forgiven," he said, because it seemed to be what she needed from him.

"Really?" Two tiny, vertical creases formed in her brow above the dark glasses.

"Yes."

She nodded once, apparently satisfied by his response or her own admission, or both. The frown disappeared. "What's in the bag? I'm starving."

He grimaced. "I suddenly realized, belatedly, I had no idea whether you have any food allergies. I didn't think."

"I don't have allergies. I eat anything. What's in there?"

"Come and find out."

Brad led her across to a bench partially shaded by a gigantic, spreading Moreton Bay fig tree, facing away toward the harbor. Gina sat down and eagerly dived into the bag he placed between them on the green painted seat. She removed two chilled bottles, one berry-flavored spring water, the other lemon and lime, and set them down carefully. "Yum, I love this stuff."

Back into the green bag she went. Like a child at Christmas. Brad smiled as he watched her investigate. Two tubs of fruit salad and plastic forks, two small, round vegetarian quiches and two with bacon, two small tubs of Greek salad, fresh bread rolls, a selection of pastries featuring chocolate, caramel, fruit, and custard. Paper serviettes.

"I wasn't sure what you liked so I tried to cover all the bases. I was tempted to put in wine but you have to go back to work."

"This is wonderful." Her smile was so genuine he had to believe her. She waved an arm to indicate not only the food but also the stretch of emerald green lawn sloping gently away to another path and more towering trees. Sunlight cascaded through the leaves from a clear blue sky, its strength diluted to balmy warmth by the canopy. A gentle breeze tickled the hair round her face. She removed her jacket displaying pale-skinned, thin arms with knobbly wrists. "And you're right, it is the most beautiful day today."

"Yes. Plus I thought we should stay away from enclosed spaces."

"Oooh! I didn't realize." She gazed at him intently for a moment. "Thank you."

"You're welcome." He saw himself reflected in her dark lenses, staring at her, his face misshapen, his own glasses round black holes. "Help yourself."

And she did. She was either being very polite or she was very hungry, because only after ten minutes of solid, predominantly silent eating did Gina pause to wipe her fingers and mouth. "Excellent," she announced. "I was starving."

"Have another quiche."

"I will in a minute." She drank some lemon and lime flavored water and screwed the top back on thoughtfully. "So, Brad. What brings you into the city? You never did tell me why the first time."

"No, that's right." He wiped his mouth. "I was delivering a petition to the Networks head office."

Gina nodded, her expression suddenly serious, interested. "Why were you going there, to the head office instead of a shopfront? That would have been more public."

A familiar anger rose through his body. Impotent, frustrated rage aimed at those senseless, insensitive, greedy clods. "To get some answers from the bastards. Or try to. They're very good at keeping their plans to themselves even when what they do affects hundreds of people. They're setting up mobile phone antennas all over the place, and one of them is planned for Birrigai. Right next to the primary school—Fifi's school—and the local shops. Plus there's an aged-care home nearby too." He shook his head, exhaling in disgust.

"And you're objecting to it?"

His back straightened. "Me and everyone else in town. No one wants one of those lethal things nearby. Would you want to live or work underneath one?" He stared at her, demanding a reply.

She gave nothing away. Her expression, behind the glasses, was remote. No teasing grin accompanied her words now. "They're a necessary part of life these days. You like having a mobile phone and the Internet and all the rest of it, don't you?"

"I don't have a mobile phone or the Internet." How pompously self-righteous he sounded. But he honestly had no need of either.

Gina laughed. "Brad, you're positively Stone Age."

"Claire certainly thinks so but, seriously, you didn't answer my question. Would you like to live or work right under one of those towers?"

"There are so many in the city I probably already am." She leaned back against the seat and raised her face to the dappled sunlight. "Aah, this is lovely. So peaceful."

"But have you read about the effects?" he cried. "The waves literally cook your brain. I don't want my daughters exposed to that! Or anyone else's kids."

"A lot of that is uncorroborated fearmongering," she said without turning her head. Her tone indicated her boredom with the subject. Typical! City people's brains were already cooked. And she had no idea what peace really was—try the untrammeled Australian bush instead of city parkland masquerading as nature.

"So you don't believe it's a problem." Joan, on the committee, had the Internet, and she'd found all sorts of horrifying information.

She looked at him then, and her voice was firmer. "I'm not saying that, I'm saying you need to be careful with your facts and make sure they are facts. Networks has invested a lot of money in providing coverage. It's part of the contract they have with government." Now she was sitting straight, her back rigid.

Brad firmed his mouth and nodded. "We get to the bottom line," he said, emphasizing each word. "Money. If big money's involved, woe betide any little people getting in the way."

Gina leaped to her feet. "Of course money's involved. And it *is* big money. This is part of the country's infrastructure. What do you want?" Both arms gesticulated wildly as she made her points. "To compete in the world we have to have this technology. People demand it."

"I don't!" Brad thumped a fist onto his thigh.

Gina glared at him, her mouth twisted scornfully. "Well, you're not exactly up-to-date, are you? Poor telecommunications is one of the biggest customer complaints from country areas."

"How do you know so much about Networks?"

"They're clients of Bright and Caulfield. I was there that day, remember?"

"You work for them?" Gina was on their side! No wonder she was immune to his argument. Here he was thinking it was because she was a typically self-centered, money-oriented, career woman with no thought for those outside her business orbit, but it was worse. Far worse. "Was that your big important million-dollar meeting? With them?"

"No, that was with the another client. But the Networks contract was definitely a good one."

Brad slumped against the seat. "Good grief."

Gina sat down. She leaned back and crossed her legs and arms. Closing herself off from him and his ridiculous, doomed, knight's quest. Her stomach churned. She turned her wrist to look at her watch. Twenty minutes left. Why was she so bitterly disappointed? She knew he was a new age greenie type right from first sight. Why did she feel guilty? Dirty, even. What could she say?

"I don't work for Networks."

"But your firm does, or did, so it's splitting hairs, wouldn't you say? Did you evaluate Birrigai as a good place for a tower?"

"I can't discuss my work with you." There'd been so many little towns on that list—Lincoln would know. Or Sophie or Cherie. They'd done most of the footslogging. The places were numbers on a page to her. Did he know the government was reevaluating all the country area primary schools as well? She couldn't tell him that either or there'd be hell to pay. If the information went public before time and she was responsible . . . good-bye career.

Sirens screamed in the distance. Horns blared. Brad looked away toward the entrance gates. He obviously wanted to go. She'd become a pariah in his eyes in a matter of seconds. Fulfilled all his expectations.

"If you had children you'd understand." He spoke with the weary tone of someone beating their head continually against a brick wall. No one understands me, no one cares. Boo hoo. Gina gritted her teeth.

"Why is it," she asked carefully, "that people who produce children expect the whole world to revolve around their little darlings? Some of us don't want children or can't have children. Some of us have other things to do with our lives, other things that make the world a better place for your precious kids. What thanks do we get? None. Just that smug, patronizing, 'You don't understand. You don't have children.' "

"You don't," he said. He began packing the empty containers into the green bag. The pastries were untouched, the chocolate and custard softening in the warm air. "Would you like one of these?"

"No, thanks. Take them home for your daughters."

He looked at her sharply but didn't reply. Gina snatched up her drink and drained the last of the water, unpleasantly tepid and sticky now.

"I'd do anything to protect my girls," he said. "To keep them from harm. Your parents would do the same for you and mine for me. We can't help but feel that way. It's hard-wiring."

"I must be wired differently."

"I doubt it. It's a matter of priorities. And timing."

"Believe me the last thing I want is babies." She pulled a face.

"What *do* you want?"

"I want to be the best I can be. Run my own firm or be general manager or director of somewhere big. I'd love to move to our London or New York office. It's cutthroat. Especially for a woman. We have to be tougher and smarter and work harder."

"What about the collateral damage in your climb to the top?"

"There's always going to be someone who doesn't like progress. This is a democracy. For the good of society in general and all that."

"What total rubbish! Networks doesn't give a damn about the good of society. Networks wants to make heaps of money as cheaply as it can. Big companies have the psychological profile of a psychopath, did you know that?"

Gina shrugged. "Survival of the fittest. Businesses have to make money. Of course they do. It's how our economy functions. *You* have to make money."

"But I don't make my money by endangering the health of people."

"That's a pretty extreme claim, Brad. They're not our only client." She shook her head in frustration. "Without Networks the country would grind to a halt. We need the communications industry. Surely you understand that?"

"Of course I understand that. I'm not against telephones and progress. I'm not anti the Internet and TV. I'm not a Luddite. I object to the way these big corporations walk all over people and justify it by saying, 'We're doing it for you,' when they're patently not. Lines need to be drawn. Clear lines."

"You won't get anywhere with your protest, you know."

"All they have to do is put the tower somewhere else."

"They're not monsters and they prefer the public to be on their side. There's always a consultation period, so maybe if you suggest that they will."

"No. They won't. They say that's the only suitable site in the area and we're too late, the deadline for objections has passed. It's bull, but we're not giving up. They rang me to come in today so they must be worried about public opinion but only in as much as we're annoying them."

Gina sighed. He was right but he was too late. Places like Networks were expert in deflecting his kind of well-meaning but inexpert and doomed protest. When they made a decision they stuck to it, especially after the consultation period had passed.

"If you're in cahoots with them," he said suddenly, "could you give me a name to ask for. Someone with clout?"

"They'll fob you off regardless. And I'm not in cahoots with them. They were clients. It's business. They pay, we deliver. Just like you when someone wants a chair or a salad bowl." Petty and nasty. The look he gave her confirmed the immediate guilt for such a childish comment. Why did she always come across as mean-spirited in conversations with him? She wasn't mean or nasty, she was tough and businesslike. There was a difference.

More sirens wailed, closer, louder, and many in number. A fire? More likely a false alarm. The intrusion provided a distraction, a way to escape gracefully. Gina stood up. "I'll have to go back now. This was a lovely idea. Thank you very much."

"I'm sorry it ended in a free-for-all. It's nothing to do with you, it's my problem. Thanks for joining me." His voice was as stiffly polite as hers.

"I enjoyed it. Really." Gina offered a tentative smile.

His mouth flicked into the semblance of a smile for an instant. He picked up the green bag and started walking slowly across the lush grass toward the further path. Gina hesitated, then followed rather than turn her back on him and go the shorter way they'd arrived. They hadn't actually said good-bye, not properly.

Unless he thought they were parting ways here. Was she chasing after him when he'd rather be alone, thought he'd said good-bye and was free of her? His silence told her nothing. Was he annoyed, disappointed, bored? Impossible to tell. He paced along, his feet swishing casually in the thick green while her heels sank into the moist ground, forcing her to mince like a prize poodle.

"I'll walk you back to your office," he said.

Of course, he would whether he wanted to or not. He was old-fashioned, a gentleman. "You don't need to, but thanks."

The sirens increased to a shrill barrage of sound, coming at them in waves, unsettling and painful to the ears.

"That's an incredible racket," he said.

"Sounds like some sort of disaster." Gina veered right, walking faster to reach the solid path. Brad took her lead without comment. "Sometimes we get bomb scares and they evacuate us."

"Nasty."

"Insane."

They reached the street. A fire engine roared past, lights flashing, siren screaming. Two police cars followed. The trio careened around the corner and dived into the CBD.

Gina and Brad crossed at the lights and walked down the sloping street toward her building.

"Not us, thank goodness," said Gina as they reached the glass-walled entrance.

"I hope it's not Networks again. My appointment's with someone called Thelma Riley at two fifteen. Know her?"

Gina shook her head. "She's probably a PR person." No point saying more. He was determined to keep bashing his head on this particular brick wall.

"I'd better go." He removed his dark glasses and shoved them into his pocket. "Thanks for having lunch with me." He held out his hand, and she shook it firmly. Then he suddenly leaned forward and kissed her cheek. The breath she'd drawn stuck in her throat. His cheek pressed on hers for an instant, his fingers gripped tightly. Memories raced through her veins, crashing into her heart.

"Thanks," she murmured. "I . . ." She swallowed. He drew away. He wasn't smiling.

"I'd like to see you again," he said slowly. "If you would."

She nodded, licked suddenly dry lips. "Yes." Barely audibly. She tried again. "Yes, I think so. I would."

His sudden smile shattered her. Brown eyes, all warm and intimate gazed into hers, plunging effortlessly to her center, stealing the breath from her lungs, rendering her incapable.

"As long as you don't discuss telecommunication towers," she gasped over the hammering of her pulse.

A grin creased his cheeks and those perfect white teeth flashed as he laughed. "We're adding to our banned topics list, aren't we?"

"Banned topics?"

"Yes. You know . . ." He held her gaze firmly. "Things we've agreed not to mention ever again."

"Oh!" A telltale flush of heat crept up her face. "You promised."

"I haven't broken my promise. Not that one. Have you?"

"No!"

Brad laughed out loud at her vehemence. Gina drew her hand from his with a reluctant smile. "I'll call you," he said.

He stuck his dark glasses back on, began to move away. An idea sprang into her head. Perfect, reasonable, and true.

She said, "I was thinking of visiting your gallery in Sunderland. I want to find something special for my grandmother's eightieth birthday." Desperate? Now the words were out did she sound like a teenager trying to interest a boy?

He stopped and nodded. "Fine. Let me know when you're coming down, and I'll meet you there."

No amusement. He seemed pleased. Gina did a rapid calculation. "It'll have to be soon, her birthday's on the seventeenth."

"This weekend or the next?" His eyebrows lifted expectantly.

"Not this weekend." Tomorrow? Too soon, too much of a rush. She needed time to contemplate the idea of Brad Harding. She also had work to prepare for Monday. "Maybe next Saturday?" Back in control.

"Great. Will you drive?"

"Yes."

"It'll take about an hour to Sunderland. Have lunch with us. I'll do a barbecue." Spontaneous and friendly. Natural for him. Unnatural for her.

"Um. I don't want to impose. I really . . ." Control was lurching away from her again. He swamped her with his good-humored openness.

He held up his hand. "If you're coming all that way you may as well make a day of it. And I'd like you to see Birrigai," he added. "It's only about twenty minutes from Sunderland."

"I get it." Gina nodded, screwing up her lips. "I can't do anything about the unmentionable topic. Seeing Birrigai isn't going to make the slightest difference to decisions being made by . . . those other people."

"It's a lovely little town," he cried with feigned injured innocence. "And I want you to meet the girls." He smiled with such genuine enthusiasm she couldn't resist. Not that she was trying to resist, just to slow him down. Keep her foot on the brake.

But there was one inescapable fact. A veritable brick wall of a fact. This man came with attached daughters. They'd be enough to remind her of the reality of the situation if she was tempted to think of . . . intimate things. A relationship with him wouldn't go anywhere. They both knew that. But he was nice, and she was in need of a revitalized social life. Why turn down an invitation to spend a day in the country? With a friend.

And she really did need to find something special for the eightieth birthday gift. Grandma would be delighted with the story behind the purchase. Edited, of course.

Chapter Six

Both girls insisted on accompanying Brad to Sunderland to meet Gina when at breakfast the next day he told them she was coming to lunch the following weekend.

"We have to give her the test," announced Fifi.

"What test?"

"You said any woman you fell in love with had to pass our test," Claire said.

"I haven't fallen in love with Gina!"

"You might." Claire and Fifi exchanged grins and began to giggle.

"Gina's a friend. She wants to choose something at the gallery for her grandmother's birthday. I invited her to have lunch with us, that's all."

"Sure, Dad." More giggles.

"Have you collected the eggs yet?" he asked Claire sternly. "And are you eating that toast or playing with it?" He frowned at Fifi, which only elicited more laughter.

"Don't change the subject," ordered Claire. "And you're eating one of the eggs I collected."

"No, don't change the subject, Dad." Fifi chewed on her vegemite toast in between spurts of laughter.

"I thought we could go to the RSPCA today," he said casually. "But if you only want to talk about Gina, well . . ." He shrugged and forked up more fried egg.

"Yes! Can we?" Both girls sprang to attention.

"They may not have what we want," he warned.

"They always have kittens," said Claire.

"I want a black one," said Fifi. "All black with a white front."

"They may not have exactly that, poppet."

"We can see, can't we?" Big eyes stared up at him.

"Of course. We'll go after breakfast."

The girls were ready in record time, sitting in the car, seatbelts buckled, excitedly discussing kittens while Brad locked the house. He slammed the car door and turned the key. The elderly Volvo wagon wheezed and groaned. He tried again. Same thing. Three more tries and the engine barely turned over.

"Darn it. I'll have to get Matt to have a look on Monday. Sounds like the battery or the starter motor," Brad said. "Sorry, girls."

"That's okay, Dad," Claire opened the door and climbed out. "Can I go round to Amber's?"

"Back for lunch. You've got that English assignment."

"Okay."

"Is it broken badly?" asked Fifi from the backseat. She began unbuckling her seat belt.

"No. It's just old and bits wear out. Matt will fix it for us."

He got out and opened the door for her. "We'll have to go next weekend for our kitten."

"Gina can come too," said Fifi. She bounced out of the car leaving Brad standing, amazed. He'd expected disappointment and maybe even a tear but not that.

"She might not want to," he called as she disappeared around the corner of the house.

"She will," came floating back. He followed slowly. How would Gina react to this wholesale and premature acceptance of her as a contender for the role of mother to his daughters? She'd made it very clear children weren't in her immediate life plan. And a mother for his daughters hadn't featured in his, either. Certainly not Gina. He gave a disbelieving laugh at the bizarreness of the whole notion, shaking his head as he selected the house key from the bunch on the key ring.

Gina drove slowly along the main street of Sunderland peering at the shop fronts and signs. "Turn first left after the Red Dragon Chinese Restaurant," Brad had said. "Go two hundred yards and the gallery is on the right. Easy," he said. Maybe it was for the locals, but she was darned if she could see a Chinese restaurant anywhere.

Saturday morning and the place barely had a pulse. A few people wandered along the footpath peering into shop windows. A trickle of cars meandered by. Country towns like this gave her the creeps. Like ghost towns. Sure they were picturesque and undoubtedly had their attractions, but they were the sort of attractions that appealed to Gina for about ten minutes. Apart from the ubiquitous Chinese restaurant there'd be an arty little coffee shop with—she'd wager a week's pay—amateurish local artwork for sale on the walls, a pretty community park with flower beds and a rotunda, an antique/junk shop, and a small museum. Very often the best feature was a fifties-style café selling properly made hamburgers, good coffee, and milkshakes. After those delights she'd be looking for the road to the city.

An intersection loomed. A white painted sign pointed left with SUNDERLAND GALLERY printed on it. So much for the restaurant landmark. Gina swung left into a residential street lined with tall shade trees which almost met overhead. The narrow road wound away toward the surrounding bush-covered hills. One block. Two blocks. A larger version of the earlier sign told her she'd arrived.

A white weatherboard house with dark green trim and a dark red painted roof sat amidst lush gardens of hydrangeas, azaleas, irises, and lilacs. A small gravel parking area held several cars. Gina parked her Golf between a battered yellow Volvo wagon and a new looking silver Honda. Nice car. She'd investigated the same model before settling on the Golf.

Was Brad here waiting for her? With his daughters? She turned off the engine and sat for a moment steadying herself for the meeting, took a quick peek in the rearview mirror. Hair, okay. Makeup, fine. Casual outfit. Jeans, deep red linen blouse worn loose. Low-heeled red pumps, comfortable for driving. Jacket on the seat next to her in case it was cooler here.

Ten twenty. She'd aimed at ten thirty. Good. Time for a quick look around before they arrived. In case his work wasn't quite the same in reality as the photographs on the Web site. She could prepare a tactful decline to buy. "Nothing suitable, oh dear."

Her shoes scrunched on the white gravel path. A lovely old house, beautifully maintained. "Converted to a gallery ten years ago," Brad had said. She stepped onto the wooden verandah and in through the open door. Internal walls had been knocked down to provide a large display area. A young couple wandered slowly amongst the exhibits. A reception desk was tucked away on the right with brochures in a pile and a smiling gray-haired woman in attendance.

"Good morning," she said cheerfully. "You wouldn't be Gina by any chance?"

"Uh. Yes, I am."

"Excellent. I'm Judith. Brad and the girls are through the back in the courtyard." Large, arty, blue ceramic earrings swung wildly as she turned her head and waved her arm toward a sliding glass door.

"Thank you." Gina smiled with uncertainty. Was her visit common knowledge? She glanced about. Beautiful, glowing pieces stood on display—all sculptures made from wood. Some were polished and smooth, others with the rough, natural bark texture featured as part of the design. "Are these Brad's?"

"Some are. There are three artists represented here." Judith handed Gina a printed catalogue. "His furniture is through that door." She pointed to the right. "Lovely pieces. He's very much in demand. By far our most famous exhibitor. We're lucky he's happy to stay with us. He could easily be selling his work in overseas galleries."

"Really?"

"Oh, yes. He had a very successful exhibition in London several years ago." She lowered her voice. "Before Elaine died, actually. Now he's devoting himself to the girls and says he's not worried about fame and fortune." She shook her head. The earrings looked about to deliver a knockout blow. "Such a tragedy."

"Yes." Gina edged away. How did this lumpy woman in the vibrant orange caftan know she knew anything about Brad's private life? And what had he told her about his new friend from the city? Were country people all such gossips? What on earth was she getting into by coming here? She'd have to be careful not to give the wrong impression. Not to seem overly interested in him. Not that she was. She was here on a mission.

She studied the list of artworks. Brad's were numbered from twenty to twenty-six. She wandered around the room until she came to his pieces. Quite abstract, they'd obviously grown from inside the timber just as he'd mentioned in the elevator. The smooth shapes twisted gracefully along lines only nature could have produced. He seemed to have brought out the inherent beauty without imposing any sort of structure—yet they were structured, in a completely natural way. Fascinating.

She moved slowly from one to the next, totally absorbed. No wonder he was so much in demand. Grandma would love one of these. In fact, she'd love one for herself. Buy two. But which ones? How could she choose? Gina studied the list again. They were all priced at $550. Very reasonable. Especially if he was as famous as Judith Orange Caftan said. Could appreciate considerably over the years. Good investment.

But she should check out the furniture.

Chattering childish voices broke her concentration. A small dark-haired girl in a pink dress burst into the room from a rear entrance. She stopped when she spied Gina and darted back to call to someone outside, "She's here."

Gina licked her lips and swallowed. That must have been Fifi. How did they all know immediately who she was? Then Brad was there smiling in the doorway with the small girl bouncing by his side clutching his hand, and another, taller one, coming through behind. At the sight of him Gina's lungs contracted, her heart lurched and settled. In self-defense she tore her gaze from Brad to the older daughter. Must be the troublesome one, Claire. Pretty. Swaggering with casual nonchalance in jeans and a cropped white T-shirt. Lovely smooth creamy skin and gorgeous dark eyes. Like her father's.

"You made it," Brad said, scouring Gina with those lethal weapons. She kept her eyes away from his. How did he make her feel so weak and wobbly just by looking at her? Since when had the sight of him made it difficult to breathe? When had that begun to happen? Think kids. Two. No way!

"Yes. I had a good run out of the city."

"Any run out of the city is a good one." He laughed, displaying those amazing teeth. And she'd forgotten those lips. And the crinkly smile lines. She looked away hastily and caught Claire's curious gaze instead.

"I'm Fiona," piped up the little one. Gina switched her attention downward. What a sweetie! Cute as could be. Fluffy mop of curls, the family brown eyes surrounded by dark lashes.

"Hello. I'm Gina."

"I know. And you have a cat called Big Al."

"Yes." Gina laughed in astonishment.

"We're getting a kitten today. Do you want to come with us?"

"Fifi! Shush." Brad grimaced. "Sorry," he said. "This is Claire."

"Hello, Claire."

Claire smiled and held out her hand. Gina shook it, conscious of a comprehensive stock take of her outfit.

"Hi."

"Have you been here long?" asked Brad.

"A few minutes. I was looking . . ." She gestured awkwardly toward the exhibits. "They're wonderful. I'd love to buy something, but I can't decide."

"Thanks, but don't feel obliged." Brad sounded equally as uncomfortable. "Have you seen the furniture?"

"No, I was just thinking I should have a look before I make a decision."

"Show her the rocking chair, Dad," said Claire. She turned to Gina. "That'd be perfect for your grandmother."

Gina laughed. "My grandma doesn't need a rocking chair yet, Claire. She'd be quite offended if I gave her one."

"Oh." Her face fell.

"Is she still active?" Brad asked.

"Very. She did the Harbour Bridge climb last year and she practices Tai Chi every morning."

"Good for her."

"Yes."

"Maybe she'd like a salad bowl or a stool," said Claire, recovering quickly. "She eats salad doesn't she? And sits down sometimes?"

"Sure does, and that sounds like a good idea," said Gina. "Show me."

To her surprise Fiona grabbed her hand and dragged her after Claire into the adjoining room. Gina threw a glance over her shoulder at Brad who was following close behind. "Are your girls always so friendly?" she half-whispered.

"No, they like you," he said.

"They don't know me at all."

"They can tell."

She was about to ask what they could tell, but Claire and Fiona had deposited her in front of a collection of three-legged stools and beautiful, elegant chairs with curved backs flowing up from the seats in a variety of ways.

"Goodness," she said.

"I was experimenting with shapes."

"Sit on one," ordered Claire.

Fiona perched on one of the stools grinning madly and swinging little sandal-clad feet.

"Can I? They look too beautiful to use."

"Of course you can," Brad said. "They're stronger than they look."

Gina tested each chair carefully, wriggling her bottom and leaning back. "Very comfortable," she announced. "But Grandma has too much furniture, she says."

"The bowls are over here." Claire beckoned from another doorway.

Fiona grasped Gina's hand and pulled her off the chair. "I'll show you," she said.

"Thank you."

Brad appeared content to allow his daughters full rein. He wandered along behind as Claire acted as tour guide-cum-sales lady telling Gina the types of wood and the techniques used in the making.

"Gosh, you know a lot about your dad's work," said Gina.

Claire glanced at Brad who was watching from the doorway.

"Can't help it," she said. "There's wood everywhere at our house."

"Are you going to buy one of my daddy's bowls for your grandma?" asked Fiona.

"I am and I'm also going to buy one of those beautiful sculptures in the other room for myself."

"Which bowl?"

"Why don't you two choose for me. I can't decide." Gina smiled at the two eager faces. They were very alike—same delicate arching eyebrows, same straight nose and brown eyes. Where Fiona's face still had the soft roundness of babyhood Claire's had begun to take on more definite lines. A strong character emerging from the cocoon of childhood.

"This one," said Fiona. She picked up a flattish bowl of a lovely dark wood, even and smooth in color and grain.

"I like this one best." Claire held up a deeper dish-shaped bowl with a striking pattern of knotholes and flaws in the glossy surface.

"Gosh. I still can't decide." Gina laughed, shaking her head. "Fiona's would suit Grandma's things best but I love that one, Claire. I'd better take both."

"Daddy, Gina's buying two bowls."

"Are you sure?" Brad eased away from the doorframe where he'd been leaning.

"Absolutely. They're beautiful. Grandma will love this one. And I love that one."

"And Gina wants a sculptor too," piped up Fiona.

"Sculpture, dopey. Not sculptor," said Claire. "Dad's the sculptor."

"Gina might want Daddy."

Brad growled, "Shush, you two." Fiona and Claire giggled hysterically while Brad chivvied them ahead of him.

Gina followed, clutching her two bowls in stiff hands. Was there an ulterior motive here? These two were lovely children, but they seemed excessively interested in her. Not that she knew much about kids of any age, but the twelve-year-old was nothing like she'd expected from Brad's description. Claire was enormously proud of her father and his work. She couldn't fake that. She was polite, well-mannered and well-spoken, and little Fiona was plain adorable, if a bit clingy.

Why was she feeling a tad uneasy and uncomfortable with such overt friendliness? Was it her? Or them?

The family had stopped in the main room in front of Brad's sculptures.

"Which one will you buy?" asked Fiona.

"I'm not sure." Gina walked slowly around the display. Fiona followed close behind.

"Look at this one, Gina. It's lovely," she said running her little hand over a tall arching, branchlike piece. "Or this one." She ran to the next.

"Let Gina think for a minute," said Brad.

"But Gina doesn't mind us helping, do you, Gina?" Fiona stared up at her earnestly.

"Well . . . I wouldn't mind having a quiet think." She flashed a quick glance at Brad to see his reaction.

"Take Fifi outside please, Claire," said Brad.

"Ooohh," began Fiona and her lip trembled.

"Come on." Claire headed for the rear door. "Let's look for butterflies."

"Sorry." Brad stood beside her, anxiety creasing his brow. "They can be a bit overwhelming."

Gina smiled faintly, but said nothing. Nothing worse than a whining child. She turned to the pieces. "Which is your favorite?"

Unhesitatingly he selected a contorted, knobbly lump with highly polished protrusions and a beautifully smooth central cavity partially hidden away. From some angles it was completely obscured, from others more visible.

"If you look at it this way," he said, "the center is completely exposed. I like the way this has different meanings and different ways of presenting itself. It's a complex piece of wood, very old and weathered, with lots of contrasting facets and I tried to bring that out. Like people. From some angles a person can be sharp and hard and tough, unapproachable, but if you come at them the right way they're the opposite—all open and vulnerable."

Gina stared at the piece. The way he described it brought a wealth of meaning to the planes and angles, the rough and smooth places, the areas left unpolished and those glossy and hard. "It's fantastic," she murmured. "I had no idea you were so . . ." She stopped, embarrassed yet again by her early tactless assumptions based on his appearance and demeanor.

He put the piece back in its place, shrugged. "I don't have much of an idea about you either," he said softly.

Gina snorted gently. "What you see is what you get with me."

"I don't think so. Not at all."

"No?"

"Definitely not."

"What do you see?" she asked curiously.

"I'll tell you later," he murmured as Orange Caftan approached, with an all-devouring smile.

"Have you found something you like, Gina?" she asked. Her other two customers had consumed her attention up until now. Having sold them a stool she was free to concentrate on this new and fascinating friend of Brad's. Her chumminess made Gina retreat into chill politeness.

"Yes. I'll take these bowls, please, and that piece." She pointed at the lump of wood Brad had just replaced.

"Lovely. They're marvelous, aren't they? I just love coming in here every day to work."

"I can imagine," Gina said.

Brad laughed. "You'd hate it. You'd be bored rigid in ten minutes."

That made her smile. She shared a glance with him. "Probably. It's very quiet."

"That's exactly what I love," said the woman. "Can't stand the noise and clamor of the city. These days, with the Internet, it doesn't really matter where the business is housed. We do quite a number of international sales from the Web site. Especially of Brad's work. He needs to clone himself and we'd all make a fortune."

"Your prices seem very reasonable. Perhaps you should charge more," Gina suggested.

Brad said, "Judith keeps telling me that, but I refuse to overprice my work."

Judith rolled her eyes. "He's hopeless." She punched figures into the cash register. "Six hundred and fifty-eight dollars, thank you, Gina."

Gina frowned. "Is that right? I thought it was more."

"It's right," said Brad firmly.

"Are you giving me a discount?" she demanded.

"Well . . ."

"You don't need to do that!"

"I always do that for friends," he said defensively. "Judith knows that."

Gina sucked in a breath, exhaled. No wonder he wasn't making any money. Still it was none of her business. She handed Judith her credit card. "Thank you. Unnecessary and unexpected, but thank you."

"I'll fetch the girls." Brad headed away through the gallery.

"Will we be seeing more of you?" asked Judith as she packed the salad bowls carefully in tissue paper and placed them in a large carry bag.

"I'm not sure." Gina clamped her mouth closed to avoid telling Judith that was none of her business.

"It's so nice to see Brad with a girlfriend, finally." Judith bent down behind the counter and reappeared with a sheet of bubble wrap. "He's such a lovely man, it's a wonder he hasn't been snapped up. To tell you the truth he just hasn't been interested in finding another woman. Too busy with those daughters." She began wrapping the sculpture, wielding sticky tape and scissors. "But they need a mother. Girls need a woman in their lives especially as they reach the teens." She lowered her voice and leaned forward slightly, a conspirator. "And it's been five years. That's a long time without . . . you know." Orange painted lips creased in a knowing smile.

"I'm not Brad's girlfriend," said Gina clearly when Judith stopped to draw breath. "I'm not interested in a relationship with Brad, and I'm certainly not interested in being a mother to his girls. We're friends." And she certainly wasn't interested in a relationship with a man whose personal life, not to mention sex life, was the subject of town gossip and speculation.

"Oh. Excuse me!" Judith's face turned a fascinating shade of puce, which clashed violently with the caftan. "I hope you make your position clear to him, then, and don't lead him on."

"I don't think my relationship with Brad or anyone else is any concern of yours." Gina produced her brain-shriveling glare. Should have the same effect on this woman, but she didn't have a chance to find out. Brad and the girls reappeared.

"Ready?" He picked up the large wrapped bundle. "Thanks, Judith. See you on Wednesday."

"Good-bye, girls. Bye, Brad."

"Thank you," said Gina politely. Judith nodded with tightly pursed, disapproving lips.

Outside Brad headed for the yellow station wagon. "Which is your car?" he asked.

Gina pressed her remote, and the Golf's lights flashed. She lifted the hatch so Brad could deposit her sculpture carefully in the back. She rested the carry bag with the bowls next to it.

"Thank you," she said.

"We're going to get our kitten now," said Fiona.

"Are you?" Where did that leave her? Was the barbecue lunch invitation still valid?

Brad said, "The RSPCA shelter is here in Sunderland, so I thought while we were in we'd go and have a look. Shouldn't take long, then we'll head home for lunch. Everything's ready."

"Can I ride with Gina?" asked Claire. "I can show her where to go."

Gina smiled at Claire who had moved toward the Golf. That was friendly of her.

"I want to," cried Fiona.

"You don't know the way," scoffed Claire.

"Can I go with Gina, Daddy?" The five-year-old voice rose in a whiney wail. Good grief. Why did people want children? The simplest things turned into sibling wars. Gina opened her mouth to say she'd drive by herself, but Brad intervened firmly.

"No. You come with me, and Claire can go with Gina. If Gina doesn't mind."

"Fine with me." What on earth do you talk to a twelve-year-old about?

Claire smirked at her sister and piled into the front seat of the Golf. By the time Gina opened the driver's door she was buckled in and investigating the CD player.

"This is so cool," she said. "What music have you got?"

Gina clipped her seat belt. Here's where her object-of-interest rating plummeted. "Nothing you'd like. Opera."

"Opera?" The look was to be expected. But not the next comment accompanied by a pleased grin. "Dad likes opera."

"Does he?" Gina started the engine and waited while Brad backed out next to her.

"I don't mind some of it," said Claire doubtfully and very politely. Brad had brought his girl up extremely well.

Gina slipped her a sideways glance. "I have a secret passion for Italian tenors. They're incredibly romantic."

"Really?"

"Yes. You must have heard 'Nessun Dorma.' Listen to this."

Gina pressed the play button, and the glorious music burst into the car.

Claire cried delightedly, "I've heard that. The winner of *Australian Idol* sang it."

"Gosh." What on earth was *Australian Idol*? The name was vaguely familiar.

"I didn't vote for him. I liked someone else. Dad wouldn't let me vote anyway. He said the show was dumb."

"What is it? *Australian Idol*." Gina rarely turned on her TV. The news and the occasional movie was her limit. She twisted around to peer out the rear window, then backed out and followed Brad as he turned right from the car park.

"It's a singing competition on TV. They audition people all over the country, and then people vote for who they think is best. They have judges first and they pick the top twelve."

"Pop music?" It must be if twelve-year-old Claire was interested in it.

"Yes."

"And one of them sang 'Nessun Dorma'?"

"Yes."

"He must be pretty good if he managed this aria," said Gina. They were back on the main street now heading on through the town. "Why was he singing opera?" Although "Nessun Dorma" had become part of the popular domain since Pavarotti belted it out at the World Cup Soccer final, years ago.

"He is good." Claire sat back with a pleased expression. Somehow Gina had said the right thing. "They had a judge's song choice show, and they chose it because they said it really suited his voice."

"I see. Which music do you listen to?" Not that she'd know any of the names.

"Me and my friends, we listen to tunes—whoever does them—not really favorite bands. But I like Pink, Guy Sebastian—he won *Australian Idol* one year, Beyoncé, Nope . . ."

"They're Australian, aren't they?" She'd seen a poster advertising their concerts and proclaiming them as the next Aussie sensation. She'd looked twice and laughed because the name contradicted the glowing PR statements.

"Yes." Another tick for Gina. "I'd love to go to a concert, but Dad won't let me go to the city, and they never come here."

"Wouldn't he take you?"

Claire snorted. "No."

"I guess he has his reasons," murmured Gina. No way was she taking sides in this obviously well-worn argument.

"Stupid ones."

"That's not very nice, Claire."

"All my friends get to go to concerts and things. I wish I lived in the city or at least somewhere better than Birrigai."

Gina said nothing. She couldn't. She wholeheartedly sympathized with Claire. The tenor had moved on from Puccini to Verdi. Another favorite aria, but two in a row might be pushing her luck.

"You can turn the CD off if you like."

Claire pressed buttons, and suddenly jangly, boppy pop music erupted into the car. She began singing along softly.

They'd left the town limits now. An orchard stretched beside the road on the right, a field with horses behind a white post and rail fence on the left.

"How far is it to the RSPCA shelter?"

"About five minutes."

"What sort of cat do you want?"

"Fifi wants a black one with a white front."

"What about you?"

"I don't mind. Dad says we should get a female because they're cleaner."

"Big Al's clean. He spends his time eating, sleeping, or washing himself."

"Turn there," said Claire.

The yellow station wagon blinked its left light, slowing for the turn. Gina followed along the dirt road, which lead up a slope to a low-lying building sprawled amongst tall gumtrees. A sign said OFFICE. Another building stood at right angles and was obviously a kennel.

Gina parked beside the Volvo. Fiona and Brad were already out and walking slowly toward the office. Barking in a variety of pitches came from the kennels.

"I feel sorry for all the ones left behind," said Gina to Claire.

"It's sad," agreed Claire. "But someone like us might come and take them home."

"They might."

Brad was waiting with the door held open. He smiled as Gina passed through. Her shoulder brushed his chest. His outstretched arm was almost around her body, almost hugging her. A familiar smell of aftershave on skin sent tingles of memory through her nerve endings. That kiss. Wild, passionate, unexpected, and unstoppable. Implanted in her brain.

She looked up. His face was close, lips smiling, eyes meeting hers. Open, warm, inviting. Remembering?

She wanted desperately to kiss him. No.

"Okay?" he said softly.

"Sure."

"We want a kitten, please," said Fiona to the man who appeared from a back room and stood behind the counter.

He smiled down at her. "Do you indeed? You've come to the right place."

"A black one with white on it."

"I'm not sure about that," he said. He looked at Brad and Gina. "Come through here and you can see what we've got."

The room was full of cages and the cages were full of cats. Big ones and small ones in every color. They pressed against the wire mesh, mewing for attention.

"They all want to come with us," cried Fiona. She squatted down to peer into the lower-level cages. "These are big ones. Hello, pussycats."

"The kittens are over here," said the man.

Claire and Fiona darted across to where he was opening a larger cage on the upper level.

"These are five weeks old. Ready to go. We have two older ones. About three months." He held up two tabby cats and gave one each to the girls. "These are harder to place. The cats are almost impossible. Everyone wants the kittens."

"They're so cute," cried Claire rubbing her cheek against the soft fur.

"Mine's purring," said Fiona. "Can we have this one?"

"I can see this is going to be very difficult," said Brad.

"Didn't you want a black one?" asked Gina. "Do you have a black kitten?" She turned to the assistant.

"No. I'm sorry. Looks like black and white is the closest.

Like this." He picked out a tiny scrap of white fur with patches of black.

"Can I hold it?" Fiona thrust her tabby cat at Gina and leaned forward to examine the kitten. "It's so tiny!" She touched a finger to its head gently.

Brad took the tabby from Gina. "Sorry," he said. "She's excited." He put it back into its cage. Claire handed him hers. She walked along the rows of cages peering into each one. Gina followed. Easy not to think about kissing when children were around. The world's best passion killer.

"This one's pretty," she said staring at a little tortoiseshell kitten sitting primly in the center of its pen. A wayward sandy stripe meandered down between its eyes, and one paw had a patch of the same on a basic body color of dark chocolate with stripes and splodges of lighter brown and sandy cream.

"Ooh, yes!" cried Claire. "Can we hold this one, please?"

The assistant opened the cage. Claire lifted the little cat out and immediately a deafening purr emerged from the tiny body.

"Goodness, that's loud." Gina laughed. "It likes you."

"This one is a female. She's seven weeks old."

"Look, Fifi." Claire carried the kitten to her sister who was still clutching the black and white one.

"I want this one," cried Fiona.

"Dad?" Both girls turned to Brad.

He drew in a large breath and glanced at Gina for help. She shrugged and grinned. "Not my problem," she said.

"Thanks a lot."

"You could always take both of them," she suggested.

"Yes, Dad!" The chorus was in perfect unison.

"Thanks even more."

"You're welcome."

His eyes bored into hers for a moment, hiding laughter. Private, just between the two of them. "We can't have two cats," he said firmly to his girls. "We came for one and that's what we'll take."

"Why can't we have two?" Fiona's voice was heading for the familiar whiney end of the scale.

"Because I don't want two cats."

"I think I'll leave you to sort this out," said the assistant. "Bring out the one you decide to take." He beat a hasty retreat. Gina watched him go. Could she sneak out as well? She took a step backward and examined a fluffy gray cat through the wire mesh.

"Why don't you want two cats?" demanded Claire.

Brad held her gaze. How could he make her understand it was a money thing without broadcasting his financial state to Gina. Although . . . Gina already knew he wasn't a millionaire, and what was to be gained by pretending he had more money than he did? She wasn't stupid, far from it, and she probably had a pretty shrewd idea of his value in dollars and cents. She only needed to take a look at the Volvo.

He'd favored her with his "money isn't important speech" in the elevator so this was pure male pride. But it was a much more difficult statement to make than he'd imagined. The sum they were discussing was half what Gina had paid so blithely for his pieces.

He glanced away from Claire at Gina's back. She was bending over peering into one of the cages. He wanted to impress her the way a boy wants to impress a girl. He wanted to kiss her. From the first moment he saw her at the gallery, he wanted to get her alone and ravish her.

"Dad? Why?" Claire asked again.

He said in a tight voice, "Because they cost a lot to look after. Vet bills and things. They both have to be desexed. And I know who's going to be looking after them. Me."

Gina didn't make any acknowledgment whatsoever. But why should she become involved? Just because she'd agreed to tag along on this excursion didn't mean she was willing to take part in family business. Or that she was in any way interested in him or his personal affairs. He'd assumed too much. By the look on her face she wanted to escape the way the assistant had. Or perhaps he'd made it very clear he was not a good prospect in any shape or form.

Claire stared back at him for a moment, then suddenly turned and put the kitten in its cage. "Take Fifi's," she said. She closed the cage door and stomped out of the room.

"Are we having this one?" cried Fiona.

"Looks like it," said Brad. Oh, Claire. He'd blown it again. She was so volatile these days. He cast a despairing look at Gina who lifted her eyebrows. "Would you . . ." He gestured helplessly toward the door. "I'd better get this sorted."

Gina gulped. Soothe a cranky twelve-year-old? How? But he looked so in need of assistance, even hers, inexpert and inept as it would be. "Sure."

Claire was standing in the driveway, staring out over the paddocks. She didn't turn when Gina approached although she must have heard her footsteps on the gravel. Gina stopped beside the still figure. The lower lip was set in a stubborn, hurt pout.

What on earth could she say? It was sure to be wrong—she had no idea.

"She always gets what she wants," Claire said suddenly. "She's the favorite."

"Oh no, I don't think so," Gina blurted in surprise. "Your dad adores both of you. When we were in that elevator he talked about you all the time."

"Did he?" The sulky face turned her way slightly.

"Yes. In fact . . ." Gina paused, weighing her next comment.

"What?" A flicker of interest replaced the pout.

"Between you and me, I was a getting a bit sick of him going on and on about you—I don't have any kids." Gina tried a grin at Claire and received a little giggle in response.

"Don't you like kids?"

"I don't know any except my friend Cathy's baby, Shelley. She puked on my favorite sweater."

"Yuck." Claire pulled a face and laughed.

"Yes." Gina nodded. "Very yuck. I had to get it dry-cleaned to get the smell out. It's a really lovely cashmere cable. Hot pink."

"Ooh, I've got hot pink shorts. I love hot pink. My friend Amber has a baby sister. She's got three sisters and they're all younger. Georgia's ten, Sarah's four, and Felicia is nearly two. Sarah threw up on Amber when she was ready to go to a party. All over her dress."

"Gosh! Poor girl." Four? The parents must be insane. "That's a big age gap."

"Amber and Georgia have a different father than Sarah and Felicia." Very matter-of-fact. Perhaps there were lots of broken and rejoined families among her peer group. "Do you have any brothers and sisters?"

"One brother, Oliver."

"I wish I had a brother."

"Why?"

"A brother would be more fun than a little sister." The lip curled in distaste.

"I always wanted a sister," said Gina. "Someone to talk about boyfriends with and share clothes and things."

"Fifi's too small to do that. And she can't keep secrets. She tells Dad everything."

Secrets? Gina's neck prickled in alarm. Was she going to be confided in about some teenage plot, or worse still, disaster? "She won't always be five," she said feebly.

"No, but she'll always be a baby," Claire said viciously.

Fiona's piping voice called, "Claire, Gina. We're going now."

"Can I ride with you again?"

Gina looked down at the pleading face. "Of course you can." Poor kid, she maybe had a point. Fiona certainly had her father wrapped around her cute little finger. Claire wasn't sweet and biddable any more. She had character and strength and she was stepping into a world Brad knew nothing about. The world of the teenage female. She needed support, and Gina doubted she was getting enough of it.

Fiona was already strapped in to her seat. Brad was placing the cat carry box carefully in the back of the station wagon. Claire stalked straight to the Golf pointedly ignoring her father. Gina clicked the remote, and she flung the passenger door open and got in. Gina waited while Brad closed the back of the Volvo.

"Thanks," he said quietly. "I don't know what to do about

Claire sometimes. I'm sorry to offload her on to you." Concerned creases appeared in his brow.

"She's fine," said Gina. And she was. Surprisingly fine. Somehow she and Claire had made a tentative connection.

"Really?" The brown eyes lightened and he smiled. He touched her arm briefly. "Knew they'd like you."

"I didn't."

Brad held her gaze. "How could they not?"

It was a glib remark, but his expression had an underlying seriousness she didn't want to deal with at the moment. Not given the way lust hovered just beneath the surface. Her surface. They were friends, light and breezy.

Gina grimaced. "Easily, believe me. I'm not a kid person."

He laughed. "Come on. Home for lunch." He turned away.

But kid person or not, she could see Claire was a girl in need of a cheer squad, or at least some special attention of the nonjudgmental variety.

"Brad." Gina licked her lips nervously but it had to be said, right or wrong. "I think you were a bit rough on Claire—about the kitten, I mean."

He frowned. "I don't want two cats, Gina."

"I know—it's just that—well, couldn't you have taken the one she liked? She feels Fiona gets her own way all the time."

Brad studied her for a moment. "Fifi doesn't get her own way all the time."

"She thinks Fiona's your favorite."

Brad sucked in a breath. His eyes narrowed slightly. He was annoyed; she'd gone too far. Cripes, what was he going to say? Gina clamped her mouth firmly closed, waited for the explosion. But she wasn't sorry she'd spoken up for Claire.

"Gina, with all due respect, you really don't know anything about us. Claire says all sorts of things that don't have much connection to reality. You know what kids that age are like. They exaggerate and take everything personally. Everything's a drama."

"Okay. It just seemed . . ." She stopped. "Sorry. You're right. Forget I mentioned it."

"I will." But the look he gave her before he got into the Volvo hinted he would do nothing of the sort.

Chapter Seven

Brad drove home with Gina's words churning in his mind. What did she know about his family? About children? Nothing. She admitted as much in the elevator. Not just knew nothing, wanted to know nothing. Wanted nothing to do with them. More interested in her career.

"Is the kitty all right in the box, Daddy?"

"Yes, it's fine," he replied absentmindedly.

"It's squeaking."

"It's fine, Fifi. Don't worry."

"Can I hold it?"

"No."

"Why? It wants me to cuddle it, Daddy."

"It's dangerous to drive with the kitten loose in the car. It'd be frightened."

"Are you cross?"

"No."

"You sound cross. Don't you like our kitty cat?"

128

"Yes, of course I do."

"Good."

Was Gina right? Claire had been so excited about getting the kitten and then walked out just when they made the decision. Gave up and let Fifi have her way. Affecting disinterest, he was sure. Did that happen often? Too often? And when she did dig in her heels, did he side with Fifi because she was smaller? Brad sighed. He glanced in the rearview mirror. The red Golf was tailing them with the two girls sitting side by side. Too far back to see their expressions. Good for Claire to talk to a woman, wasn't it? As long as Gina didn't undermine his authority with her well-meaning but misguided, inexperienced opinions.

"Why are you frowning?"

"Fifi, how about we let Claire name the kitten?"

"Claire wanted the other one."

"I know. That's why it's fair if she chooses the name."

"It was pretty, but I wanted this one."

"Yes."

Brad drove straight into the garage when they reached the house. Gina pulled up behind him in the driveway. He helped Fifi out and then went to open the back and retrieve the now more-than-squeaking kitten.

"Claire, Daddy says you can name our kitty," cried Fifi.

Claire closed the door of the Golf. "Can I?" A tremulous smile hovered. She looked at Gina, who grinned.

"Better have a proper look at it first," she said.

Brad, carrying the cat box, led the troupe to the back door. "Open up, Claire, please," he said.

She took the keys from his outstretched fingers.

Gina stood back as the girls and Brad took their new pet

inside. She held the door for Fiona and then closed it behind herself. They were in the laundry. Quite large. White tiles, black border pattern, washing machine, sink. No dryer. A mop, a blue bucket, and a broom leaning against the wall in the corner, several pairs of boots and shoes in different sizes in an untidy heap by the door.

"This might be a good place to unload," Brad said. He squatted down and put the box on the floor. The girls hovered anxiously while he unclipped the foldover lid. The kitten mewed and tried to climb up the sides.

"It's all right, kitty, don't be frightened," crooned Fiona.

"We'll leave her in there while we set up a bed for her," said Brad.

"It's all ready," said Claire. She darted away and came back with a cut down cardboard box lined with a towel.

"She'll need a saucer for milk too," said Gina.

"We've got one already." Fiona all but hopped up and down in her excitement. "Can I hold her?"

"Gently lift her out and put her in her box," Brad said.

Fiona clutched the soft round body in two little hands and carefully placed her on the towel. The kitten stood uncertainly gazing about with wide, blue eyes. It took two tottery steps then sat down abruptly. The girls laughed.

"What will you call her, Claire?" asked Gina.

"I don't know. I'll have to think about it." She knelt beside the box and touched a very gentle finger to the fluffy little body. Immediately a loud rumbling purr started up. Fiona chortled with delight and clapped her hands.

"She likes you, Claire."

Gina glanced at Brad. He was watching his daughters with so much love she had to look away. She could never be part of such a family. She'd never experience the joys of parent-hood. Telling herself she didn't care always worked before.

"I'd better get the barbie started," Brad said.

"I'll help."

"Make sure you keep the back door closed so she doesn't get out. We'll keep her indoors until she gets used to us."

"Okay, Daddy." Neither girl looked up.

Gina followed Brad through to the kitchen. Compared to hers it was a mess. No cleaning lady here. Breakfast dishes stacked in the draining rack, an untidy pile of what looked like accounts mixed with brochures sprawling on the cream laminated bench. A child's picture book fallen open on the floor. A soft floppy doll leaned against the bread bin, and sundry colored crayons, textbooks, and the newspaper were strewn randomly about the floor and table. The fridge was adorned with postcards, reminders, Post-it notes, magnets, a school excursion letter, and photos.

On closer examination the floor was clean, the bench was clean, and the dishes were ready to be put away, but still . . .

If Brad noticed her critical perusal he didn't comment. He went to the cupboard over the bench and took out a box of matches.

"We'll go out the side door," he said. "Oh, sorry. If you need it, the bathroom's down the hallway and second on the right."

"Thanks. I'll go."

"Come out to the garden through the dining room—just there." He pointed to an arched doorway leading into another room.

Gina went down the hallway and discovered the toilet and separate bathroom next to it. They were both scrubbed clean and a neatly folded yellow guest towel sat on the vanity unit. She washed her hands and splashed cool water onto her face, patted it dry, and refreshed her lipstick.

Nice old house sitting in the midst of a large block of land. High ceilings, cool in summer—especially with the overhanging trees and shrubs giving shade. Lovely, old-fashioned molded plasterwork around the cornices. Neat white paintwork, the doorframes were the natural timber, stripped back and varnished. Brad was obviously a handy man; he would be, of course. The mess was superficial, caused by children.

Gina headed for the dining room, peeping into the living room opposite on the way. Two large squashy sofas faced each other. A TV perched on a cabinet in the corner, a lovely wooden coffee table labored under magazines, more children's books, mail both open and unopened, sundry small items of Fiona-sized clothing, a coloring book and pencils. A teddy bear lay on his back on the polished wood floor.

She shook her head and turned to join Brad. French doors opened from the dining room onto a verandah. Hands on hips in the middle of the lawn, Brad was studying a Weber barbecue. Heat shimmered up from the heat beads. A green all-weather outdoor table and six chairs beckoned invitingly from a corner of the large garden, which was enclosed by the L-shaped building. A slate path lined with brightly colored azaleas led away around the side of the house to the driveway, the garage, and the back door.

"My brother has one of those," Gina said as she stepped down the few steps onto the grass.

"I use it a lot in summer." He turned with a smile. Warm and inviting. His eyes were such a lovely deep brown. They caressed her face, made her stomach drop, and her breath catch. Think! He had those two children he adored. Mess-makers.

She plastered on her professional, social smile. "It's a lovely garden. It's one thing I do miss about my apartment."

"I couldn't stand not being able to go outside."

"I have a balcony." With a view of the street and the apartment block across the road. She could see the tops of the trees in Hyde Park if she leaned out far enough and looked to the left.

Brad raised an eyebrow. "Not quite the same. Like a drink?"

"Yes, please."

"Apple juice, tropical juice, or mineral water?"

"Tropical juice would be lovely."

"Take a seat. I'll be right back."

Gina wandered across to the chairs and table and sat down. A stone birdbath nestled in amongst the plants behind a little cluster of birch trees. She leaned back and looked up through the canopy of leaves, breathing deeply. Lovely. Fresh air with a faint hint of florally springtime perfume, warm, very relaxing. A bird twittered nearby.

The screen door banged, Brad's feet swished across the grass. He placed a tray with a jug of juice tinkling with ice cubes, two glasses, and a dish of nuts on the table.

"Those two will be occupied for a while," he said. "Give us some time to ourselves." He poured juice.

Gina took her glass thoughtfully. "I'm sorry if I interfered—about Claire." She glanced at him as she spoke. He didn't seem to be mad at her. He sat down and picked up his own glass.

"I don't pretend to have all the answers," he said. "I'm just bumbling along like every other parent."

"You seem to be doing pretty well."

"Thanks."

He smiled across at her. Gina returned the smile. Her hand shook. If he kept staring at her that way she wouldn't be responsible for her actions. How could a man like him engender such incredible desire? A father, a man who hated everything she held important, a casual laid-back man who didn't bother himself over money, status or anything else from her world. What was the aphrodisiac? What chemistry was exploding here? Why was red-hot lust flooding her body? Would he think she was mad if she grabbed a handful of ice from the jug and rubbed it over her scorching neck?

She raised the glass to her lips and allowed the cool liquid to flow into her mouth. Brad leaned forward and placed his glass on the table.

"You've no idea how much I want to kiss you right now," he said.

Gina spluttered and coughed, barely managed to swallow the remains of the mouthful. "We weren't going to talk about that!" she cried.

"We're not talking about *that*, we're talking about now," he said. "I want to kiss you now."

"You can't," she gasped.

"You'd object?"

"No—yes—no, not that—the girls." She gestured helplessly toward the house. Kiss her? Had he read her mind? No, he couldn't have or he wouldn't be thinking she might object.

"So you think it's a good idea," he continued, smiling serenely. He didn't appear to be going to act on his idea.

Gina met his gaze. "Yes," she said. "I do."

"Good. Later, then." He raised his glass and laughed.

Gina's hand lifted of its own accord and clinked her glass against his. He was infectious, contagious, and totally irresistible. She was laughing, too, diving into his eyes. Forgetting everything, anticipating, remembering.

"You know we have absolutely nothing in common," she said as a form of sanity returned.

"We have one thing."

"What's that?"

"We enjoy kissing each other."

"Brad!" He was also totally irresponsible.

"What? It's true."

Gina frowned at his grin. "Maybe, but that's all."

"So far. We don't know each other very well yet."

"But some things are too obvious." She waved an arm around. "For a start you live here, and I live in the city. You hate the city, I hate the country."

"You've never lived in the country, how do you know?"

"I know, believe me. I'm a city girl. That's where my work is. My life."

"What else?"

"You have children." May as well be clear about it. Kissing and lusting after each other was one thing. A serious relationship with all the attendant dependants another thing entirely.

He grinned. "They're a bonus."

She smiled, but said nothing, toyed with her glass, then reached for a selection of the nuts in the little wooden dish.

"You don't think so?"

"They're lovely girls," she said. "But I'm not a kid person."

"When you have some of your own you will be," he said. "You can't help it. They win you over, take you by storm."

"I won't have children of my own, Brad."

The laughter faded at the tone of her voice. He was as serious as she now. He leaned forward slightly, emphasizing his words. "Again, how do you know? It may seem that way at the moment, but nothing's set in stone, circumstances change." He paused, dropped his gaze. When he met her eyes again his expression was somber. "Look at me, the way my life changed. In an instant."

"This won't." She wished he'd drop the subject. He was forcing her hand going on and on about it. It was none of his business anyway; they were barely acquaintances whatever he might be thinking, or hoping. She stood up. "Show me where you work."

He took her cue. "My workshop is behind the garage. Sort of an extension to it. Sometimes the old car has to sit outside."

The smell of timber was first, then an overlying tang of polish—oil of some sort—invading Gina's nostrils. Next her astonished eyes took in stacks of wood, planks, blocks, and smaller pieces ranged along the walls on shelves and the floor. A large machine sat at the far end of the room, and another sawlike contraption stood nearby. Unidentifiable tools of all shapes and sizes were arranged neatly along the spare wall space, hanging on wire hooks or between strategically placed nails. Pigeon hole wall cabinets held jars and boxes of things Gina couldn't even guess at. Woodworker's secret equipment. Two half-completed chairs similar to the ones in the gallery stood on the long work bench. Curly shavings crunched underfoot as she stepped further into the room.

Brad said, "These are more bowls. I've just finished turning them on the lathe."

He pointed to six bowls at one end of the bench, similar to

the ones she'd bought. Unpolished as yet. He picked one up and handed it to her. "From a walnut tree we used to have. It fell over in a storm a few years ago. Lovely pattern in the wood."

Gina ran her hand over the smooth surface. "It feels lovely."

"Has to be sanded down and then stained."

"I love the smell in here." His skin had a hint of the same. Now she knew why, what made his scent special.

"I don't notice it much anymore. This is what I'm going to use for the sideboard. Australian red cedar." He drew a plank from a pile and stared at it with a kind of reverence. It looked like any other plank to Gina.

"Haven't you started it yet? You were talking about that in the elevator weeks ago."

"You remembered." He turned to her with a pleased smile.

"An old bloke died and gave you the wood," she said with a grin and just the hint of a smirk.

He laughed as he slid the plank back into place. "Bert's not dead yet. Still forging ahead at eighty-six."

"Good for him. I should introduce him to my grandma."

"Yes, except Betty's still forging ahead with him. She's eighty-three with a jealous streak."

"So why haven't you started the sideboard?" Gina prowled about the workshop peering at the tools, the lathe with all its shiny little wheels and knobs and gauges, the saw with lethal-looking teeth. Anything to keep her distance from Brad. If she looked at him she'd throw herself on him and be completely wanton and abandoned and disgraceful.

"Things keep cropping up. Trips into the city. Visitors. Those bowls for the gallery and someone wants a set of six chairs. I've just started, as you can see."

"Nuisances," said Gina. She turned around. He'd snuck up behind her while she was studying a group of chisels arranged in descending order of size. "Especially those darned trips to the city." Her feet were virtually nailed to the floor. Or glued.

He stepped closer. "Not to mention those visitors."

"I won't." Even if her feet weren't glued to the floor her brain wasn't sending any meaningful signals. It had virtually shut down leaving her body on auto respond.

"Add it to the list," he murmured. His fingers traced gently down her cheek, cupped her chin.

Her arms automatically slipped around his neck as his lips came closer, hovered, brushed hers ever so gently. Smiled. Touched again. Gina's eyes closed. Pure sensation. Fingers caressing her face, holding while lips tantalized, sweet pineapple mango tasting, soft.

The back door banged. "Daddy, Gina. Where are you?"

Eyes flashed open. Brad sighed, released her.

"Bonus?" she murmured.

"Later," he said as her hands slid down his shirtfront.

"Daddeee."

"Probably better not," said Gina.

The puzzled, concerned look he threw her was short-lived. Fiona burst into the workshop. "There you are," she cried in her penetrating voice. "I didn't know where you'd gone."

"Your dad was showing me his workshop," said Gina. "What's the kitten doing?"

"All curled up sleeping. When's lunch, Daddy? I'm hungry."

"I'm about to start the sausages right now." Brad took the outstretched hand in his and led the way to the garden. "You can help bring the salad outside to the table."

Gina followed. If she needed any reminder of the colossal

stupidity of beginning something with this man, no matter how gorgeous, here it was. He would always give his child preference over any woman—other than the child's mother. And despite what Claire thought, that meant both his children. Gina would always be the one following along behind the family—figuratively speaking—never quite belonging. If she was able to produce a child of her own to balance the equation something might change, but given the situation and her condition, it wasn't going to happen. Not here, not with this man.

Better to head off trouble before it began. Look ahead, anticipate. The key to survival.

Brad prodded a sausage with the barbecue fork. Nearly done. Juice squirted out and sizzled into the glowing coals. Going well so far, this visit, this trial run. The screen door opened and closed rhythmically as Gina and the girls ferried food from the kitchen. Fifi carefully placed a pile of paper serviettes and the tomato sauce bottle on the table, then turned and ran back inside. They all seemed to be getting along beautifully. Fifi always charmed everyone, she couldn't help it—part of being five.

Claire appeared next with a tray of cutlery, plates, and glasses. Worrying whether Claire would cooperate had been unnecessary. Far from the sullen, antagonistic rebel he'd come to expect these days, she'd made a return to the Claire of old, the sweet, lovely, helpful girl.

She came and stood beside him examining the sausages with a critical eye.

"All right?" he asked, fork poised.

"Turn that one," she said and pointed.

"I meant with the kitten. And Gina." But he did as she ordered. The sausage hissed and complained.

"The kitten's asleep. Gina's nice." She grinned at him and looked away quickly, hiding laughter. They'd been discussing her, those girls, giggling together in the laundry with the kitten.

"What?"

"Nothing." But the smile was still in place.

"Mmm." He narrowed his eyes as he studied her, smiling.

"What?" Her eyes narrowed in return copying his expression.

"Nothing. Got a name for the kitten yet?"

"Fiddles, maybe. Or Misty."

"That'd suit a gray one better, wouldn't it?'

"Probably."

Gina and Fifi came down the verandah steps together. Gina held two covered bowls of salad. Fifi had the salt and pepper shakers.

"Nearly ready," he called.

"Goody, goody gumdrops." Fifi dumped the shakers on the table, skipped across to the barbecue, and hugged him with fierce intensity.

"Careful, poppet." Brad laughed. He slipped his free arm around her shoulders and squeezed, dropping a kiss on the top of her head. Claire walked away and joined Gina at the table.

He piled sausages onto the platter he had ready. "Here we go. Sit down, Fifi."

She scampered to the table and dragged a chair round next to Gina, the legs catching and scraping on the grass. Claire already sat on Gina's other side. "Give Gina some room, Fifi," said Claire, scowling.

"I want to sit next to Gina." She scrambled onto the chair.

Brad looked at Gina's expression—unconcealed trepidation—too close an encounter for comfort. He deposited the platter on the table, strode around and picked Fifi up, chair and all, and carried her to the opposite side. The shriek of outrage turned into a squeal of delight as she was swung through the air.

"You sit here next to me," he said.

Claire picked up the fork and speared a sausage. She dumped it on her plate and reached for another.

"Claire! Let Gina go first, please."

"It's fine," Gina said. "Claire, go ahead. I'm having first serve of the potato salad."

"I made that," Claire said while Brad muttered, "Here I am trying to instill some manners into the barbarians," shaking his head. Gina helped herself to two sausages and passed the platter to Brad.

"What's a barberarian?" asked Fifi.

"You," said Claire.

"A barbarian is a wild person with no manners," said Brad.

"I've got manners," Fifi said. She stuck her fork into the sausage Brad had placed on her plate and began chewing on one end.

"You have not," said Claire. "You shouldn't eat like that. Cut it up."

"It doesn't matter," she replied with a mouthful. "Does it, Gina?"

Gina swallowed her own mouthful of food. Her expression was polite in the extreme. Not a kid person, she'd said and here were Claire and Fifi busily reinforcing that opinion. But five-year-olds were like that. Unpredictable, lovable works in progress.

"It's nicer for the other people at the table if you learn some table manners—eat with your mouth closed and don't put too much food in at once. Things like that."

"See." Claire smirked at her sister. Fifi poked out her tongue.

Brad said, "Stop it, both of you." He passed the green salad across to Gina. She took it and served some to Claire then to herself.

"Thank you." Claire spoke to Gina with more respect than he'd heard come from her mouth in months. At least she was still capable of civilized behavior.

"This potato salad is really good," Gina said.

"I put sour cream in with the mayonnaise." Claire cast a pleased glance Gina's way.

"Makes it very creamy and smooth." Gina dolloped some more onto her plate.

"How do you keep so slim?" asked Claire.

Brad opened his mouth to protest the personal question, but something in their manner, the way their heads turned, engrossed in their conversation made him put in a forkful of sausage instead. A sense of completeness enveloped him. This was how it should be. Two adults, two children. A woman with his daughters, sharing and caring for them. A woman who fit into that hole in their lives. A hole he did his best to fill, but was there nevertheless. Was it Gina or would any woman do? Was his incredible attraction to her lust alone, or was he tapping into something far deeper? Something the girls instinctively sensed in Gina—that she belonged with them.

Gina said, "It's inherited. Doesn't matter what I eat I don't put on weight. Mum's the same and so is Grandma."

"You're so lucky."

Gina inclined her head skeptically and shrugged. "Can't do much about it."

"I inherited fat genes," Claire said. "All my friends take a size smaller clothes than me."

"Claire, you're not overweight and you're far too young to be worrying," put in Brad. "It's all those teen magazines you read and the rubbish on TV telling you a girl has to look like a stick insect to be attractive." Not to mention the influence of those girls at her high school. The ones he didn't know but was sure were a negative force. She'd never mentioned her weight until recently.

"Childhood obesity is becoming a major problem," Gina said mildly. "But Dad's right, Claire, there's absolutely nothing wrong with your body. Looks to me as though you all eat well." She gestured at the food spread before them. "Not take-away and junk food. Do you do any sport?"

"At school I do. They make us go on runs and stuff. I want to take dance classes, but there's none here, and I'd have to stay late in Moss Vale."

"Makes it awkward," added Brad. "The class times are all wrong for us."

"I don't get to do anything after school. All my friends do. It's because we live in this stupid town."

That was too much! She was making it sound as though she was in prison. "You play tennis on Sundays with some of the kids."

"Yeah." She poked at her food. "I don't like tennis much."

"Where did that come from all of a sudden?"

"I'm not very good at it."

"You have to practice," said Fifi solemnly. "If you want to get better at something you have to put in the hours and do the yard hards." Brad looked at her in surprise, only just preventing the burst of laughter.

Claire glared at her. "Shut up, Fifi. Who told you that?"

"Claire!" The admonishment was met with a stony stare.

Fifi, unfazed by her sister's harshness said, "That's what Pop told Mick about cricket training when he didn't want to go."

"Important to do the yard hards. Who's Pop?" Gina asked. Her lips were trembling, straining not to laugh. Brad caught her eye for a moment before she concentrated on her plate. Lucky, or he would've cracked.

"Maybe I don't want to get better at tennis," said Claire.

"Pop is our neighbor Melinda's father," Brad explained. "He lives with them. These two are there so much they call him Pop the way Mel's boys do."

Gina recovered enough to ask, "Where are their real grandparents?"

"Mummy's parents live in New Zealand," Claire said quickly. "We don't ever see them."

"Daddy doesn't have any parents," added Fifi.

"Of course he does." Claire rolled her eyes.

"Dad died when I was fourteen. Mum remarried fairly soon after but died nine years ago."

"Oh, I'm sorry." No laughing now.

He felt Gina watching him as he helped himself to more salad. What was she thinking? Too much death in this family? Too much grief and trauma and emotional upheaval? Keep away.

Couldn't blame her when it was all added up. And she didn't know how Elaine's parents had blamed him for their daughter's death—not in so many words—more an unspoken accusation. How could you let this happen? You knew another pregnancy was dangerous. They hadn't ever really approved of Elaine's choice of husband, wanted better than an impoverished artist for their daughter. Didn't approve of her choice of painting as a career. And they couldn't face the girls, preferred grandparenting from a distance. Cards and gifts on birthdays and Christmas arriving in the mail. At arms length.

Yes, this little family had more than enough emotional complications. Especially for a woman who enjoyed her freedom. Free as a bird and liked it that way.

He poured more juice for himself, offered the jug to Gina. She shook her head. "No, thanks. I mustn't stay too long. I don't want to hit the traffic from Centennial Park. There's a game today."

"You can stay," said Claire. "We've got a spare room."

Gina gulped. Stay? She glanced at Brad swiftly to see his reaction. Blank-faced, sipping his drink nonchalantly.

"Yes, you can sleep over," cried Fiona. "But if you want to marry our daddy you have to pass our test."

Bam! Marry? Test? What was this?

Gina froze in the warm, midday air. Everything stopped for an instant as total and utter shock rippled through her body. One hand held her fork an inch from her mouth, one foot stopped scratching the other ankle, her brain paused in the midst of considering and discarding the spare room offer.

"I don't want to marry your daddy," she said after a moment of reorientation and a mental and physical reboot.

"Why not?" Almost a wail from Fifi. Cute yes, but in small doses.

"She hardly knows him," said Claire. "People don't marry people they don't know."

"Exactly." Gina glanced at Brad. He hadn't said a word, probably because his shock was as evident as hers.

"Although," Claire continued thoughtfully, "other cultures do. In India they have arranged marriages where the bride and groom sometimes don't even meet before the wedding. The families arrange it. We learned about it at school."

"We could arrange it," said Fiona. "And Gina's grandma could help." She grinned happily at Claire who actually seemed to agree because she laughed and nodded.

And Gina's grandma no doubt would leap right in there and conspire with them given half a chance. Ridiculous.

"No. You couldn't," said Brad firmly. "This isn't India, and neither Gina nor I want to get married at the moment."

"But you might," said Claire. Persistent.

Brad met Gina's eye across the table. She looked straight back into those gentle, chocolate brown orbs. Marriage to this man had never entered her head, and it wasn't on the horizon now. If he was unencumbered, lived in the city and had a different outlook on life, an affair would definitely be on the cards. But marriage? Never.

"No," she said.

"No," said Brad. "We're too different."

The way he said it, clear and unequivocal, sent a sharp and completely unexpected pang of disappointment arrowing through her body. Different they may be, but he didn't mind kissing her. Kissing and flirting.

Chapter Eight

"What do you do in the city?" Claire asked, changing the subject with an abruptness Gina found disconcerting, swamped as she was by images of kissing Brad. Why couldn't she just stop herself from thinking about it? "Do you work in an office?"

"Uh . . . yes. I work for a company that works out the value of things that other companies own or want to buy. Clients ask us to do a valuation for them."

"To see if they're getting a bargain?"

"Yes, or if it's not a good deal and they'd be better off investing in something else. Sometimes they need to know how much what they own is worth for other reasons too. Tax or insurance or something."

Silence greeted this statement. If it was part of the test, she'd failed it with brilliance. Too much unintelligible and boring information for children. Brad didn't look particularly interested either. But she already knew he wasn't. Too bad.

"Do you work in a great big skyscraper?" asked Fiona.

Gina smiled. "Yes, I do. It's twenty-eight-stories high, but I only work on the eighth floor. My building's round. It looks like a tube or a great big pencil. It's the only round one in the CBD."

"I'd love to work in the city one day." Claire sighed.

"No reason why you can't."

"I'll never get out of this hole."

Brad snorted. "That's silly."

The telephone shrilled from inside the house. Claire leaped to her feet. "I'll get it." She ran across the grass, bounded up the steps to the verandah, and disappeared inside. The ringing stopped.

Brad said, "Had enough to eat, Fifi?"

"Yes. Can I go and check on the kitty?"

"Yes."

She was gone in a pink flash. Gina placed her knife and fork neatly side by side on her plate. Brad sighed.

"I didn't warn you, I'm sorry," he said.

"That your daughters are on the lookout for a wife for you?" she asked dryly.

"Yes."

"What's the test? Is it like in *Turandot*? Do they set riddles and behead the suitors who get the answer wrong?"

"Do you like opera?" The worried expression fled replaced by one of delight.

"Yes. Don't avoid the question."

"I've no idea what they've thought up. I told them once

that if I ever fell in love, the woman would have to pass their test before I married her. I was joking."

"Oh, nice!" A coil of anger stirred deep inside. What was she? Some sort of guinea pig? A crash-test dummy? Or just a plain dummy? Did he bring all his female friends here for inspection?

"I'm sorry. This whole situation is embarrassing—for me too. I'm not even thinking of marrying anyone, and I know you aren't either. They seem to have got it into their heads that because I invited you for lunch we have something."

"We don't."

"No."

Gina fiddled with the placement of her cutlery, rolling the knife over, leveling the handles. "That woman at the gallery told me not to lead you on." She glanced up, straight into his eyes. They were staring at her in a kind of wide-eyed, stunned shock. "Does this whole town and surrounds know about me?"

"No! Judith is—"

"A gossiping sticky beak?" It just slipped out borne on the confusion and annoyance. She grimaced. "Sorry. She's your friend." Pressed fingers to her forehead. "Sorry. I'm not used to this."

He leaned forward urgently. "Neither am I, Gina."

"I just wanted a gift for my grandma and lunch with a friend. A simple, uncomplicated day in the country." To her surprise her lips began trembling. She couldn't meet his gaze. He pushed his chair back and stood up, moved around the end of the table toward her.

The screen door banged. Claire came down the steps in one excited bound.

"Dad. Guess what? Nope is playing in Sydney and everyone's going. It's their first big concert. Can I go? Please, Dad?"

Brad stopped. He flung an exasperated look at his daughter. "Claire, don't interrupt like that. Gina and I were talking."

Claire threw an apologetic glance Gina's way. "Sorry, Gina. But can I? Everyone's staying at Amy's aunt's place."

"Who's everyone? Do I know any of them?"

"You know Tamsin."

"Not really. Is Amber going?'

"She can't. She has some family thing she has to go to."

"How many?"

"Five."

"And who's taking you to the concert?"

"Amy's aunt will drop us off and pick us up."

"No way, Claire. I'm sorry but I wouldn't dream of letting you go to a show like that without an adult."

"But we'll be perfectly safe."

"No."

"But Daaaad."

"No. Don't argue."

"Gina?" The distraught face turned her way.

"It has nothing to do with Gina," snapped Brad.

"But Gina would you let me go?" she wailed. "Did your parents let you go to concerts with your friends?"

"Well, I did go to a few shows."

"See, Dad. Gina was allowed. Everyone else is allowed. You're so unfair. You don't want me to have any fun at all."

"Claire, you're twelve years old. When you're older you can go to things like that. Not yet."

"If we lived in the city I'd be allowed to go. I hate it here.

There's nothing to do. I hate it!" She spun around and charged for the house, sobs of rage issuing forth and lingering in the still air like black clouds even after the door had slammed behind her.

Gina swallowed. She began to collect the dirty plates and stack them on the tray. Brad slumped into his chair. "Leave that," he said.

"I think I'd better go soon." He didn't reply, didn't try to dissuade her or reiterate the suggestion of staying the night. Not that she would. "I'll use the bathroom before . . ." He nodded.

Gina lifted the tray and carried it to the kitchen. Claire was nowhere to be seen. Fiona's voice came from the laundry chattering softly to the kitten. She took her purse from the bench and headed down the hallway to the loo. Pop music suddenly blared from behind one of the closed doors, loud and brash. Claire expressing her feelings again. Gina washed her hands, deliberating on the wisdom of becoming involved in this situation. She wanted to say good-bye, couldn't leave without. Should she mention the fight, try to say something soothing? But Claire was vulnerable and very bruised at the moment. She may see it as interfering. Another adult messing up her life.

Gina dried her hands on the little yellow towel and drew a breath for courage. Tapped on the door. Again and louder. That music was raucous. Horrible. Knocked again even louder. If it was Nope, no wonder no parents wanted to go.

"Come in," called a sulky voice.

Gina pushed the door open and stepped inside. Typical teenager's room. Posters of pop stars on the walls, clothes on the floor. Books and magazines scattered haphazardly. A soft, stuffed toy dog and a teddy bear sat on the one chair. Claire was sprawled on the bed. She leaned over and pressed a button on a portable CD player. The music stopped abruptly. She regarded Gina through tearstained eyes. Sniffed and rubbed her hands across her face.

"Sorry. I wanted to say good-bye."

"Are you going now?"

Gina nodded. "I think I'd better."

"You don't have to leave because of me."

Gina instinctively moved closer. "I'm not leaving because of you!" She sat on the end of the bed. "I have to drive home and I want to get back before dark."

Claire straightened and sat up. "Can't you stay? You can sleep here."

"Claire, I can't. I have to go home and feed Big Al."

"Oh. That's right."

Something about the miserable expression, the perceived isolation, the memory of the desperate aloneness of a twelve-year-old against the world made Gina open her purse. "Look. If you ever need to . . . here's my card. That's my phone number."

Claire took the proffered business card and studied it. "Georgina Tait. Bright and Caulfield. Cool," she said. "Thanks."

Suddenly she'd scrambled down the bed and flung her arms around Gina. Gina hugged her gingerly. Sweet kid. She patted her on the back and extricated herself gently. She stood up. "I'd better go."

"I'll come and wave to you."

Brad was in the kitchen unloading the tray of the remaining

dishes from outside. His curious glance flew from one to the other, but he didn't say anything.

"Thank you for lunch. You do a very good barbecue sausage. And lovely potato salad." She looked down at Claire and smiled.

"I can give you the recipe if you like." Big hopeful eyes still red-rimmed and teary looking gazed back.

"Yes, please."

Claire dived for the bench and scrabbled about in the mess looking for a pencil and paper.

"Here." Brad handed her a pen.

She took it with outstretched arm and no eye contact and began studiously writing a list of instructions.

"I'll say good-bye to Fiona." Gina walked across to the laundry.

Fiona had the kitten in her lap, pink skirt stretched across her knees as a kind of hammock, talking to it as it tried to climb up her legs.

"I'm leaving now," said Gina.

Fiona looked up. "Bye bye, Gina. Kitty says bye bye too."

"Bye bye, kitty." Gina smiled.

"Are you coming back?"

"I don't know."

"You'd better."

"Should I?"

"Yes. You have to see how kitty is."

"Maybe. Good-bye."

But Fiona had already returned her attention to the kitten. "Kitty, don't scratch."

Claire handed Gina the piece of paper with *Claire's Potato Salad* printed carefully at the top.

"Thank you." Gina folded it and put it in her purse. "I'll make some soon."

"Claire, come and see what the kitty is doing," cried Fiona from the laundry.

"Bye bye, Gina." Claire hurried to answer the call.

Gina slung the strap of her bag over her shoulder. She walked to the door leading to the garden. Brad followed, and they walked down the steps to the path leading around the house to her car in the driveway. They reached the Golf in silence.

"Do you think I was too hard on her?" asked Brad.

Gina, leaning in to throw her purse across to the passenger seat, turned in surprise. "What do you mean?"

"You thought I was hard on her before. Do you think I should let her go to this concert?"

"It's not my decision, Brad." Why was he asking her? Why did he give her opinion any credence? For heaven's sake.

"But you think I'm wrong."

"I'm not saying that! I don't think I'm saying anything. I don't know."

"She's twelve."

"There'd be a group of them," she said slowly, doubtfully, only speaking because he was so insistent. It didn't sound too good to her, but how would she know?

"But no adult."

"No. I agree that's a worry." The memory of that music made her grin slyly, "You could go."

He snorted. "I couldn't stand it. And what about Fifi? It'd mean staying overnight."

Gina said nothing. Not her problem, thank goodness. Her face gave her away again.

"Not your problem," he said disconcertingly. How did he know exactly what she was thinking?

He touched a finger to her cheek. "Wrong time, wrong place," he murmured.

"Pardon?"

"Us. It's the wrong time and wrong place for us."

Gina's heart jumped and thudded in her chest. "Do you think there could be a right time and place?" she whispered.

"Oh yes, Gina Tait." He bent and brushed his lips across hers quickly and her pulse leaped. "But not in this lifetime, perhaps. Our paths have diverged too far, and I think they're headed in different directions, up different mountains."

Listening to his words Gina's world shifted and slid. Her eyes closed against the intensity of his, boring into her heart and soul. Breath rushed from her lungs as she released the muscles tensed against his message. It was true, every word was true, but she didn't want to hear it. It was so final and undeniable coming from his mouth. She breathed in slowly, trying to calm the thud of her disappointed heart. She didn't want to hear him state what she'd already decided was right. He didn't need to agree so definitively, so easily. He didn't need to feel the same.

"What are you? A guru?" she murmured just before some control mechanism snapped inside and she reached up to grasp his face between her palms. How could she bear never to kiss him again? So easy to make a decision like that. Impossible to keep to it with him so close, touching her, bathing her in his gaze. He smiled, and she pressed her mouth on his before he could say a word, or pull away, or object, or anything else that may occur to him.

This kiss would have to last a long time. The memory, at

least. Brad seemed to feel the same because he drew her into his embrace, fell into the kiss with her, willing and eager. His arms wrapped around her and almost lifted her from the ground. Or maybe it was her, floating on the rapture of it.

If this was all there was to a relationship with him, they'd be made. But it wasn't. They couldn't kiss each other forever, perfect and desirable as that may be. Reality hovered in the background, harsh and ever present.

Brad slowly released his hold. Her feet landed on firm ground. Conscious thought returned. His lips left hers. He stared into her eyes. "Safe trip," he murmured.

"Thank you. For everything."

She got into the Golf without another word and backed down the driveway paying careful attention to where she was going. Avoiding looking at him watching her go. If she did she'd cry. And she didn't want that. Not at all. She reached the street and spun the wheel to straighten and turn for home. She changed gear and risked one short, quick look to where he was standing, her hand half raised ready to wave. Friends.

But he'd gone. Walking his different path.

"You must take me to meet this woodturner of yours when I come to Sydney at Christmas," said Grandma, turning her salad bowl over again and studying Brad's mark on the underside. Her knobbly arthritic fingers stroked the smooth wood gently. "Bradley Harding."

"He's not *my* woodturner, he's a friend." And hadn't he made that very clear? Not a call, not a word in response to her polite thank you for lunch message left on his answering machine. A week ago. Probably better that way. She certainly wouldn't crack and call again. He wasn't going to call her, obviously. Much better. No point pursuing anything in that direction. She'd be running on an unfamiliar path, stumbling and ultimately falling.

"He's very good, isn't he? This is beautiful. Thank you very much, Georgina." She placed it delicately on the coffee table beside the teapot and the plate of left over birthday fruitcake.

"I wanted something special, Grandma. I knew you'd like it."

Grandma poured milk into her tea cup. Almost a third of a cupful. She added tea, turning the liquid a very pale version of beige. Angel's Piss her daughters called it.

"Top up?" Gina held out her own cup, and Grandma refilled it. "You need some milk in that. Black tea turns your innards brown."

"If I can't see them, it won't worry me."

Aunty Joyce and Mum appeared in the doorway having finished restoring the kitchen to pre-party order. As the years passed they looked more and more alike. Thin frames, squarish jaws, and wide-set, clear blue eyes. The eyes inherited from their father and passed on to Gina and Oliver. Joyce's children missed out. They took after their father, the squinty-eyed wife deserter. Long gone and good riddance according to family wisdom.

"All cleared away now, Ma," said Joyce.

"It was a lovely party. Thank you very much for doing all that work. It was quite unnecessary."

"Yes, it was." Mum sat down next to Gina with a frowning

smile at her mother. "Don't know why we bothered about you at all." She took a piece of cake, broke off a chunk, and ate it.

"Have a cup of tea," said Grandma. She looked from one daughter to the other.

"No thanks, I need a lie down. I'm knackered," said Joyce. She headed off down the hallway to the bedroom she was sharing with Mum for the few days of their stay. Gina had the narrow, hard couch in the room Pa had used as a study.

Mum poured herself a cup and took another piece of cake.

"Georgina was telling me all about her woodturner friend."

"You should have invited him," said Mum. "I told you to bring someone."

Gina sighed. "He couldn't come to Brisbane, and I'd never ask him," she said patiently. Now she'd have to try to deny or rather, explain, a relationship that fell far short of such an intimate connection. Any remotely available man she met was automatically elevated to the status of prospective husband. *Man, Gina*, and *friend* didn't go together in the same sentence in their rose-tinted world.

"Why not?" Two inquiring faces watched her expectantly.

"I hardly know him."

"You said he was a friend," retorted Grandma. "And you went to his house for lunch."

"He might have enjoyed seeing where one of his bowls was going," added Mum brightly, earning a chuckle from Grandma.

Good grief!

"If I'd invited Brad, and for some wild reason he'd agreed, or could afford to come to Brisbane for a weekend with someone he'd only recently met, he'd have had to bring his daughters along. It's a package deal."

"Daughters," exclaimed Mum with redoubled interest, while Grandma said, "How many does he have?"

"Two. Twelve and five."

"Perfect." Mum smiled happily.

Hating herself for biting, Gina asked, "Why perfect?"

"I had two—Joyce and Irene. Irene had two—you and Ollie. It's a good number," announced Grandma. No mention of Joyce's three.

"Ready made family. Past the baby stage with nappies and feeds and no sleep and all that, but young enough to need mothering."

"Mum!" Gina could only shake her head in stunned disbelief. Without a doubt Brad's girls and these two had to be kept apart. But that wouldn't be a problem—she kept forgetting. He was difficult to dislodge from her thoughts, constantly hovering there in the background.

"We're only teasing," said Grandma.

"Look, love," Mum said gently placing her hand on Gina's arm. "You know you won't have children of your own so a man with a family is the ideal solution."

"Solution to what?"

Gina sat back in her chair. Darn it! Teasing they may be but there was an undercurrent of truth here. She should have left earlier with Ollie and his girlfriend, Christine. Taken them up on their offer to have a drink somewhere first instead of meeting for dinner later.

"Children." Mum could be succinct when she chose. They hadn't had a chance to corner her beforehand with preparations in full swing. Now there were cups of tea and plenty of time to focus on their favorite subject. Good thing Aunty Joyce had gone to her room for a lie down or it'd be three against one. Grandma was running on adrenalin and showed no signs of flagging.

"Maybe I don't want children," Gina tried, defiantly.

"Of course you do," said Grandma. "Maybe not yet but when you hear that clock ticking . . ." She nodded her head.

"Won't make any difference to me, though, will it?"

"I'm sorry, Gina," Mum said with a seriously woebegone look and a complete change of direction.

"It's not your fault my ovaries don't work, Mum. POF's not a genetic inheritance," said Gina in surprise. "And it doesn't worry me, really. I focus on other things."

"I feel it *is* my fault. I suppose mothers always feel responsible for the health of their children. Things that happened in the womb—that they have some sort of control during the cooking. I don't know . . ." She trailed off, sipped her tea.

"Don't be silly, Irene," Grandma said. "You didn't smoke or drink or take drugs and you were the picture of health through both your pregnancies. Sometimes things just happen."

"Things don't happen for no reason," insisted her mother.

"But they do, Mum," said Gina. "Sometimes stuff just happens and there's no reason. Brad's wife died having their second baby. She was young and healthy, too, but something went wrong and she died."

"Oh dear, how tragic." Both faces turned from laughter and teasing to sorrow in an instant.

"Yes."

"Is he raising the girls on his own?"

"Yes. He said he has help. There's a neighbor, but no family from what I can gather."

"He sounds like quite a man." Grandma smiled innocently. "Good-looking?"

"Very," said Gina before she thought, because the image of Brad's smiling face was sharp in her mind. Just before she kissed him, or he kissed her.

"Like I said. Perfect, Gina." Mum drained her tea cup with satisfaction plastered all over her face.

Gina studied the list of figures in the interim report Sophie had compiled. Valuations of government school sites in the southeastern district. The team was slowly working its way through the country areas designated by their clients, the State Education Department.

The enrollment figures and total capacity were in brackets beside the name of each school. Not that the enrollment figures played a part in their own calculations. They were simply calculating the value of the land and assets. They were asked to do the number crunching, and that's what they were doing. What the client chose to do with the results had nothing to do with her.

But the way some of these results were stacking up didn't bode well for about seven schools and preschools, as far as she could judge. Couple that with the results from other areas, and if the government went ahead with the closures this seemed to be predicting, there'd be an awful public outcry. Gina compressed her lips. Not her problem.

Birrigai. The name leaped from the page. The land in that whole area had appreciated considerably in the last few years as people chose to commute to the city from the surrounding country districts. It was certainly a beautiful part of the world. Good rainfall and climate keeping it lush and green even when most of the state was gripped by drought. Tall stately gums, rolling hills. Quiet—if you liked that kind of thing.

Gina frowned as she made sense of the figures. Low enrollment: fifty-two was very low considering the school was capable of holding one hundred thirty. She skimmed down to find the Sunderland School—they'd be closest. Much healthier: one hundred sixty-three enrolled, capable of holding two hundred. But the Birrigai school land was worth a packet. It was a large parcel with playgrounds plus an oval used by the whole community, although that might be community property. Opposite Brad's house. She remembered thinking what a lovely place to go to school. Walk across the road, over the oval, and there you were. Fiona's school. Claire would have gone there too.

Still, not her decision. And these things had to be decided upon for the good of everyone. Pouring money for staff and upkeep into a tiny school didn't make sense when other bigger schools needed funding. Wonder if Brad knew this was underway? Doubt it. Secrecy went with the job, and this type of information was always sensitive.

It'd give the residents committee something to complain about. The Networks tower protest bid had failed as she knew it would. Hopeless from the start. All those new residents flooding into the once-sleepy rural areas brought with them money and expectations. They wanted city-style conveniences, sent their kids to expensive private schools, and had the clout to get what they could pay for. People like Brad had to take a big step forward into the twenty-first century.

Lunchtime was imminent. Gina closed the program. She

had her eye on a pair of shoes in a shop in the Queen Victoria Building and today she'd have time to try them on. She didn't really need more shoes, but what else would she spend her money on if not little indulgences like that? She'd wear them to dinner at Cathy's on Friday night. And hope baby Shelley didn't puke on them.

Gina sauntered back to the office swinging the carry bag and a take-away salad roll to eat at her desk. How would little Fiona react to the news of her school being closed? She'd have to bus to Sunderland. Long, tiring days for a little kid. Or Brad would have to drive her in and pick her up every day. Inconvenient and expensive in terms of time and gas.

But it might not happen. Who knew what the Education Department bods would decide? They did seem keen to cut costs, though. Governments always did and country areas usually were the prime targets. Not enough voters to make a difference. Sure they'd kick up a stink, but the bottom line was they didn't have the numbers—too spread out in too vast a country.

For the first time an unease settled around Gina as she sat in front of her computer. Helping decide the fate of many small children's educational future had suddenly become a lot more personal. Primary schools and preschools—all young children like Claire and Fiona. All had parents like Brad who loved them and tried to give them the best start in life and the best education they could. Governments were supposed to help people, not make life harder for them. Governments were supposed to invest in the future, and children were the future. She may not want her own, but the importance of educating children was a self-evident truth.

Education spending should be a priority, for the good of the country. And she'd bet that was one thing, maybe the only thing, she and Brad would agree on.

How was he doing? How was Claire? And the kitten. Did it have a name yet? It was a month ago she'd been there with them at the shelter. A month and not a word from any of them.

If there was to be a next move, he had to make it.

Friday afternoon in the conference room breathing stuffy, warm, turgid air. Air-conditioning not working properly again. Gina glanced surreptitiously at her watch. Nearly five twenty. With any luck she'd be out of here in half an hour and could leave work relatively early. Have time for a leisurely shower and change for dinner at Cathy's. Fred and Craig were discussing the details of the last meeting with the Education Department people. Gina hadn't been involved. Her job wasn't liaison, her job was making order from the data her team supplied. She didn't really even need to be there, but Fred insisted. She shifted her bottom and crossed her legs in increasing irritation.

They didn't care in the least that schools would be closed. Craig was marveling at the price some of the sites would fetch on the open property market.

"They'll make millions," he said. "Land out there is a veritable goldmine."

"Schools were allocated massive blocks of land in the old days," agreed Fred. He removed his reading glasses and rubbed the bridge of his nose. "Cheap and plentiful."

"Doesn't it worry you that these are schools we're talking about?" asked Gina suddenly.

Two faces swung toward her in surprise.

Craig said, "Overfunded, unviable schools. Why should tax payers pour money into places where only a handful of children are enrolled?"

Why? Why indeed. She hadn't really thought it through, it just felt wrong. "Because it's their right to have a public education and a school close to where they live. At least for primary-age kids."

"Totally irrational, economically, Gina, you should know that," Fred said dismissively.

"Serves them right for living out in the sticks," said Craig and laughed. "Anyway we don't make these decisions, luckily for them. I'd shut most of those tinpot schools and send all the kids to a central superschool in each area. Much more efficient. Centralize the facilities."

"Like those gigantic pig and cattle farms, you mean? Cram as many in as possible and force feed them information?" Gina tapped her fingers on the desk top, the nails clicking loudly, earning a glare from Fred. She folded her arms. Craig and Fred shared a pointed look. Fred replaced his glasses.

All right for Craig, his children went to expensive private schools where the students were nurtured and coddled with the latest in technology and innovative teaching methods. What about people like Brad? Single parents, single-income parents, low-income parents. Their children deserved individual, personalized attention too. Disposable income should have nothing to do with the quality of education. And Fred's daughter had been to . . .

Tap, tap. This time on the conference room door.

"Yes," Fred snapped.

The door opened a crack. Sophie's head appeared. "Sorry to interrupt. Gina, there's a child here to see you."

Gina sat bolt upright.

"A child?" exclaimed Craig. He looked at Gina and laughed in astonishment. "Didn't think you knew any. It's not yours, is it?"

Sophie grimaced. "She's a bit upset—bit of a mess, really."

Gina said, frowning, "Who is it?" Her mind scrambled for names, possibilities. No one she knew in the city had children except Cathy. Who?

"Claire someone. Hardy?"

Claire? Brad's Claire? Impossible. She pushed her chair back.

"Tell her she'll have to wait until the meeting's over," said Fred. He scowled and picked up the paper he'd been referring to before the diversion into the moral question of school closures.

"What am I supposed to do with her?" demanded Sophie.

"Give her a glass of water and a magazine and sit her in a corner," said Fred. He flapped his hand. "Go. This is important."

Gina stood up. "I'd better see her, Fred. She must be in trouble somehow; she doesn't live in the city."

He glared at her over his glasses. "Two minutes."

"I'll be right back. Excuse me."

Sophie closed the door behind them, eyeing Gina curiously. "She rang the buzzer and I let her in. Who is she?"

"A friend's daughter," Gina said. "Thanks, Sophie."

"No problem." Sophie shrugged and went off to her cubicle.

Gina turned the corner to the small foyer area just inside the glass office door. They had no receptionist. Visitors rang a bell and were met either by Sophie or whoever was expecting them. Two black leather armchairs sat in the small waiting area. One was occupied by a tearstained, very upset Claire.

Chapter Nine

She leaped to her feet when Gina appeared, her relief emphasized by the gasp and smile of delight.

"Claire! What on earth are you doing here?" Gina strode forward.

"Gina, I'm so glad . . . I didn't know where else to go . . . I was lost and . . ." Tears started dripping down her cheeks as her face crumpled. She groped for a tissue.

"Hey, it's all right, you're here now." Gina studied Claire in bewilderment. Her hair was pulled back in a high ponytail, she wore a white top with sparklies around the neckline, tight low-slung jeans. Not school wear. "What are you doing in the city? Where's your dad?"

"At home," she mumbled.

"Does he know where you are?" Alarms sounded in Gina's head. Claire had run away. Cripes! They'd had a massive fight and she'd run. But—Gina glanced down—she hadn't packed anything much. All she had was the school backpack lying

169

on the floor by the chair, its straps sprawled untidily on the carpet.

"He thinks I'm staying tonight with a friend. With Tamsin."

"Where's Tamsin?"

"Going to the Nope concert."

"But I don't understand, Claire. What's going on?" Nope concert? Claire wasn't allowed to go. Unless Brad had changed his mind. Doubtful.

Claire sniffed and blew her nose.

"Look. Sit down for a minute. I'm in a meeting. I have to . . . just wait here. Okay?"

Claire nodded, her ponytail swinging as she turned. Gina smiled and patted her on the shoulder briefly. "It'll be all right."

Fred glared at her when she slipped back into the conference room. "Right. We're up to the plan for the next—"

"I'm sorry, I have to go. This girl is in trouble. I think she's run away from home. I'll have to sort it out."

"Can't it wait until we finish?" The glare turned to a scowl of disapproval.

"No. I don't think it can," said Gina slowly, the realization dawning that it really couldn't wait. Or even if it could she wasn't sticking around. Claire needed her. Her! She'd come to Gina for help, and Gina wouldn't let her down. "I'm sorry. I'll see you on Monday."

Gina left Fred and Craig muttering all sorts of things she didn't want to know about. Stuff them! Claire was more important than numbers and reports. Gina almost ran to her desk and grabbed her purse and jacket. She closed down her computer and locked away any stray files in her desk drawer.

She stared at the phone. Call Brad? He wouldn't be worried because he thought Claire was at her friend's place. The last thing Claire needed at the moment was a father attack. Take her home to the apartment, calm her down, have dinner. Find out what was going on first. Then call.

Claire sat in the leather chair, small and very young, very vulnerable. She straightened when Gina appeared, jumped up and swung her backpack over her shoulder. The tears had gone; she smiled and was instantly the confident girl Gina remembered.

"Let's go," said Gina. She pressed the release button and pulled the heavy glass door open.

"Where?"

"To my place."

An anxious expression flitted briefly across Claire's face. "Did you call Dad?"

"No, I will later. After you tell me what's going on." Gina raised an eyebrow and pursed her lips in an expression she remembered her high school English teacher using to good effect. It seemed to work.

"Okay."

They rode down in the crowded elevator in silence. Gina led the way to the street and across to the bus stop where they joined the throng of home-going office workers.

"How did you get here?" she asked when they were on the bus, strap-hanging side by side, lurching backward and forward as the bus shuffled and stopped and started, jostling bodies and elbows with other passengers.

"On the train. But when we got to Central we went to catch another train and the others got on, but I couldn't before the doors closed. There were so many people." Claire glanced about the bus. Every seat was taken, the aisle jammed. Her face was on a level with everyone else's chest. "It's so crowded here." The bus jerked to a halt, and she grabbed the nearest seat for support. Her backpack slammed into the woman beside her who turned with a scowling, "Watch out!"

"Sorry," she gasped.

"It's rush hour," said Gina.

"And everyone's really pushy. No one helped me, they all just ignored us even when my friends yelled to hold the doors open." Gina offered a sympathetic expression to the indignant cry. Welcome to the city. "So I got on the next train, then I got off at Wynyard where we were meeting Amy's aunt, but I couldn't find them." The brown eyes widened at the memory. Scary stuff for a kid unused to the city.

"They didn't wait for you?" Claire had done the best thing under the circumstances. The others should have realized. But they were twelve-year-olds—from a country town, albeit a larger one than Birrigai. Brad was right. Not a good idea at all.

"No. They might have, but it was so crowded I couldn't see anything and I didn't know where to go properly. I waited, then I came up onto the street, but they weren't anywhere. I didn't know what to do so I walked around a bit. Then I saw your building."

Wynyard was a very confusing station even when you knew it—lots of entrances—impossible at rush hour. What sort of arrangement was that?

"Where does Amy's aunt live?"

"Lane Cove."

"That's across the harbor." Gina edged forward. "We get off next stop."

They stepped down onto Oxford Street opposite the supermarket. She needed to buy something for their dinner. Dinner! Gina snatched her mobile from her purse and dialed Cathy's number ready to make heartfelt apologies.

"Working back?" asked Cathy in a resigned voice.

"No! It's nothing like that. It's . . ." Gina glanced at Claire standing beside her as they waited for the pedestrian lights, relaxed now and almost cheerful. Excited by her adventure. Gazing up and down the busy street with its array of cafés, restaurants, bars, and clothing boutiques, not to mention the parade of local characters that gave Darlinghurst its flavor and reputation. The gay center of Sydney. "A friend's daughter turned up unexpectedly at work." She lowered her voice and turned away. "She's twelve and I think she's lied to her father about where she is."

"Run away from home?" Cathy's interest level shot up.

"No, I don't think so. She wanted to go to a rock concert and wasn't allowed so she came anyway, but it all went wrong and she lost her friends somewhere in the city."

"And she came to you."

"Yes." A wave of pleasure flooded through Gina. "Yes, she did."

"Smart kid."

"I'm sorry about dinner, Cathy. I was really looking forward to it. Even bought new shoes."

Cathy laughed. "As if you needed an excuse to buy shoes. Not to worry. You've got a pretty good reason for not coming."

"Sorry, I'd better go. Thanks, Cathy."

She dropped her phone into her purse. Claire stepped closer, curious. "Were you going out?"

"Yes, but it's all right."

"I'm sorry, Gina." Uncertainty now. Realizing how much of a mess she'd made, how much of a nuisance, an imposition, she might be.

The pedestrian lights changed. Gina headed across the road with Claire striding beside her. "What would you like for dinner?"

"I don't mind." The voice was much more subdued, anxious to please.

"We can order take-away. There are some really good restaurants around here. What about Thai or Indian?"

"Either."

"We'll go in to the supermarket first for a few things."

Claire trailed obediently behind Gina, carrying the shopping basket and trying hard not to be in the way. Walking to the apartment they shared the load, each lugging a plastic carry bag.

"Dad has green bags," said Claire.

"So do I, normally," Gina replied. Brad didn't have a monopoly on eco-consciousness. "We'll order Thai in here." She swung into Three Sisters Thai, a favorite of hers. Quick, cheap, high-quality food and very friendly. A twenty-minute wait tonight.

"We'll go home first and come back," said Gina to Claire.

In the apartment Claire put her plastic bag in the kitchen and stared around in awe. Quite a contrast to her place. No mess, the decor cool grays and blues with large scatter cushions of burgundy, black and jade on the leather lounge suite. Brad's sculpture sitting in one corner, a focal point. Big Al rose from his spot on the armchair. He jumped to the floor and stretched his hind legs one at a time. Then the naughty boy clawed at the carpet briefly before heading for the kitchen at a trot.

"Big Al!" cried Claire in delight. "He's beautiful." She squatted down as he approached, but he skipped sideways and darted around her.

"He wants his dinner," said Gina. She opened the fridge and took out a plastic container of fresh minced chicken. "Give him about a third of this in his bowl. There's a spoon in that drawer. Thanks."

Claire did as she was instructed while Gina unpacked the groceries. "The bathroom's there," she said pointing at the relevant door. "And there's another loo and washbasin through the door near the front door."

"Thanks." Claire rinsed the spoon under the tap and replaced the mince in the fridge. She disappeared into the bathroom. Gina went to change into jeans and a casual shirt.

Walking back to collect their dinner Gina said, "So. You lied to your dad."

Claire's brow wrinkled and she bit her lip briefly before replying, "Just a little bit. I really wanted to go to the concert, and everyone else was going."

"It sounds like an odd arrangement to me. Meeting the aunt at Wynyard. It's such a big station. What if she couldn't find any of you?"

"Amy rang her on her mobile when we got to Central. They have a meeting place. Her aunt works near there, and we were all going home to her place with her." She was emphasizing the validity of the plans trying to justify the safety of the trip. Bar one overriding flaw. No permission. Two flaws. No backup plan for disasters.

"You need a mobile," said Gina.

Claire leaped on Gina's comment with self-righteous indignation. "I know! Dad won't let me. He says I'm too young, and I don't need one."

"You needed one today. We should call Amy and tell her you're all right." Good grief! The aunt was probably panicking after losing someone else's child. Especially one she didn't realize shouldn't be there in the first place. What a mess! The first thing the aunt would do, of course, Gina now belatedly realized, would be to phone Claire's father. In which case he'd already know she was missing. He'd already be frantic with worry.

"I don't know her number. I thought of that before, but I couldn't find a pay phone to call *anyone.*"

Gina whipped out her mobile. "What's your number? We have to call your dad."

"He'll be really angry."

"Yes," said Gina grimly. "And I don't blame him. Do you?"

His line was busy.

While Claire doled the fragrant spicy food into bowls Gina rang Brad again. Six attempts and still busy. Not surprising. He'd be phoning everyone he could think of including the police. She looked at the clock. Five past seven. Maybe not the police yet. He may wait to see if she came home by herself on the train.

"What time does the last train get in to Birrigai?"

"It doesn't go to Birrigai, it goes through Moss Vale. The last one is about nine o'clock."

"Your dad might think you've caught that."

"Maybe. He'll still be mad, though."

"You're not going to avoid getting into trouble."

"But you're not mad at me."

Gina carried bowls to the table. "No, not really. But I know where you are. He doesn't. And you haven't lied to me, have you?"

"No! I wouldn't." Claire's shocked expression almost made Gina laugh.

"But you'd lie to your dad." The contorted logic of a twelve-year-old rebel.

"He doesn't understand." Claire sat down and began spooning rice into her bowl.

Gina sighed. "I'll try him again."

Brad snatched up the phone the instant it rang. "Claire?" he barked.

"It's Gina Tait," said a calm voice.

"Gina?!" Gina whose voice he'd dreamed of hearing again, whose image invaded every waking moment. Whose kiss . . . What particularly rotten timing that she should ring now when he was beside himself with worry, sick to the stomach with visions of the horrors his daughter could be suffering. "I'm sorry I can't . . . I have to get off the phone, Claire's missing. I'm . . ."

"She's here," interrupted Gina loudly. "She's fine. I'll put her on."

"There?" Brad struggled to comprehend the news while alternating cascades of relief and joy streamed through his body. Fifi clung to him, teary eyed and worried. "Claire's at Gina's," he said to her weakly, leaning against the wall as his legs turned to rubber. Her face split into a massive smile. She clapped her hands and danced about the room.

Then Claire was on the line. "Hello, Dad."

He straightened with a jerk. "Claire, where are you? I've been frantic ever since Brenda Lowe rang over an hour ago. Are you all right? What did you think you were doing going in to the city that way? I rang Tamsin's mother. You lied to me."

"I'm sorry. I'm at Gina's place."

"How did you get to Gina's?" He frowned. Had there been more than twelve-year-olds involved in this conspiracy? "Did she know you were going to that concert?"

"No, of course not! I'm trying to tell you."

"Okay, okay. I'm sorry. I'm upset, that's all. Upset and furious."

"I know." He recognized the tone. Defiant and angry with it. How dare she? But this was no time to have a slanging match. He moderated his voice.

"How did you get to Gina's? I didn't know you knew where she lives. *I* don't know where she lives."

"I went to her work. She gave me her business card before."

Brad sucked in air, bit his lip. Took another deep breath. "Okay, I understand. I'm glad you're safe, but it was a very, very stupid thing to do. Anything could have happened to you. Anything!" The rage simmered despite his attempt to control it, and she heard it.

"I know, Dad. I'm sorry." She didn't sound it. She sounded resentful that he should be angry.

"Put Gina on, please."

He heard the murmur of voices, then Gina was there in his ear again. "Hello?"

"Thank you for dealing with this, Gina," he said stiffly. "I'm sorry she dumped herself on you. It must be very inconvenient, especially at your work." Thank goodness she was a workaholic, staying after hours on a Friday evening. What if she hadn't been working? Where would Claire have gone then?

"It's all right. We're not at my work now. We're at my place just about to have dinner."

"Dinner?" Brad looked at the gold carriage clock on the bookcase. Ten past seven. Brenda had rung at about twenty five to six. "When did she turn up at your office?"

"Umm, probably at about five thirty. I was in a meeting."

So cool, so unruffled. So completely oblivious! All the pent-up anger rose like lava. "But why didn't you call me straight away, Gina? I've been frantic here. Have you any idea what it's like to know your child is lost?" He didn't wait for an answer, if she had one. "No, you wouldn't, of course. How could you wait an hour and a half to let me know? Even someone with your lack of interest in parenting should understand that's a bit excessive. Did you even think?!" The last words were shouted into the receiver.

"It's taken me at least half an hour to get through to you, Brad," she shot back. "If you had call waiting on your phone you'd know that. And if you gave your daughter a mobile phone she could have called you herself and vice versa, and you wouldn't have had to worry at all."

The phone went dead in his ear. It rang again almost immediately. "Claire can stay here tonight unless you want to come and collect her—if you don't trust me. She says the last train has already gone." Ice cubes virtually dropped from the phone.

"Thank you," he said, stunned. Before he could say another word the line clicked and he was holding a disconnected phone again.

"Is Claire coming home?" asked Fifi. She stared at him curiously. "Are you angry with Gina?"

"No, yes." He rubbed his hand across his face. "A bit."

"Why?"

Why? Brad closed his eyes briefly and heaved a vast sigh. "Because Claire has been with Gina for ages and she didn't tell me."

"We were very, very worried." Fifi clamped her tiny hands to her hips and frowned.

"Exactly. But we're not now. Claire's safe." Brad leaned down and scooped Fifi up for a kiss and cuddle. She wrapped her arms around his neck and deposited a big wet kiss on his cheek. He put her down. "I'd better phone Amy's Aunt Brenda and tell her where Claire is." And all the others he'd called in his panic.

Rain began falling as they left Sydney. Gray and dismal, it mirrored Gina's mood. She felt as guilty as Claire. Why hadn't she phoned Brad straightaway? Ironically it was because she wanted to spare him some worry, not add to it the way he seemed to think. Well, too bad! If that was his attitude, tough. Her first thought had been for the girl, finding out what caused this breakout. Or rather breakdown. Brad had a few things to sort out in his relationship with his daughter.

He had no idea what went on in her head, he'd admitted it freely in the elevator, and she'd seen it in action on her Birrigai visit. Last night, too, for example, seeing Claire using her computer to create amazing graphics for a school project. "I can't do anything at home," she'd said. "We don't have a computer, and the ones at school aren't nearly as good as yours."

She'd been engrossed for hours playing with the graphics program. Did he know how talented she was?

Claire sat beside her staring out at the rain-soaked paddocks. Facing Brad cast a pall of gloom over both of them, which thickened the nearer they came to Birrigai, and the heavier the rain fell.

He'd rung this morning, early, to say he wouldn't be able to collect Claire until late because a man was coming about a set of chairs, and he had to be at home.

"Put her on a train," he said. How could he suggest sending her home on a train all by herself after what had just happened? He spoke with a coolness she'd never heard from him before, a withdrawal from their previous flirty intimacy. It hurt. More than she could have guessed. She wanted to see him. Explain face-to-face. Surely if he saw her, looked into her eyes . . .

"No. I'll bring her myself."

"It's not necessary."

"I'll bring her. We'll be there about two." She hung up and faced Claire who'd appeared from the spare room wearing one of Gina's oversized cotton T-shirt nighties.

"Can't I stay longer?" Big Al came and wound himself around her ankles, and she bent to stroke him, then looked up at Gina with a pleading expression.

Gina smiled and said with complete honesty, "I'd like that but I don't think we'd better this time."

"Does that mean I can visit you again and stay? During the holidays? Next holidays?" She jumped up, startling Big Al into a dash for the kitchen.

Gina raised her hands in mock protest. "Hey, slow down. We have to get you home first, talk to your dad. I don't think he's going to look very favorably on any holiday plans from you at the moment."

The eager expression collapsed. "No, s'pose not. But you can talk to him about it. He likes you." She grinned cheekily. "He likes you a lot so he'll listen to you if you invite me."

That had become highly unlikely in a very short space of time.

Gina slowed as the rain suddenly drummed down harder on the roof. She leaned forward peering through the sheeting gray for a glimpse of the taillights of the car ahead. She flicked the windshield wipers onto high but they only made marginal inroads into the deluge flooding across the glass.

"Gosh," cried Claire. "This is freaky." Her voice was all but drowned out by the thundering raindrops pelting onto the car.

"I'll have to pull over," Gina yelled. "But I can't see the side of the road." The last thing she wanted was to slide off onto the soft grassy verge and become bogged.

They crawled along, Gina's hands gripping the wheel so tightly her hands ached. The twin red lights ahead wavered and faded, then grew stronger briefly as the car alternately accelerated and slowed. The thrumming on the roof dimmed slightly.

"We must have driven through a cloudburst," said Gina in a more normal tone. She drew in a deep breath and exhaled shakily. "Wow!"

"I can see the side of the road now. Heaps of people have stopped."

"I think we'll keep going." Gina accelerated ten miles an hour faster bringing their speed up to thirty. A four-wheel drive whooshed by in the next lane spraying them with water. "Cretin!"

Then the deluge was upon them again.

"It's hail," cried Claire. Small lumps of ice skittered across the windshield now, but the wipers brushed them aside. The taillights in front had disappeared.

"Keep a lookout for the turnoff. We don't want to miss the exit for Moss Vale," Gina shouted. "I've no idea how far we've come in this, but it should be fairly close."

Ten stomach-churning minutes later a large green sign loomed through the downpour. "There!" they shouted together and laughed in relief.

Gina eased the Golf to the left exit ramp. Water cascaded down the slope on either side, but the car was no longer plowing head on into the driving rain. It pelted into the driver's side now making visibility better. Gina could see about twenty yards of road ahead instead of just the front of the Golf.

She flexed her hands and rolled her shoulders up and down. They didn't need to drive through Moss Vale, the Birrigai road went off at right angles just before the town limits. Every dip was filled with water, but Claire insisted none of the puddles were deep.

"I come on this road in the bus every day," she said.

"We're not in a bus," Gina said under her breath.

Although the rain had eased to a steady, heavy, drenching downpour, the wind had picked up. Gigantic gums waved regally in the gusts blasting across the paddocks. Several large branches were down although none lay across the road, as yet. Gina eyed the roadside trees uneasily.

Finally the Birrigai town sign appeared through the

grayness. The rain was lighter here, but the wind was building, buffeting the Golf each time they passed through an open space in the trees.

"Go next left," cried Claire. Gina swung the wheel and they plumed through a vast puddle spreading halfway across the intersection. She recognized the road with its half dozen houses nestled in thick gardens, the vast expanse of the oval opposite, a patchwork of massive gray puddles against the green grass. Big trees along the nature strip loomed threateningly, but nothing had fallen here.

Birrigai only boasted a couple of roads. The main one had a shop, the ubiquitous hotel, a couple of residences, the primary school, oval, a church, and the community hall. Evidence of a once-thriving population. The Sunderland road ran off to the right next to the hotel. She'd followed Brad in on it from the cat expedition. Farther along was the old people's home—a modern, new building—the first indicator of progress in this backwater. Somewhere nearby must be the controversial Networks tower site.

"Here. Go up the drive as far as you can."

Gina edged the car forward. Brad's driveway was gravel, squishy and slippery in the wet. The trees and shrubs had closed in under the weight of the water. Branches bowed low, scraping the side and roof. But she was close to the path leading to the front door, and they could make a dash for it. Claire opened her door, her side closest to the house.

"I'll get an umbrella," she said. The door slammed. Gina watched her race across to the verandah, head bent, clothes soaked before she'd gone three steps. She'd left her backpack on the rear seat. Gina twisted around and dragged it through to the front. She collected her purse and waited.

What was an enraged Brad like? He wouldn't become physical with Claire, would he? No! Never. Gina shook her head. Of course not! But was Claire all right in there? They should've gone in together. She needed backup even though she deserved to face her father and take the consequences of her silliness. Maybe he was so annoyed with Gina, he wasn't even going to come out and invite her in!

Gina flung the door open, grabbed the two bags and struggled out of the car. Rain hit her like a dumper at the beach. Cold, stinging, soaking rain, making her gasp with shock. The lilac branches scraped and clung as she struggled along the side of the car stumbling and slipping. Her shoes were drenched, her toes sliding against wet leather. She rounded the front of the Golf and headed for the house, shoulders hunched, chin down against her chest, hugging the bags against her body for a measure of protection.

Thud! A solid object barred her way. A solid chest clad in a slicker. An arm pulled her hard against the chest and half lifted, half dragged her along the path and up the steps. An umbrella vaguely shielded her head. Suddenly she was completely undercover, and the rain was pelting onto the verandah roof instead of her. But the arm still held her tight. She raised her head to discover Brad gazing into her face. His expression was stern, forbidding, and angry. No trace of the warmth and good humor she'd come to associate with him.

"I was coming to get you." He turned and propped a big black umbrella against the wall. "Come in."

Gina took one squelchy step into the house and reversed quickly. "I'd better take these off." They were ruined, her expensive red leather pumps, water stained and muddy. Her bare feet were chilly on the wooden floor as she followed Brad through the living room to the kitchen, conscious of the trail of drips she was leaving. Claire was nowhere to be seen.

"I'll put that in the laundry." Brad took the sodden backpack from her grasp. "Would you like a hot shower?"

She placed her purse on the kitchen table. "I don't have any other clothes." Gina pulled her wet blouse away from her body and gave an involuntary shiver. Her hair was plastered to her head.

"We'll find something," he said tersely from the laundry. "I've sent Claire to change." He came back into the kitchen. "I was getting worried. You said two o'clock. It's nearly four." He stared at her accusingly.

"It poured the whole way. I could only go about twenty miles an hour." Gina stared right back at him. "Hail too. The roads are flooded."

He dropped his gaze, licked his lips. "Sorry, it must have been a rough trip." He looked up again. "You didn't have to drive her. I told you to put her on the train. She must have a return ticket."

"Probably, but I didn't ask her because I didn't think it was a very good idea."

Eyes locked for a moment. Hers defiant, challenging—his implacable, stonewalling.

"I'll get you a towel and some clothes," he said eventually. He turned abruptly and headed down the hallway toward the bathroom. Gina picked up her purse and padded after him.

Claire's bedroom door opened, and Fiona burst out along with the kitten, which had grown sleek and long-legged. It dashed away toward the kitchen.

"Hello, Gina!" she yelled. "You're all wet. So's Claire." She covered her mouth with both hands and giggled.

"Hello, Fiona. I know, I'm soaked. I have to borrow some dry clothes."

"Mine won't fit you."

"Claire?" called Brad. He opened a door at the end of the hallway and pulled a towel from a neat pile in the cupboard. "Have you got something Gina can wear?"

"Track pants," she said.

Brad handed the blue towel to Gina. "Her tops won't fit you, I'll get you a shirt of mine."

Gina went into the bathroom clutching her purse, the towel, Claire's baggy, gray track pants, socks, and a red-checked flannelette shirt of Brad's, which was enormous by comparison, but looked cozy and warm.

Thank goodness she had makeup and a hairbrush in her purse along with a small perfume spray. She also carried extra nylons now after the elevator disaster, but she wouldn't need those here.

The hot water was marvelous. Gina emerged from the bathroom refreshed and warm, ready to hold her own in any confrontation with Brad.

"You can use my hair dryer," said Claire who was hovering by the door. She shoved the item into Gina's hands and took the wet jeans and shirt. "I'll hang these in the laundry."

"Thanks." Gina grinned and stuck one hand on her hip, model style. "How do I look?"

"My pants are a bit short and Dad's shirt is massive." Claire smiled. "But it looks fine."

"Boy, what a trip!" Gina took the hair dryer and plugged it in while Claire watched.

"Yeah. I've never been in rain like that."

"Me neither."

"Claire go and hang up those clothes, please." Brad's voice cut through their conversation like a knife. Claire darted away.

Gina switched on the dryer and concentrated on her hair. If he was trying to make her feel like a naughty schoolgirl, one of Claire's little friends, he had another thing coming.

Chapter Ten

"There's coffee when you're ready," he said loudly.

Gina lowered the dryer. "Thanks. I'll only be a minute."

He hovered a moment with a blank expression, then turned away. Gina continued combing and drying.

When she entered the kitchen the girls were sitting at the big wooden table drinking something from mugs.

"We've got hot chocolate," said Fiona. "Yummm." She flashed Gina an ingenuous smile. Friendly and sweetly non-judgmental.

"Lucky you," said Gina returning the smile. She touched the soft curls gently.

Brad poured coffee from a plunger pot and slid a red mug across toward her. Gina spooned in sugar from a wooden bowl with a neat little lid. She sat on a chair next to Fiona who grinned at her over the top of her mug as she slurped a mouthful of chocolate. The kitten wound its way through the chair legs.

Gina looked down. "Gosh, the kitten's grown. What's her name?"

"Miss Mistoffelees," said Claire.

"From Cats?"

"Yes. 'Cept it's Mister Mifstoles in Cats," said Fiona. She had a chocolate milk mustache.

"Good name. I like that." Gina smiled at the girls, then glanced at Brad who'd said nothing since she'd appeared and seemed overly concerned with drinking his coffee.

"Are you staying with us?" asked Fiona.

"Only until my clothes are dry enough to wear home."

"But you can stay longer," she cried. "You can stay tonight."

"I don't think so, Fiona. Thank you for the invitation, though."

"You might have to if it floods," said Claire. "Or a tree falls on the road. I wouldn't want to go out in that again. Too scary."

"Oh! Gosh, you're right. There were lots of branches down." Gina cast Brad a worried look. Would he insist she head off into that horrible stormy weather?

"Gina can stay, can't she, Daddy?" said Fiona.

"If the storm hasn't died down," he said reluctantly as though Gina in the house was akin to inviting a plague carrier. "We'll catch it on the six o'clock news."

Gina sipped some coffee. Claire caught her eye and mouthed something that looked like "Should I ask now?" Gina shrugged imperceptibly. Now was as good a time as any, especially if Brad threw her out as soon as the rain stopped.

"Dad, Gina said I can have her old mobile phone if you say it's all right." Claire stopped, almost holding her breath. Waiting for the explosion.

Brad put his mug down carefully. A mobile phone? How dare Gina go behind his back that way? And Claire. Although she already had with spectacular results and she'd be unlikely to say no to that offer.

"I don't think you deserve any sort of reward, Claire, for your recent behavior. Especially an expensive mobile phone." He turned to Gina. "Thank you for the offer, but I don't say it's all right and I'd rather you'd asked me first."

Gina kept her voice level. "I apologize, Brad, but Claire accepted the proviso you had veto power."

"That's right," interjected Claire, her face as thunderous as the weather. "But didn't I tell you what he'd say, Gina? It's so unfair."

"Unfair?" Brad rounded on her. "Unfair? I was sick with worry about you. Was that fair? Sneaking out, lying . . ." He bit down on the rage before he said something he'd regret. "Just go to your room."

Claire gave Gina a teary look and headed out the door.

"Fifi, go and read a book or play with the cat, please. I want to talk to Gina."

"Yes, Daddy." Fifi meekly slipped off her chair and followed Claire.

Brad stared at his coffee mug. How could he possibly make Gina understand what was going on here? It was blindingly obvious she had no idea of the seriousness of the situation and was clueless about discipline or punishment. Sitting there with her holier-than-thou, I-know-best face. Swanning in thinking she could change the life he'd built for himself and his girls.

"I'm sorry you got dragged into our business," he said. "But you must understand, Claire needs to be punished for what she just did, not given a gift."

"It's not a gift so much as a necessity, Brad."

Her tone made him look up in surprise. Far from remorse or indifference she was intensely angry. With him? Her eyes flashed with a dangerous light he'd never seen before, even in the elevator when she was so annoyed.

"Has it occurred to you Claire needs a mobile phone for her own safety? She travels to another town every day. What if she misses the bus or gets into some sort of trouble. It's not just the city where perverts and weirdos hang out. Anything could happen to her and she'd have no way to call for help. Like today. Plus you could call *her*. If she were my daughter I'd have given her a mobile as soon as she went to high school."

His eyes narrowed, his voice emerged in a hiss. "But she isn't your daughter and you've freely admitted not wanting or knowing anything about children."

Gina didn't flinch before his anger. She wasn't accustomed to backing down. That was her problem. She was used to getting her own way—no compromises, no responsibilities.

"True. But I'm not blind and I can see what's happening here. You freely admitted to me you knew zip about teenage girls and you were losing touch with Claire. Well guess what? You've not only lost touch, you're on another planet as far as she's concerned."

Brad glared at Gina's furious face. "So what you're suggesting I do is allow her a mobile phone, pay all the costs involved—and believe me you don't know the length of her phone conversations—and give her the impression that the stunt she just pulled is fine and dandy. Is that how you'd deal with her?"

"Of course, what she's done isn't fine and dandy. I never

said that, but I can understand why she did what she did, whereas you won't listen to her. You can't listen to her without judging and dismissing her, so you'll never understand. You have no idea what she's interested in."

"That's ridiculous!" He slammed his hand on the table with a slap of palm on wood.

"Is it? Do you realize she's very good at computer graphics, but she can't do anything at home because you don't have a computer? She spent hours on mine, and I was amazed at what she was producing. She said her school doesn't have very up-to-date programs so she can't do what she wants, but she loved what I had."

"So I have to buy a computer as well, do I?"

"It would be a very good idea if you want Claire and Fiona to have any sort of chance in life."

"They can use the ones at school, can't they?" He was losing ground here. Attacking him by using his daughters' future was exposing a vulnerable weak spot.

She knew it. She was ruthless. "Sure. Except most schools don't have the latest software and the kids have limited time on them. Claire told me. Especially country area schools— they're all starved for funding and the government's looking to make cuts . . ." She stopped, moderated her tone— reasonable—now she sensed he was weakening. Appealing. "She's really frustrated, Brad."

"Isn't that part of being twelve?"

Gina smiled wryly and shook her head. She raised her hands and let them fall. Was he so dense or so stubborn he couldn't see how Claire needed this support? Thank goodness she hadn't blurted out the primary school closures thing. Birrigai was almost certain to be on the list. She eased her bottom off the chair and rose, suddenly weary of the whole thing. "I'll check how dry my clothes are."

"Why do you care so much?" His expression was different now. The anger had faded. He seemed genuinely curious.

Why did she care? She didn't know Claire very well, had only met her twice. Was it because she was Brad's daughter, or something else?

"I don't know that I do care. Like you said it's not my business."

He was insistent, pressing the point, pinning her down. "But you do care or you wouldn't waste your time driving all this way, and you wouldn't get all hot and bothered about whether I'll buy a computer, or let Claire have a mobile phone."

Gina opened and closed her mouth. She hadn't thought about the why, she just did and said. Not much thought involved. "I don't like to see talent go to waste, I suppose. I hate to see a girl with such potential being held back because her father is—"

"What?" He was almost smiling, daring her to say it.

She met his gaze, laughed softly. "Stuck in the last century."

"Oh, really?" He stepped round the end of the table, closer. "I think you care because despite all your protesting you do have a few maternal instincts buried in there."

Gina steeled herself against him. If he touched her she'd collapse into his arms and they'd restart the whole pointless merry-go-round thing. She said quietly, "Don't confuse maternal instincts with stating the blindingly obvious. That girl's crying out for help." She pulled the sleeves of the shirt up. The cuffs covered her hands completely otherwise.

When she looked at Brad again, he'd stopped, leaning

against the bench with his arms folded, brown eyes studying her. Mustn't get distracted by how attractive he was. This was about Claire, her future. "My father trained me to always learn as much as I possibly could, always strive for knowledge. About anything and everything. We didn't have a computer when I was small, but Dad bought one as soon as they were available. He said they were the way of the future and he wanted us to be prepared."

"I'm not that sort of person," Brad said. "I don't push my girls hard. I want them to enjoy their childhood. I don't want them to be worried about their futures when they're still young. There's time enough for that later."

"Don't get me wrong. I had a great childhood. Dad didn't whip me or lock me in my room to do my homework. He just encouraged learning."

"So you're saying I don't encourage my girls to learn."

Dangerous ground. Gina licked her lips and considered her reply. "I think Claire and Fiona are incredibly lucky kids to be living here with you in this house, but I also think a place like Birrigai doesn't necessarily suit a teenager just because it suits an adult. You've rejected a lifestyle on her behalf which she finds very exciting and which as a young person she needs to understand in order to hold her own in life. The world's changing incredibly fast, Brad. You owe it to both of them to prepare them as well as you can."

"I think I'm doing that."

"Right." There was nothing more to be said. Rain drummed down outside. Through the kitchen window Gina glimpsed the trees lining the driveway thrashing about hellbent on uprooting themselves, or at very least tearing themselves apart. Would he insist she leave in that? Was there a motel in Birrigai?

Definitely one in Sunderland, she'd passed it coming here from the animal shelter. Would she make it there?

"How much will that mobile phone cost me?" His voice startled her.

"Nothing. The phone is an old one, not worth anything, and I bought her a thirty dollar prepaid number. She can pay to renew it herself when she uses up the credit. It'll teach her not to overuse it."

"I'll repay you."

"You don't need to."

"I'll repay you."

Gina didn't argue. One victory was enough.

"But she can't have it until I say so."

"Fair enough." Gina scooped her bag from the floor by her feet. She handed him the phone and the card with the number on it.

"Thanks."

"I'll check my clothes."

Gina escaped into the laundry where Claire had hung her damp jeans and blouse on a wooden clothes horse. No dryer, of course. Brad wouldn't indulge in one of those energy guzzlers. She fingered the jeans. Turned them around. Still wet. They'd take all night. She could drive home in what she was wearing—as long as the rain stopped, otherwise she'd be soaked again before she made it to the car.

The back door rattled in its frame. Wind howled around the eaves with an eerie wail. Rain still smashed down on the roof. Gina shivered involuntarily. She was stuck there.

Brad had cleared away the coffee mugs and stood at the sink peeling a potato. He glanced round when she entered the kitchen.

"Still wet," she said.

"They'll take ages to dry in this weather. Too damp." He returned his attention to the potato.

"I could wear these home and send them back later."

"Too dangerous to drive tonight. Stay," he said in a very stiff voice.

Gina walked right up close to him. She put her hand on his arm. "I don't want to stay if it's going to create too much tension. You already have a problem with Claire. My being here will just make it worse."

"Could it be worse?" he asked with a tiny snort and a wry twist of the lips as he shot her a swift look.

Gina shrugged. "Probably. She could have really run away."

"Good grief! She's not that unhappy, surely." He dropped the peeler into the sink in his shock.

She smiled. "Of course not. She's not going to run away. Calm down. She was pretty scared when she turned up at work, and remember there *were* plans, they'd just gone wrong. The whole expedition went wrong one way or another. I'm just saying—there are worse things than sneaking off to a rock concert." Gina hesitated. There was something else he needed to know about his daughter. Something she was fairly certain he didn't know but should. Would he see it as more interfering? "Umm, did you know she started her periods?"

His expression changed from shock to bewilderment. "No. She hasn't said anything to me."

"She's too embarrassed. Periods aren't the sort of thing she's likely to discuss with you. Especially as you two aren't really . . . her friend Amber's mother helped."

"Oh," he groaned. "Why didn't *she* tell me?"

"It's all right. She's only just started . . . last month."

He heaved a vast sigh. "Should I mention it to her? Or maybe you could tell her you told me?" The brown eyes gazed at her in male bafflement.

"If you like."

"That way I won't seem to be prying."

She smiled. "It sure is a minefield."

Brad grimaced. "Tell me about it."

"And you've got two of them." She picked the peeler out of the sink and nudged him aside. "I'll do this. What are you cooking?"

"Pot roast chicken."

"Delicious."

"It's easy, and popular in this house." He turned on the gas under a large black pot, poured in olive oil, and began to chop an onion.

"You're a very good cook," said Gina. "I'm not."

"Claire doesn't think I am."

"What are you going to do to her?"

"Do to her? After I've thrashed her? Lock her in her room and feed her water and crusts of bread." He scraped the onion pieces into the oil and stirred with a wooden spoon. "If she's lucky."

Gina rinsed the last potato and placed it on the draining board. She bundled the peelings and dumped them in the bucket Brad indicated the under the sink. For compost, of course.

"Keep going." He put garlic, carrots, a parsnip, and two large zucchini in front of her. "She's grounded for fifty years, at least. Extra chores, maybe. I don't know. She's never done anything like this before."

"Are you finished talking to Gina, Daddy? Can I come in now?" Fiona peeped around the doorframe.

"Yes, poppet."

"Are you staying, Gina? It's storming outside."

"Yes, I am."

"Goody. Will you read me my story tonight?"

"Oh." Gina glanced at Brad. He smiled. "All right."

Gina finished the vegetables. She wiped her hands on a handtowel hanging on the oven door.

"Can I have a drink, Daddy, please?"

"Of course. Apple juice, Gina?"

"Yes, please."

He placed glasses and the juice on the bench. "Would you mind pouring?"

Fiona scrambled onto a chair. "What about Claire?"

"Claire's in trouble." Brad took a whole chicken from the fridge, rinsed it, and placed it in the pot. He added the vegetables, stock, wine, and a lid and slid it into the oven. "Done," he said. "Just in time to catch the news."

Gina and Fiona followed Brad into the living room.

Storms headlined with graphic pictures of fallen trees, unroofed houses, and flooding. Gina watched in amazement as the presenter outlined the devastation. A swathe of destruction across the area from Sydney stretching down as far south as Nowra and inland to Mittagong.

"You were lucky to get through at all," said Brad. "They must have closed the highway just after you came along. Run and get Claire, Fifi."

Claire came in silently and watched, sitting on the floor near Gina on the couch. Fiona settled herself next to Gina. Close.

"You'll have to stay," Claire said when the news moved on to a political program. She grinned at Gina, pointedly ignoring Brad.

"She is," cried Fiona. "Aren't you, Gina? Come and see my room." She leaped off the couch and began pulling at Gina's hand.

"Leave her alone," said Claire crossly.

"It's all right." Gina stood up and allowed herself to be dragged down the hall to Fiona's bedroom.

Claire rose to follow them. Brad said quickly, before she had time to escape, "You can have the phone, Claire." She stopped. "But not for two weeks and only on the condition you pay for the calls yourself. And that you behave yourself. You're to come straight home from school and stay home for the next month. No going out anywhere unless it's with us or to a school function. Not even to Amber's."

She nodded vigorously. He said, "And don't think of this as a present from Gina. It's not. I'm paying her for it and I'm only letting you have it because what she said made sense. It's for your own safety."

"Yes, Dad. Thanks." She smiled quickly and darted away to find the girls. Brad slumped into his armchair. Bursts of laughter and Fifi's excited chatter echoed down the hall. For someone who wasn't a kid person Gina had somehow managed to enthrall both his daughters. But it would be the novelty value of an overnight visitor as much as anything else. Certainly as far as Fifi was concerned.

As long as everybody involved realized this was just a friends thing. Nothing more. Brad clicked the news off and roused himself to find a pillow, blankets, and bed linen and take them to the spare room-office-come-study. Fifi's door was closed and he paused for a moment listening to the murmur of voices before chiding himself and moving on. He dumped the pile on his desk chair and began clearing the bed which he more or less used as a storage shelf.

What were they talking about in there? Girl stuff he had no clue about. Like Claire and her periods. He'd failed her badly but what could he do short of questioning her and snooping about in her room for evidence? Naively, when the thought had crossed his mind, he'd assumed Mel would help, or that Claire would turn to her. Not that he'd thought about it much at all. Difficult to accept that his little girl was growing up. And it wasn't something a man had in the forefront of his mind.

He spread the sheet and tucked it in. Computer graphics. She'd inherited the artistic talent from Elaine. He knew she drew well. He'd boasted to Gina about it but Gina had discovered in the space of twenty-four hours something, again, he had no clue about. How could he have missed that? Claire didn't confide in him anymore, that's how.

He stuffed the pillow into a pillow slip and dropped it onto the bed. Two blankets should be enough. It wasn't cold at night now. And any talk of a computer or new technology made him defensive. Poor Claire. Brad sat on the newly made bed. What sort of father was he? Out of touch, old-fashioned, and grumpy. And he was only thirty-six.

"You didn't need to make my bed for me." Gina stood in the doorway, smiling. "Thank you."

"I'm used to doing beds," he said with a grin as he stepped toward her. That red shirt of his suited her, and wearing Claire's slightly too small trackpants and socks made her softer and even sexier. Cuddly. "I'd better check on the chicken."

"You'll make someone a wonderful wife one day," Gina said with a laugh. She moved aside to let him pass, but he stopped so they were jammed in the doorway together. That familiar fresh fragrance teased his nostrils.

"Oh yeah?" He looked down at her with a raised eyebrow. "Will you?"

"No way! That's something I do *not* aspire to—housewifery."

"Uh-huh." Why did she equate marriage with housework?

"Absolutely. I can't think of anything worse than being stuck at home vacuuming and cooking."

"Is that all you think I do?" He headed for the kitchen.

"I know you don't." She padded after him in Claire's thick wool socks.

"We share the load in this house."

"Glad to hear it."

"Elaine and I did too. Equals. She had her career as an artist. More juice?" Gina nodded and he poured refills. "It's all about balance."

"Except she was happy to be a mother and I . . ." She stopped abruptly.

"Don't want to be," he finished, handing her the glass.

"I was going to say can't." Her voice was so low he almost didn't hear the words. She turned away sipping the tangy juice. Sat at the table.

Brad busied himself with the oven and the chicken, his mind full of the implications of her confession. "How tragic and how very sad" was his immediate reaction, but he knew Gina well enough to know she wouldn't want pity or condescension. It explained a great deal, though, and he suddenly understood much of her antipathy to children. A defense mechanism, hiding the hurt, pretending childlessness didn't matter, that she didn't care. Or maybe she really didn't want children. Interesting revelation, though. Very personal. And they weren't stuck in an elevator, either.

"No comment?" she asked as he slid the pot back into the oven. "That smells delicious by the way."

He straightened up. "It's looking good."

She stared at him, tense but trying hard not to let on. Brad sat opposite her at the table. Her face was tight, the jaw rigid. Her fingers caressed the smooth glass.

"Accident or medical problem?" He kept his voice as non-committal as possible. How much of a deal was it to her? Her eyes skittered away.

"My ovaries don't work properly." A smile flicked on and off. "At all, actually. Lucky I don't want kids, isn't it?"

Was it? Brad was beginning to doubt that stance. "Especially as you don't like them," he said carefully.

She screwed up her face in annoyance. "I don't dislike kids, I don't know any. Except yours, and a friend's baby."

"They like you. Mine do." He grasped her hand. Her fingers returned the pressure for a moment, then relaxed. "I think you're very good with my girls. Claire, especially. She's not easy to get on with at the moment, but she trusted you, and even though I don't think you did . . . well, even though I would have handled it differently, I'm grateful she went to you."

"Whether kids like me and vice versa is irrelevant though, isn't it, Brad?" she cried suddenly, violently. "I can never have a baby of my own, so any man I marry isn't going to have a child either."

He kept his voice calm, rational, gripped her fingers firmly even though she tried to pull away. "Not every man wants children, just as you say you don't. And two's plenty for me."

She sat back, frowning, and eased her hand from his. "What are you saying?"

What *was* he saying? "Nothing. I'm simply stating facts," he said. "Just because you can't have children doesn't mean you can't marry someone you love. And it doesn't mean no one will love you." He lowered his voice. "If you let them."

"I'm not stopping anyone from loving me. It's just that nobody does."

"When's dinner, Daddy? I'm starving!" Fiona's voice cut through loudly from the living room where she was watching TV.

"About half an hour," he called.

Gina said, "I could never properly belong in a family where there were already children. I'd always be the extra one, not really belonging. They'd always compare me to their real mother. I'd be the *stepmother*."

She smiled as she said the last words, giving them a portentous emphasis, but Brad wasn't fooled. She was serious, she really believed she was destined to be single.

"They wouldn't if they didn't have their own mother." He leaned back in his chair. "My girls would leap at the chance to have a mother. You've seen the way they carry on. Fifi crawls all over you." He laughed and met Gina's startled gaze. "But I don't want to get married. And neither do you. And we've already decided we couldn't possibly marry each other so their plans are doomed to failure as far as you and I are concerned. Right?"

Gina nodded.

"But," he continued, "hypothetically speaking there's nothing to prevent you from marrying a man who already has children, doesn't want more, loves you, and needs a mother for his kids." He picked up his glass.

"Right," said Gina. "I feel so much better now." She raised her glass and clinked it against his. "As long as he doesn't expect me to give up my job to be this mother."

"No modern man would stand in the way of his partner's fulfillment in life."

"So where is this paragon?"

Brad stood up with a grin. "Who knows? He might be right under your nose."

Gina watched Brad lift plates from the cupboard, and the realization hit her like a thunderbolt. The perfect man *was* under her nose. Perfect in every way except one—lifestyle. She could no sooner live out there in the sticks than he could live in the city. Any attempt at melding such vastly different lives would end in disaster for all concerned, including the girls.

"What about you?" she asked. "What, hypothetically speaking, is your ideal woman?"

Brad set the plates on the table, opened a drawer, and counted out knives and forks. "Someone the girls love and vice versa. Someone I love and vice versa."

"That's it?"

"Need there be more?"

He shot her a look quite at odds with the lighthearted tone of the conversation. A searching look, diving deep into her eyes and her heart.

Gina swallowed, groping for sense amid a rush of emotion. "Heaps more I would've thought."

"Such as?"

"Lifestyle choices, education, ambitions, similar tastes in art, etcetera. World view."

"Sometimes differences in those things can add spice."

"To a point. Or they can just mean two people completely at odds. Like us."

"I think if we truly, deeply loved each other we could work any of those things out." He passed her a handful of cutlery.

"Oh" was all Gina could come up with, and it was a very small, almost inaudible sound at that, because her lungs had virtually stopped functioning from surprise. She stared at the knives and forks. Set the table. Right.

Brad had turned his attention to the oven.

Did he really think that? Her brain began to work. She positioned the knives carefully—blades facing in. Forks on the left. Plates in between. Hadn't he been telling her very convincingly they were traveling on different paths? Even climbing different mountains?

"You've changed your tune," she said. "You said 'wrong time, wrong place' for us and added some esoteric stuff about diverging paths."

He lifted the black pot onto the bench. "Times change. You have to be prepared to adjust."

"What?" Gina burst into incredulous laughter. "That's rich coming from you."

"I've recently made some adjustments in my thinking," he said calmly.

"Not without a fight."

He grinned. "This is ready. Would you mind calling the girls?"

"Sure." Gina withdrew, shaking her head in amazement. So what did that mean?

And he had said *if* we truly, deeply loved each other. A tiny word with a massive meaning. Did she truly, deeply love him? And more to the point did he love her even the teensiest bit? No, appeared to be the answer to that question. The whole discussion was clearly hypothetical. He, as a friend, was pointing out a way she could incorporate a family into her life. Very kind. Very helpful of him.

Something thumped intermittently against the far side of the house, branches clawed at the roof. Rain still drummed down. The old house creaked and groaned under the stress but nothing leaked, nothing gave way. Dependable, solid, reliable—like its owner.

Gina ate dinner at the table with Fiona sitting by her side, facing Brad and Claire opposite. Just like a family. Cozy and secure while the storm raged outside.

"Your dad's a good cook," said Gina. "I haven't had pot roast for years. It's delicious."

"I love meatballs best," said Fiona. "But I love pot roast second best."

"Gina and I had Thai food last night," said Claire.

"Do I like Thai food?" Fiona wrinkled her smooth brow.

"No, you wouldn't because it's spicy." Uttered with disdain.

"I might." Uttered with defiance.

"If you come to visit me sometime you can try it," said Gina quickly.

"Gina said I can come to stay during the holidays, Dad," said Claire. Gina concentrated on her chicken. That was pushing things a bit. Surely Claire knew to keep a low profile for a while.

"Can I come too?" came the inevitable question.

Brad said sternly, "Claire, you have a lot of ground to make up before I consider allowing you to go anywhere. Don't you forget it."

Claire dropped her eyes to her food.

The lights went out. Fiona squeaked, Claire screamed. Gina felt a little body crushing against her. She put an arm around Fiona and hugged her close. "It's all right. The wind blew something onto the electricity wires and broke them," she said into the blackness.

"We've got candles somewhere," said Brad. "Stay put everyone." A chair scraped on the floor. His darker shape became outlined briefly against the window. A cupboard opened. A match flared then a gentle yellow glow sent shadows dancing over the walls.

"Oooh," breathed Fiona. She smiled up at Gina. "It's pretty."

Brad lit several more candles, placing them on saucers on the table and bench.

"There's a flashlight in the laundry," cried Claire. She leaped up and darted away.

"Finish your dinner," said Brad.

Claire reappeared and placed the flashlight on the bench. She sat down and resumed eating.

"We get blackouts occasionally," Brad said. "Have to be prepared."

The wind howled around the eaves. Branches smacked against the roof. Gina shuddered. "It's very dark out here, isn't it? When the power goes off at home it's usually only the building, rarely the whole area. There's always light coming from somewhere."

Something crashed down outside with a tearing and rending of tortured wood and metal, and unmistakably, breaking glass. Close to the house. Gina sprang to her feet.

"That sounded like my car!" she cried.

Chapter Eleven

Brad grabbed the flashlight and ran for the front door. He flung it open letting in a blast of wild, wet air which swirled into the house intent on destruction. "Shut the door!" he yelled. "Stay inside, girls!"

Gina shivered next to him on the covered verandah as he swung the beam of light toward the driveway. The Golf had disappeared. In its place was a tree, an enormous mass of sprawling branches and wet leaves reflecting the light in crazy patterns. The huge trunk lay half on the driveway, half on the fence, and muddy twisted roots reached skyward through the lashing rain and wind. The topmost branches had fallen a hairsbreadth from the house.

"My car!" shrieked Gina.

Brad grabbed her arm as she started down the steps. "You can't do anything," he shouted. The soles of her borrowed socks were instantly soaked through.

"My car," she cried again, tears springing to her eyes.

"Come inside." Brad bundled her back in through the front door and closed it firmly against the wind.

"What happened?" Claire, holding a candle, and Fiona, hovered anxiously.

"A tree fell on my car," Gina said. Total shock. Disbelief. It couldn't be true. Her lovely little Golf. Crushed.

"The big gum," Brad said quietly behind her.

"Bits are always falling off that," said Claire.

"Why didn't you warn me not to park there?" Gina rounded on Brad in fury. "If branches fall off all the time, surely you'd expect something to happen in a storm like this!"

"I'm sorry. I didn't think." He gestured helplessly, and his candlelit shadow danced grotesquely on the wall. "These things happen everywhere. Half Sydney was hit too. You saw the news."

She strode through to the kitchen for her purse. Probably useless trying to phone anyone for assistance in this storm. If the power was out the phone lines would be too, and the emergency services stretched to breaking—if they even had any within fifty miles.

She jabbed a furious finger at the mobile. No signal. Naturally. Out here in the sticks. That's why Networks needed to put a tower in town, so these yokels could join the twenty-first century.

"Can I use your phone? Where's the phone book?"

Brad pointed, but said nothing. Wise man. He'd have his head bitten off if he so much as opened his mouth. Sure cars and houses were damaged in Sydney but there most people had no choice where to park. Here was different. How could it not occur to him to tell her to move the car? He lived here and was supposed to know things like that. She didn't; she was a city girl whose car lived in a secure underground space. And the sooner she got back there the better. The girls kept well away as she flicked through the phone book for the number.

Busy. Constantly. She tossed the phone down in disgust. "I'm stuck here."

"Go and sit in the living room. I'll make coffee," said Brad quietly. "Take some candles in, Claire, please."

Gina sat on the couch. Her feet were wet through Claire's wool socks. They were cold. She stared at her feet as the realization dawned, and slowly pulled the socks off one by one. Claire took them silently and disappeared.

Fiona crept in quietly and crawled onto the couch next to her. She snuggled up and put her two little arms as far around Gina as they'd reach. Good grief. What was this? A cuddle wouldn't fix her car. But it was comforting in an odd way, and after a moment Gina lifted an arm and draped it around Fiona's slight body.

"Daddy didn't mean the tree to fall on your car."

Gina bit her lip which had unaccountably started trembling. "I know," she murmured.

Claire came back with another pair of socks.

"Thanks." Gina detached herself from Fiona and slipped them on. Claire sat on her other side.

"You can stay with us as long as you like," she said.

"Thanks, but I need to be at work on Monday. Goodness knows how I'll get there."

"The train?" suggested Claire.

Gina nodded. She had no choice. Brad couldn't get his car

out with her wreck and that tree in the way. "Is there a bus to the station?"

"Yes."

Brad came in with a tray. "Lucky we have a gas cooktop," he said. He handed Gina a mug of steaming coffee. The girls had hot chocolate again.

"You're insured, of course?"

Gina nodded. "It'll be a write-off."

"What does that mean?" asked Claire.

"They'll give me money to buy a new one instead of fixing it."

"Oh, poor car," cried Fiona.

"Yes." Gina looked at Brad. "I'll try to get something going tomorrow but I'll have to leave the car here obviously, until someone can tow it."

"I can start on the tree in the morning if the rain stops. Neighbors will help."

"Shouldn't emergency services do that?" What sort of place was this? Surely people paid rates and taxes to cover these situations.

He shrugged. "They'll have plenty to do. Might take days to get around to us."

"Days?" Who'd choose to live surrounded by dangerous trees, miles from anywhere, at the mercy of whatever the elements chose to throw at you? She couldn't phone anyone from this backwater, and there was no way of knowing if the roads were cut. The buses may not even run on a Sunday.

Brad met her exasperated gaze with calm detachment. "You saw the news. It's a massive storm front. We're not the only ones affected, and yours won't be the only car hit. Plenty of people will have homes damaged and be in far worse situations. Remember those storms a few years back?"

She did. Half of Sydney was unroofed, cars were pounded with massive hailstones, roads turned to rivers. The damages ran into millions. But she'd been snug at home and her car safe in the underground car park. Her building was unscathed. Brad was making her feel selfish and guilty for having such a minor thing as a crushed car, wanting assistance, and expecting the authorities to come up with the services she paid her taxes to provide.

Enough. She'd had enough. Gina stood up. "I think I'll go to bed."

"Take a candle," said Claire.

The way things were going at the moment her candle would probably burn the house down in the night.

A chainsaw woke her in the morning, ripping through sleep with an earsplitting roar that made Gina wince and curse before her eyes opened and she remembered where she was. And why.

Sunlight cascaded in through the partially closed blind. She blinked and focused on her watch. Eight ten. Her body jerked up straight in astonishment. She'd slept almost eleven hours. Last night when she crawled into the narrow bed and dragged the blankets up under her chin, listening to the wind raging outside, with thoughts and emotions churning inside, she'd been positive she'd never sleep at all. Eleven hours was amazing.

Gina pulled the blind aside and peeped out. Her room faced the back garden. Nothing happening out there. It looked peaceful if damp, with evidence of the storm in small branches and leaves strewn about the lawn. Still windy, but nothing like yesterday.

Brad must be attacking the tree already. A cracking, rending sound followed the burst of chainsaw noise. Claire's voice called something. Someone replied. Not Brad. Gina opened the study door. The house was quiet. She flicked the light switch experimentally and the bulb glowed. Thank goodness for that. She padded barefoot to the laundry to retrieve her clothes. Dry. Thank goodness for that too.

Ten minutes later she emerged onto the front verandah.

Brad didn't notice her coming across the lawn. He was intent on his task. T-shirt straining across his shoulders as he held the saw steady on a branch, jeans clad legs braced. Claire had her back turned dragging debris away down the drive toward the rear of the house. Two strangers, a man and a teenage boy armed with saws attacked smaller limbs. Fiona was nowhere to be seen.

The Golf was partially exposed now. They'd cleared the branches lying over the front, but the bulk of the trunk had fallen diagonally across the roof, squashing it flat. It had been a massive tree. Far too big and dangerous to have in a yard. Could she sue? Whose was it? Gina walked around to where the roots reached for the sky. Muddy clods of earth hung suspended, swinging gently in the breeze. The fence and bushes had been crushed in the fall but a gaping hole showed the tree had been in the neighboring garden. Worth checking out.

The chainsaw stopped abruptly. "Morning," called Brad. He wore orange ear protectors against the noise and clear plastic goggles against flying splinters. He rubbed a muddied hand across his brow, unsmiling. The two neighbors stopped what they were doing and approached warily.

"Hello."

Brad said, "This is Stan and Mick, from two doors along. Gina." The boy grinned, spotty faced and shy.

"G'day, Gina." Stan, thin and gangly like his son, stuck out his hand. Gina shook it. "Bit of bad luck, this," he said. "Devil of a storm."

"Mmm." Gina nodded. *Bit* of bad luck?

"I'll cut that trunk into sections next so we can move it easily." Brad started the chainsaw again. Gina watched for a few moments from a safe distance. Claire grabbed another branch and dragged it away. Gina followed.

"Where's Fiona?"

"At Mel's having breakfast. Dad didn't want her to get in the way."

"I could've kept her safe."

"You were asleep, and he said we weren't to annoy you."

Gina drew in a startled breath. "Claire, neither of you annoy me. Don't ever think that." Was Brad keeping her away from them after her anger last night? Protecting them from her?

Claire grinned. "Okay. But Fifi can be a real pest." She tossed the branch onto a pile she'd made near the workshop.

Gina smiled. "When does the bus go to Moss Vale, do you know?"

"Ten, twelve, and another at three."

"Where from?" They started walking back to the car.

"The main street outside the general store."

"What about trains to Sydney?"

"On Sundays they're every two hours from about ten but you change in Campbelltown."

"All right. So I could leave here at twelve and get a train about two?"

"Yes."

"Fine." Gina turned to go back inside. The chainsaw hurt her ears. Horrible racket.

Claire said breathlessly, nervously. "I'm sorry, Gina."

"What for?" Gina stopped in surprise.

"This." She gestured at the disaster area. "It's my fault."

Gina managed a smile of sorts. "Hardly."

"But if I hadn't gone to the city this wouldn't have happened."

"Claire, there are way too many ifs for you to say that. If it hadn't stormed, or if I hadn't parked right there, or if almost anything you can think of . . ."

"I s'pose."

"It's not your fault."

Gina went inside and tried calling the insurance company. She was placed in a queue so she hung up and made tea for herself, chose a banana from the bowl on the bench, and ate it sitting at the table. Big Al should be all right. She'd be home tonight. He had his dry food dispenser and water. He'd be cranky, though.

The chainsaw revved and roared outside. Should she help? No. The neighbors were handling it. She wasn't made for heavy lifting. So much for doing good deeds. So much for karma. The sooner she was home the better.

Gina finished her banana and rinsed the mug. She stripped the bed and folded the blankets, took the sheets to the laundry. Miss Mistoffelees rubbed against her ankles.

"Too noisy for you out there? Me too."

A couple of hours to fill before the bus left. She switched on the TV hoping for a news report on the storm damage. She made herself more tea, tried the insurance company again, rejoined the queue, and sat in the living room drinking it with the TV on mute. A calm voice periodically assured her she was progressing in the queue. Would they demand proof a tree had damaged the car? If Brad removed the evidence before an assessor came, what then? Gina raced outside with her mobile and the phone.

Brad turned. He shut off the saw and lifted his ear muffs. "What's wrong?"

Gina slammed down hard on the intense rush of attraction. "I'm taking a photo for the insurance. Just in case," she said in her most cool professional voice.

She raised her mobile. Brad, tough, competent and outdoorsy in dirty jeans, paint stained T-shirt and workboots, faint scowl, all of which made her want to rub her body against his. The tree, mostly dismembered, but still clearly squashing her poor crushed car. Broken glass sparkled gaily in the bright sunlight.

"Stay still," she said. "Another one." This one was more Brad than car. Something to remember him by after she left here because chances were she'd never see him again after this combined and mostly disastrous effort. He stared straight at her, stern faced, annoyed at the interruption. Annoyed with her. She closed the mobile. "Done."

He turned. She held the other phone to her ear. Still in the queue. "I'm leaving at noon on the bus," she said. "I'll train home."

"Fine," he said over his shoulder.

"Will it be all right to leave this here?" She gestured at her car even though Brad wasn't looking at her. She caught Stan's sympathetic eye. "I'll organize a tow truck as soon as I can."

"It's all right. We'll push it back onto the nature strip out of the way," he said. "Or I'll bring the ute around and tow it clear."

Brad restarted the chainsaw and began on the trunk proper. Gina obviously blamed him for this disaster. She'd said as much last night and she couldn't get away from them fast enough today. As long as her vitriol didn't spill over onto the girls. No telling what she'd say in her rage. This rotten tree. Old Ralph should have cut it down years ago. He should have insisted himself. It was dangerous and could easily have fallen on someone or on the house. Trouble was no one wanted to cut down the ancient giant. It was part of the natural beauty and attraction of the area. They were all lucky it was only a car in the way.

Gina wouldn't see it like that, though. Just when they'd begun to relax and enjoy each other's company properly. And she'd confided in him, such a personal thing. She wouldn't tell many people something like that. He'd begun to feel, tentatively, she just might fit into their lives, all three of them. The girls liked her and she liked them now she'd gotten to know them better.

He stepped back as a chunk of timber rolled free of the car. But wasn't that how it went? A thunderbolt from the blue to keep you in your place, stop you getting too happy and contented with your lot? Gina wouldn't be coming back to visit them in a hurry. Birrigai had confirmed all her prejudices. He bit back on the rise of disappointment. Bitter disappointment, if he let it assume full proportions. He couldn't wallow. She wouldn't ever feel comfortable out here. He knew that, and it was stupid and pointless to hope otherwise. A woman like Gina choosing to live out in the sticks . . . never.

"We'll get this clear soon," said Stan coming up beside him and studying the Golf. "Reckon we can push it out of the way?"

"Maybe." Brad squatted down and peered underneath. "The wheels don't look damaged."

"If you cut it here and here." Stan pointed. "That should be enough to get her free. We'll clear the drive, then you can get your car out and drive Gina to the station."

"She said she'll catch the bus."

Stan shook his head. "Drive her, mate. Believe me. Drive her."

"She blames me for this. I don't think she'll want to be that close to me for a while yet."

"She'll get over it."

"Mmm." Brad remained unconvinced by Stan's confident assessment of things female. Stan and Mel only had sons. Mel was easygoing and straightforward. Gina was anything but.

Half an hour later the tree was cleared. A neat stack of heavy, sawn logs sat along the fence and a pile of branches lay in the backyard ready to be cut up for winter firewood and kindling. A couple of logs he'd keep aside for the work-shop. Make nice bowls when the wood dried out. Leaves and debris lay everywhere and would need raking up later. A job for Claire this afternoon.

"We give it a go?" asked Stan.

"She probably left it in gear with the brake on," said Brad

after some heavy shoving failed to move the Golf an inch. Impossible to get at either with the roof crushed flat and broken glass and metal everywhere.

"I'll get the ute." Stan headed for home with Mick trailing after. Claire ran into the house.

"Bring Fifi back with you, will you, Stan? Thanks, mate."

Stan waved an arm in acknowledgment.

Brad went inside and discovered Gina in intense discussion with the insurance company. She glanced up blankly as he came in, but continued her conversation. He went to the bathroom, showered quickly and changed his filthy jeans and T-shirt for clean jeans and a shirt. Music emanated from Claire's room. He tapped on the door before sticking his head around the frame. She was sitting at her desk writing. With any luck it'd be homework.

"I'm going to drive Gina to Moss Vale for the train," he said.

Claire turned the music down. "No trains," she said. "The track's washed out somewhere."

"How do you know that?"

"It was on the news. Gina checked on the TV."

"I thought she was on the phone," he said.

"Dad, she can do two things at once." No doubt she could manage more than two.

"I'll have to drive her home," he said.

She sprang up. "Can we come?"

He shook his head. "I'd rather you stayed here and did some homework. You've already had a trip to the city. I'll be back by four at the latest if we leave soon."

"Are you taking Fifi?" Her eyes narrowed beneath the resigned frown.

"Probably not. She'll be too tired tomorrow. She can stay with Mel."

For once there was no argument. Claire returned to her work with barely a grumble. Gina had coffee ready in the kitchen. She poured him a cup.

"Thanks," he said, surprised by the gesture.

"I have to leave in a few minutes. Claire said the bus goes at twelve." Her voice was noncommittal and reserved, reminiscent of Ms. Red Suit from the elevator episode

"But there are no trains," he said.

"No, but I'm more likely to catch another bus from Moss Vale than here. Or I might get a train to Wollongong and then up from there." In other words any means of escape would do.

"Stan's getting his ute to move your car." He swallowed some coffee.

"Will that work?'

"Yep. If not I'll borrow the ute and take you home in that."

"You don't need to."

"Yes, I do, Gina." An engine sounded outside. "There he is now." He put his coffee down. "Either way I'll drive you home."

"No, definitely not!"

He ignored her and strode to the door, marched across the verandah and down the steps.

Gina followed him out. He was clearly determined to make some form of recompense for her trials. She'd be mad to turn down his offer. And apart from the convenience of driving, the idea of his unadulterated company for a couple of hours was, quite honestly, very appealing.

Fiona climbed out of the ute and ran across to her. "Hello Gina, I've been playing with my friend Joey."

"Hello."

"Your poor car's flat as can be." Fiona slid her hand into Gina's, and they stood watching as Brad and Stan hitched a tow rope to the rear of the shattered Golf. The insurance person said they'd organize a tow to the nearest registered body shop where their inspector would assess the damage. In Moss Vale. A forty-five-minute drive. Everything was so far away and slow in the country. Time-consuming and tedious. And that was assuming the road was open.

Claire came and stood with them. "Dad's driving you home," she said. "But he won't let us come. Can we?"

Gina said, "It's his decision, not mine."

"But . . ."

"Claire, I can't interfere." Gina snapped her mouth closed. She didn't mind either way whether they came or not, but no way was she weighing into this. Brad had made it clear he was in charge of the family. She was an outsider and should not interfere. She knew that.

The Golf began to move with a screeching of tortured metal and a scraping of wheels on gravel. Stray twigs, leaves, and mud flew into the air. Stan dragged the corpse clear of the driveway and left it at an odd, forlorn angle on the nature strip. He and Brad untied the tow rope. Stan wound it up.

"Ready to go?" Brad asked Gina.

"Yes. I'll get my purse."

Brad looked at his daughters. "You two go to Mel's for lunch. Claire, you can come home as long as you're doing homework. If you need a break you can rake up all this." He waved his arm at the leaves and storm litter.

"Fine," she muttered.

Gina hugged each girl in turn. When she bent to embrace Fiona she received a warm kiss on the cheek and a surprisingly strong hug from such a small pair of arms. Claire kissed her too. "Thanks, Gina," she said.

Gina touched her cheek gently. "I'd say anytime, but next time do it differently, okay?"

"Yes. Can I come in the holidays?"

"Me too?"

Gina glanced at Brad. "It's up to your dad."

"We'll discuss that later." He opened the passenger door. "Go straight to Mel's."

"Yes, Dad."

Gina waved out the window as Brad backed along the driveway and onto the street. She kept her eyes averted from the Golf. Too painful. That must be why her eyes were wet. Nothing to do with those two beautiful little girls waving wildly and running along the path as the car pulled away. Would she ever see them again? Would Brad allow them to visit? They'd wriggled their way into her heart as easily as could be. Not just Claire, but Fiona, too, with her loving, trusting nature and her warmhearted childish sympathy offered in complete honesty. She sniffed and quickly pulled a tissue from her pocket.

Brad glanced at her.

"They're lovely children," said Gina defensively.

"Yes." They left the Birrigai town limit, and Brad accelerated.

Gina stared out the window. Not much evidence of the storm here. A few branches down, but the floodwater covering the road yesterday when she and Claire had driven in had disappeared completely.

"Not a kid person, eh?" he said.

"I'm allowed to change my mind." Gina shot him a quick look, but his eyes were focused on the road. "Times change. You have to be prepared to adjust." She waited for his reaction, hoped he'd remember.

To her relief Brad's lips curved. "That's rich coming from you."

"We live and learn," she said piously.

"Some of us take longer to learn than others," he said.

"Which of us would you be referring to as a slow learner?"

"Me." His tone was serious now. "I'm sorry I was so rude to you about Claire, Gina. All you did was help, and I'm very sorry about your car. Not much of a way to be repaid for your kindness."

"The insurance company will cough up. They said the water damage would be the clincher. It ruins the interior. But I did like my car. And it's such a gigantic nuisance on top of everything else. I must have bad karma," she said.

He laughed. "Never thought I'd hear you say something like that."

"Neither did I. You must have a bad influence on me," she said dryly.

He chuckled. "It's the fresh country air. Clears your brain."

"My brain is clear. No one can ever accuse me of foggy thinking. Especially at work."

"True. I bet you're sharp as a tack."

Gina studied him suspiciously. Was he having a go at her? "I am, actually," she said. "I'm beginning to think about changing jobs."

"Really?" He darted a sideways look at her, then concentrated on the road again. "Why? I thought you love what you do."

"I do like that sort of work, but I'm not all that happy with . . ." What was it she didn't like at Bright and Caulfield? Craig, for one thing, but she could put up with him. The corporate attitude? The projects themselves? Was that it? How they'd reacted to Claire annoyed her intensely, and not least because they were expressing what would have been her own opinion a few months earlier. But even before that the insensitive, callous comments about the school closures and funding had pushed a newly sensitive nerve. The Claire thing had crystallized something, a discontent that had been slowly forming.

"Not happy with . . . ," prompted Brad.

"I think I'd just like a change of environment. Different type of work. I'd like to travel. I might start looking for something overseas."

Brad hooted with delight. "You've developed a social conscience!"

"Not so as *you'd* notice," she retorted. "It's nothing to do with Networks. Surely you can see the need for a tower in your area. You're totally cut off when the power fails."

"Let's not start that again."

"You don't want to talk about it because you know I'm right," she said smugly.

He ignored that crack. "So what's the real reason you want to switch jobs?"

"Some of the people are annoying. It's very narrow in focus, that world. I think I need a change."

"I don't have the problem of annoying work mates," Brad said. "It's one of the benefits of being self-employed.

"That Judith woman annoyed me." A sudden burst of laughter erupted from deep inside. "You know she warned me not to lead you on and toy with your emotions? What nerve!"

"Had you planned on toying with my emotions?" Brad asked with a grin.

"No more than you had with mine. I figure you can look after yourself. Even if you do live in a town where everyone knows your business. Personal included."

"It's not quite that bad."

"Yes it is. I couldn't live like that. I like my privacy."

"I do too."

"Hah. Fat chance you've got in that place."

"People respect the boundaries you set up," he said. "When I needed help it was given freely and generously, and still is, but no one interferes with my family. Apart from Judith who's just a sticky beak. They're everywhere."

"True. My grandma's another one."

"You can't have it both ways," he continued seriously. "You can't expect help from people and then keep them away later on when you don't need assistance anymore. And you can't expect people to help if you lock yourself away and insist on being self-sufficient."

"Is that what you think I do?' she demanded.

"I didn't say that."

"You didn't have to."

"All I meant was that country people do things differently." His tone was patronizingly patient. "We have a stronger sense of community. We have to work together because we don't have the services and support networks that cities do."

"You can say that again."

"But I'd take Birrigai with its lack of services over the city with its lack of humanity any day!"

Brad slowed as they reached the on-ramp to the freeway. Not much traffic. He accelerated into the left lane ahead of a distant semitrailer. Gina looked out the window with lips firmly closed. Mustn't start an argument on a topic they would never agree on. He seemed to feel the same way because he said suddenly, "You could set up your own company, couldn't you?"

"Doing what?"

"I don't know. Accounts or something. Giving people business advice."

Gina tilted her head, considering. "I suppose. If I had to I could be a freelance consultant. But I'd rather pick up a good salary from someone else."

"I'd hate to be accountable to someone else."

"You already are." She smiled at him. "Two someones."

"Yeah, and it's a life sentence." He turned the sides of his mouth down glumly.

"You're lucky to have them," she said quietly.

"I know." Brad looked across at her. "You could share them." Husky voiced.

Gina's throat clammed shut. What was he suggesting? How could they share them when they lived in different worlds, and what did *share* mean? She swallowed, forced herself to breathe. "I already said they could visit in the holidays," she said cautiously.

He smiled. With relief? The moment, whatever it meant, had gone. "Yes, and they won't let us forget."

"I don't want to forget."

"I'm glad. I wasn't sure you'd want anything more to do with us after what just happened." The glance he sent her this time was definitely relieved.

"Brad, I'm grown up enough to be able separate people's actions and decisions from acts of God. I might have over-reacted and I'm sorry for that, but I truly don't blame you for anything. Claire thought she was responsible somehow because she went to the city in the first place. It's crazy."

"Did she say that?" Alarmed. His body stiffened.

"It's all right, I told her that was insane thinking."

The hands on the steering wheel relaxed, his shoulders settled against the back rest. "Thanks. But you're right, I should have told you to move the car."

"Maybe but it's too late now. I *was* thinking about suing the owner of that property next door." Gina's voice hardened as the image of her flattened car flashed before her eyes again. Only one year old.

"What?!" Horrified, now.

"He should have made sure it was safe. What if a branch had dropped on one of the girls? Or smashed into your house?"

"I'm as much to blame as Ralph. I should have insisted he trim it."

"Yes."

"But what's suing him going to achieve? He's seventy."

Gina sighed. "Nothing, I suppose." Except make her look like the evil witch of the west for targeting an old-age pensioner, and probably get her face on some vigilante-style current affairs show.

"Right. Nothing. Suing people—money—isn't the answer to everything." He added in disgust, "Maybe you should sue God for creating the storm. Makes as much sense."

"Now there's a thought," murmured Gina. But she caught his shocked glance and couldn't hold back a laugh at his expression.

Chapter Twelve

Brad didn't laugh. Gina could be hard as nails. Always looking for the angle. Surely she wasn't serious about suing Ralph? Looking at her determined face and hearing the tone of her voice—that Ms. Red Suit, professional, tough-woman voice—he wasn't so sure.

"I don't think I'll buy another car," she said suddenly. "I'll put the insurance money into my mortgage."

"Won't you need a car?" Thank goodness they were on to a safe topic. Safer, anyway.

"No. It was nice to have it, but I don't need one in the city. And if I leave Australia I'd have to sell it anyway."

"Were you serious about looking overseas for a job?" His heart sank unexpectedly. Friends a few hours' drive apart was one thing. Gina not in the same country was another. Somehow, over the weekend he'd developed the comfortable notion they might slowly develop a deeper relationship. Given time and reasonable proximity.

"I've always wanted to go to New York," she said eagerly.

"It's a great place."

"Have you been there?" She couldn't hide her amazement. She must think of him as a real, clod-hopping hick.

"Yes."

"When?"

"Before Claire was born Elaine and I went together, and then the second time I was alone. When I had the exhibition in London. I went to the States as well. Mainly for the jazz clubs."

"I've never been."

Brad hid a smile. She sounded as though she'd been one-upped and didn't like it. Competitive. "Will it be easy to find another job?"

"Shouldn't be too difficult. I'm very well qualified and experienced. I've already been approached a few times by other firms." That was said matter-of-factly, not a hint of boasting, just stating facts. She was good with facts, clarity of vision. No messy thinking with Gina.

"Headhunted?"

Gina nodded. "Sounds terrible, doesn't it?"

"Sounds impressive." It was impressive. She said she was good at her job and he believed her, but being wooed by others in the same business meant she was seriously good at it. Maybe she would pack up and leave. She'd be in a different country, meet someone new. Some wealthy high flyer who also didn't want the burden of children. Someone who thought and moved as fast and precisely as she did.

"I might just quit and take a break. Travel and see what turns up."

Brad didn't respond. He couldn't very well tell her what he really felt, that he wanted her to stay in Sydney so he could maintain contact. That he didn't want her to go anywhere except closer to him. What was he offering? Beyond friendship, nothing at the moment. He knew what reaction that would get from Gina. She wasn't interested in him with all his dependents and responsibilities. She may have gained a new and positive awareness of the girls, but that was a far cry from . . . what? Love? Loving them. Loving him.

Was he thinking about loving her? He thought about her all the time and those thoughts warmed his heart. Nourished his soul.

Conversation ceased and traffic increased as they approached the city. Gina stared out the window. Brad concentrated on driving. She fished coins from her purse for the M5 toll and told him to stay on the expressway until they reached the Cleveland Street exit. Half an hour later he parked in a Darlinghurst street outside a building with a private, orderly garden surrounded by a high, cream-painted brick wall.

"Come in," she said.

"I won't stay long. Have to get back for the girls." And he wouldn't see her again. No point prolonging the agony. His agony.

"Time for a cup of tea?"

"Yes. Thanks."

Brad got out and stretched. Gina was already heading through a pair of ornamental wrought-iron gates in the wall. She waved a key card in front of a panel to gain access through the glass front door. Brad followed her into the cool, spacious foyer. What do they do if the power goes off, or their cards stop working? City living was so complicated.

"Stairs or elevator?" she asked, flashing him a grin.

"Either."

"Elevator. My shoes are wrecked. They've dried all stiff and uncomfortable."

"I'm game if you are."

"We'll risk it."

She stepped boldly into the small space. Brad stood beside her and tried to keep his thoughts on the present and not that other occasion. The same perfume wafted into his nostrils, enhancing and sharpening the memory. He kept his gaze away from her. Away from the rise and fall of her breathing under that crumpled blouse, the gentle curve of her hips in the jeans. His eyes slid sideways and down. The bare skin of her neck was tantalizingly close. A small pulse beat in her throat. He looked away quickly.

This elevator functioned rapidly and perfectly, disgorging them at the fourth floor with a barely perceptible sigh. Gina turned left and left again, walked by two doors and opened the third. Mid-blue door number four hundred and eight.

"Come in," she said over her shoulder. "Meet Big Al."

Brad stepped into a small entry way that opened onto a large pastel gray room obviously used for dining and lounging. Filmy white curtains billowed from the breeze slipping through a partially open sliding glass door in the living room end, which led onto a balcony. Dark-blue curtains pulled wide on either side. Two medium sized prints hung on one wall—purple/blue-toned abstracts in slim silver frames—a pair chosen to blend with the décor. Black dining table and six ladder-backed chairs, a dark blue couch with white, teal, purple, and black cushions sitting neatly in place, dark gray carpet soft underfoot. She liked blues. His sculpture sat in a corner on a small white box, nicely placed, a focal point.

A large fluffy white cat lay by the floor-to-ceiling windows, staring at the intruders.

"Hello, Al," called Gina. "I'm home."

"Hello, Big Al," Brad said as he moved farther into the room. Big Al continued his scrutiny. His tail flicked once then he got up, stretched, and disappeared through to the balcony.

Gina laughed. "He's cross because I've been away. He's pretending not to care. If you need it, the bathroom's through here on the right." Gina indicated a short passageway with two doors at the end and one on the side. "Or there's another toilet there." She pointed to a door in the entry area to the left of the front door and opposite the kitchen. "Excuse me. I need a wash. Put the jug on?"

"Sure."

A high bench separated the living area from the kitchen. In stark contrast to his home everything was meticulously neat. Like a display show room. A crystal vase of daffodils was the only occupant of the dining table. They usually had to clear books, papers, toys and heavens knows what other junk off the table at home before they could eat. Gina must have thought she'd entered a pigsty.

The kitchen bench held a telephone, answering machine, and notepad with pen neatly lying on top ready for action. In his house, no one could find a pencil when they needed one. Pencils went on walkabout. If one did appear it would probably be yellow or purple from Fifi's coloring set. Or a stub of crayon. Why would Gina want to live with that?

He filled the gleaming silver electric jug, flicked the switch, and went to use the guest washroom.

Big Al turned his head regally when Brad joined him on

the balcony. The cat sat close to the wall, well away from the strip of hot, sunbaked concrete and the remaining puddles leftover from the storm. Gina hadn't reappeared. Brad ran his hand along the cat's soft back, earning a burst of purring and a demand for more, evidenced by a determined shove of the face into his palm.

"Like that, do you?"

Big Al twined around his ankles, Brad straightened. Her building was taller than the surrounding rows of terrace housing. Gina had a view northeast over rooftops. The ocean would be away in the distance to the east hidden by a bank of leftover storm clouds. Too far to see even on a clear day, and the land sloped up and away from where they were. Nice in the morning to sit out here for breakfast.

A little potted garden of herbs flourished at the other end of the balcony. Various flowering plants trailed blue, white, and pink blooms at this end with storm-damaged petals and leaves strewn about. Petunias? Pretty, whatever they were but it was obvious, if this was the extent of last night's damage, why Gina was so upset by her exposure to the wildness in Birrigai.

Gina emerged from her room, and he turned and went inside. Her creased shirt had been replaced by a looser, long-sleeved white one that hung out over her slacks in orderly casual style. Red brocade Chinese slippers were a surprisingly incongruous addition to the ensemble. Too gaudy for the Gina he knew. Or didn't know.

Big Al skipped ahead and nearly tripped him. Typical cat. They were all self-centeredly the same.

"Al wants his lunch, don't you, my boy?" Gina opened a cupboard and removed a small can of cat food. She bent and scooped the contents into an orange plastic bowl on the kitchen floor.

"What will you do with him if you leave?"

"I'm not leaving tomorrow. I haven't decided anything yet." She rinsed her hands. The electric jug clicked off and she began making tea. "Go and sit down."

Brad did as he was told. She was so cool and calm. Had the previous month without any contact between them passed as slowly for her as for him? When he heard her voice on the phone, just for an instant, he'd been overjoyed. Then, in the anxiety about Claire and the ensuing dramas he hadn't had time to think, to contemplate the meaning of that deep hankering to see her, hear her. Touch her. Kiss her. But he did now.

Gina placed a mug of tea before him on the coffee table. She sat opposite.

"Quiet with no kids," she said.

"Yes." Hoarse, barely audible. He cleared his throat. "Thanks."

He sipped the scalding tea and realized her eyes were fastened on him, her own tea untouched. Desire surged. He should leave. Plan was to stop in for a few minutes then head on home. She was probably waiting for just that. Fed up with Hardings. He put the mug down and stood up. She hesitated then rose as well. He stared into her gorgeous blue eyes and completely forgot everything.

Her lips parted slightly. Her skin dewy fresh after her wash, no makeup save for a brush of shadow around her eyes that accentuated the blue. The same perfume. Memory swamped him. Holding her body against his. His gaze dropped to her throat, the V of her blouse. He knew how her body felt under his eager fingers. He knew her lips.

Could he kiss her? Should he?

They were alone. No interruptions in the shape of children. No imminent danger of death by falling elevator. The urge to kiss her became a tangible force. To follow on from where they'd left off in the elevator and in the street in front of his house. Better still, start again. In broad daylight. Eyes wide open. If she threw him out, so be it, he had to try. See if her desire was still as strong. A match for his.

Her lips trembled. He stepped closer and she came into his arms instantly. Soft and pliable, mouth seeking his, arms reaching for his body, finding and holding.

Minutes, or perhaps it was hours, days or even months later, Brad drew her down to snuggle beside him on the couch.

"I guess that was inevitable," he said.

"Was it?" she murmured. She raised her head and kissed his chin, rested her cheek on his chest. "I didn't think so."

"Did you doubt I wanted to kiss you again, properly, right from that time we kissed in the elevator?"

"Maybe you did, but that doesn't make it inevitable."

"It does if we kept on seeing each other."

She lifted herself up and twisted around to hold his face between her palms. "You said you wanted to be just friends. Friends don't kiss like that."

A slow satisfied smile. "I lied."

"I believed you." She pulled his arm around her again. "This makes everything very complicated."

"Does it?" Not wanting to think about the time, about having to leave. A ninety-minute drive away from the warmth of her. How long till the next time? Too long.

"Of course it does." She punched his thigh lightly with her fist.

He sighed. "I suppose a weekends-only relationship will be a bit frustrating."

"Is that what you're envisaging? I go to Birrigai every weekend to visit you?"

He frowned at her tone. "It's a bit hard for me to get away," he pointed out.

"Me too. Especially as I have no car."

He leaned over to kiss her. "You might need to buy another one."

"What?" She sat bolt upright, pushing him away. "Just because we spent half an hour kissing doesn't mean I'm completely changing all my plans, Brad."

"You mean you'd still look for a job outside Australia? Even now?"

"What do you mean *even now*? This doesn't change any of our problems."

He sat up straight as well. "I thought you might reconsider."

"Reconsider what?"

"Your future," he said helplessly. "I thought you might like to consider we'd be in it."

"You mean because of this I'll change my whole life for you, all my dreams and ambitions?"

Brad stood up and looked down at her, staring up at him defiantly.

"Gina, I kissed you because it meant something to me. Something important. I haven't felt this way about any woman. Ever. Including Elaine. I don't kiss women at random. Maybe you do men. I don't know what city girls think is the norm, but I know what I think."

"Don't give me that. You enjoyed it as much as I did. You didn't need much prompting."

"You invited me up here, and you know it wasn't just for a cup of tea." Injured innocence. "You wanted me to stay."

"Sure I did. Why not? We both know we're attracted to each other. But it doesn't mean I want to give up my life to be a mother to your girls. Much as I might like them," she added.

Brad glared at her. No words would come. He'd virtually told her he loved her. Given her his heart on a platter, confessed she meant more to him than Elaine, and she didn't care. Her career meant more to her than he did. Or the girls. This had just been entertainment to her. A diversion. Scratching an itch. He shook his head in numb disbelief.

"Oh, I see," he murmured before turning and stumbling away to find his keys discarded in the kitchen. He didn't know whether he'd ever find his heart again.

Gina listened to the sounds of his departure too disappointed and angry to stop him. What a gigantic mistake that had been. Blame the weakness of the flesh. Kissing him that way hadn't been inevitable as far as she was concerned, but the aftermath was. She knew becoming more intimate wouldn't solve anything. Was he so naïve he did? Had he really expected her to undergo a complete transformation? Had he planned this, thinking everything would magically be all right between them? No, he wasn't cunning or manipulative. That's why she loved him.

The front door clicked shut.

"Don't go," she cried. She leaped off the couch and raced to catch him, flung the door open and yelled down the empty corridor, "Brad. Stop." He couldn't have caught an elevator that quickly. She always had to wait ages. "Brad."

She held the door ajar with one hand, disastrous to be

locked out, no time to find her key, and peered anxiously at the far end where the corridor turned for the elevators. He appeared slowly round the corner and stood silently staring at her.

"Come back. We need to discuss this," she said.

"I have to get home."

"A few minutes won't make any difference. Don't leave like this."

He hesitated a moment, then started toward her. She turned silently, held the door for him to enter, then walked into the living room and faced him.

"What do you want to say?" he said flatly.

Gina faltered under his sternness. "I don't know." Her fingers fiddled with buttons of her the shirt—clumsy, shaking. Her eyes sought his, pleading. "I didn't want you to go, to leave angry."

He ran a hand through his hair, frustrated. The sternness, a façade, had gone. The underlying hurt and confusion on his face broke her heart, but this was crucial if they were to have any sort of relationship. She couldn't give in and let sentiment undermine her position.

He said, "It's obvious you don't want anything more from me and you don't want anything I can offer you." A shrug. "What else is there to say?"

"You said we could work things out," she whispered.

"With one proviso—that we truly loved each other." He stared into her eyes. "You don't love me enough, Gina, do you?"

There it was. The dragon lurking in the background had stormed center stage.

"Do *you*?" she asked, evading, sidestepping the question she'd carefully pretended would never be asked, would never be an issue.

He shook his head. "I asked first. You wanted to talk," he reminded her.

Her lips wobbled. She dropped her gaze. "I don't know."

He stepped forward and embraced her gently, holding her against his body as though she were fragile. A precious thing.

"I love you," he said softly. He tilted her chin up and kissed her, soft and tender so she almost melted. "Think about it."

"Do you love me enough to change your life?" she asked with her lips against the roughness of stubble on his cheek. "Would you come to live in the city?" She didn't move, savoring the magic of his arms around her, knowing it couldn't last longer than a few minutes.

"It's more than just my life," he said slowly. "I have Claire and Fifi to consider."

"See?" she murmured. He kissed her again and she clung to him, knowing this was the end. They'd finally faced the dragon and he'd defeated them. Easily. "We can't work this out. Neither of us would be happy and we'd all end up hating each other. You have a happy family at the moment. Don't spoil it."

"I love you," he said again. But he released her and headed for the door without turning. She watched, motionless, as it clicked shut behind him.

"Hope you'll be able to give us your full attention today, Gina," said Fred on Monday morning, when all the upper echelon staff filed in for their regular meeting. Given the amount of sleep she'd had last night, and the cause of that deprivation her full attention was highly improbable.

"No more children likely to appear?" Craig sniggered and a few people laughed.

Gina sat down. "I had a terrible weekend," she said curtly. "I had to go to Birrigai in that storm and a tree fell on my car." And her heart had suffered a severe blow. A surprisingly debilitating blow. One it may not survive.

"Were you hurt?" cried Valerie. Her visits occurred several times a year when she blew in like a mini tornado from the Melbourne office. This time she was in Sydney for a week, in connection with something another team were working on. Gerard's team.

He'd frowned when Fred made his opening remark. He was even more of a nitpicking stickler for the rules than Fred. Gerard had his long-term eye on the Managing Director's office. So did Fred, and Fred was in his way.

"No, I wasn't in it. It was in the drive at my . . . where I was visiting."

"Much damage?" asked Craig. Property damage would interest him far more than an injury to a person. Particularly herself.

"It'll be a write-off."

"More convenient in a way than messing around with major repairs," he said, and he even looked sympathetic for a moment.

Gina nodded. For once she agreed with him. This way she wouldn't need to go anywhere near Birrigai. Tempt fate. Torture both herself and Brad.

The meeting commenced. Fred talked, Gerard talked. Occasionally someone else commented, or suggested, or reported.

Then it finished. Gina got up and headed for the tearoom, intent on coffee. Valerie followed, chatting cheerily about how much she loved visiting Sydney. Gina listened vaguely and made interested noises. Valerie, she knew from experience, didn't need much encouragement to keep her going.

"Shall we have lunch together?" Valerie asked finally. "I'd really like your opinion. I need something classy to wear to my brother's wedding."

"Of course. Love to." Gina smiled. This was her world. This, she knew about. "I need some new shoes. Mine were wrecked in all that rain. Too much mud in the country."

"Lovely." Valerie picked up her coffee. "We'd better go and look as if we're doing something."

Lunch was a quick sandwich at a nearby café so as to have more time to shop.

"Shoes or dress first?" Gina asked as they headed toward the Pitt Street Mall.

"Doesn't matter. We can reconnoiter today and come back later. Maybe Thursday night? That's late shopping, isn't it?"

"Yes."

"We could have dinner."

"Fine."

Valerie frowned. "Is everything all right, Gina? You're positively monosyllabic."

"Sorry. It's just . . ."

"Oh, your car! Of course, you'd be upset about that. I'm so stupid." She tucked her arm into Gina's. "Retail therapy, that's what you need."

"Maybe." Gina allowed herself to be towed along. What did it matter where she went, what she bought, or who she was with. It wasn't with Brad so it suddenly all seemed meaningless. A memory slammed into her, making her gasp with the shock of it. Brad gazing into her eyes just before he kissed her. The intense delight, the closeness, the rightness, the love.

"Will you buy another car?"

Gina concentrated hard on the question. Car? New car? "I don't think so. I don't really need one in the city."

"I don't own one. I travel so much it'd be a waste of money."

"I'd like to travel," said Gina, alert once more. Get on with life as planned. "I've been thinking about heading overseas."

"Holiday?"

"Or work, if I could find a job that suited."

"A friend of mine just left for Hong Kong," said Valerie. "Her firm has Asian offices, and they're always sending people over there to work."

"Wow. That would be great. I've been thinking more of New York or London rather than Asia."

"Yes, but I'm pretty happy where I am. My job's good."

"Mmm. What's your friend's firm called?"

"Interested?" Valerie cocked an eyebrow.

"Maybe. This is in confidence, of course."

"Absolutely. A girl's got to do her own thing these days. I'll give you his name and e-mail. The company's called The Harwood Group."

"I've heard of them. Financial."

"Yes."

They paused to study the shoes in a shop window. "What are you after?" asked Valerie.

"Flat, casual. The others were red, but it doesn't matter."

"Want to go in?" Did she need more shoes? She had dozens of pairs. Far too many. Claire had loved trying them on, and discussing makeup.

"No, let's look for your dress. There's a nice boutique in this arcade." Gina swung Valerie left. "The Queen Victoria Building has some lovely shops too."

"You could switch to the Public Service—Foreign Affairs. The pay's not as good, though." Valerie laughed. "Then there are those aid organizations. A girl I was at school with works for one of them. She trained in the military, then switched."

"What does she do?"

"Not sure. Something to do with how relief work is done, how they distribute aid."

"I'm not sure I'm cut out to do that sort of thing." It hadn't entered her head. Ever.

"I'm certainly not. Is this the shop?" Valerie charged through the door and began trawling through the racks.

Gina followed, running her fingers idly over the silky fabrics, touching lace and sequins lightly. Long, fluffy feather boas trailed over a hat stand. Overseas aid. She'd never considered something like that. Her focus had always been on herself and her career. Brad would be impressed if she became a foreign aid worker. He'd accused her of selfishness when they first met. When he didn't even know her. He'd summed her up very accurately. Shallow, self-centered, superficial, socially uncaring.

She'd been completely wrong about him.

Valerie pulled out a deep red floaty number with a low neckline and lopsided hem. "Gorgeous color. What do you think?"

"It'd suit you. Try it on."

"Do we have time?"

"If you're quick."

Valerie yanked aside the change room curtain and disappeared within. Gina smiled at the assistant who hovered hopefully for a moment, then went back to the counter. Aid agencies would need financial advisors. Careful and discreet investigation might be in order. Interesting concept. Would Greenpeace be going too far? Yes. Don't get carried away. They'd prefer volunteers, and she had a loan to cover. A cut in salary would make life very difficult.

A fortnight later Gina answered her phone at work and was surprised to hear a familiar young voice say, "Hi Gina. It's Claire."

"Hello. Where are you? Not in the city, I hope." Amazing how that fresh, girl's voice lifted her spirits. The link with Brad.

Claire giggled. "No. I'm at school. It's lunchtime. Dad let me have my phone today, and I'm ringing to tell you. And to say thanks for giving it to me."

"I'm glad you have it. How are you? And Fiona?"

"We're fine. How are you?"

"Bit sick of work, but otherwise all right."

"I thought you liked your job."

"I do but . . ." Gina lowered her voice and shaded the mouthpiece with her hand. "I've put in an application for another one. I have an interview on Thursday."

"Oh. A better one?"

"Maybe. It sounds good. It means I'll get to travel around a bit. If I get it."

"You will," Claire said confidently. There was a slight

pause. Her breath feathered into the phone. "Dad's not very happy."

"Oh?" The memory hit like a punch in the stomach. His face, his voice. His expression when he left her. "Is he well?"

"I think he's still mad at me."

"I doubt it, Claire. What makes you think that?" Gina's voice rose. She sat back in her chair.

"He's been pretty grumpy ever since that weekend."

"Has he actually said anything? He gave you the phone so he mustn't be too angry with you."

"But he promised he'd do that if I behaved myself, and I have. He never goes back on his word."

"Maybe it's something else entirely." Like a woman who told him he wasn't good enough for her. Or as near to as possible. In his eyes, anyway. A woman whom he'd just told he loved. "His work."

"No." Quite definite. "He always tells us about things like that. When he's having trouble figuring out how to make a chair or something. He says we help him think. Can you come and visit us again, Gina? He likes it when you come. So do we."

"Oh, but Claire . . . I couldn't. I haven't been invited. I can't just turn up . . ."

"Yes, you can. I've invited you and Fifi has too."

"But I can't do anything. It's not . . ."

"But he likes you Gina. He was so happy when you were coming to lunch that day. And he was really happy after he met you, when you got stuck in the elevator. Please come. You can ring up and say you want to visit us, if you like."

"No, I don't think I can, Claire. I'm sorry, but it's too

difficult for me at the moment. I don't have a car and I'm job hunting . . ."

Claire sighed. "All right," she said sadly. "I have to go. Is it all right if I call you sometimes?"

"Of course, it is. Any time you like."

"Bye, Gina."

Gina hung up with salty tears in the back of her throat. Brad was right. It wasn't just him involved in this. There were four, and two of them were innocents, guilty only of loving their Dad and wanting the company of someone they regarded as a friend. Some friend.

Chapter Thirteen

T WENTY-THREE SCHOOLS FOR GOVERNMENT AXE.

The headlines screamed at Brad when he studied the paper over breakfast. He scanned the article, turned the page to skim the list of doomed schools. Birrigai Primary. He went back to the beginning and read the whole thing with growing fury.

"Bastards!"

"Who?" Claire came to read over his shoulder.

"The government wants to close twenty-three schools, and our primary is one of them." The girls stared at him in horror.

"My school?" cried Fifi.

"It's on the list."

Claire said, "It says here Bright and Caulfield did the valuations. That's where Gina works."

"She must have known all about it," muttered Brad. He hissed through his teeth and folded the paper, slamming it onto the table.

"Will my school be closed, Daddy? Where will I go?" Fifi's bottom lip trembled.

"I wish they'd close my school, I hate it," said Claire. She unfolded the newspaper and continued reading.

"But I like my school. I won't have anywhere to go," wailed Fifi.

"Poppet, don't cry. It's not happening for ages, if it happens at all."

"They'll make you go to another one," said Claire, studying the report. Probably Sunderland. It's not on the list."

"I don't want to go to pooey old Sunderland."

"That's enough," said Brad. "Get a move on, Claire, or you'll miss the bus."

What was happening to Birrigai? Once an idyllic little country town removed from the stresses of modern life, it was now embroiled in one traumatic event after another. So much for progress. Gina told him he'd have to face up to changes. Then there was Claire and her inadequate school. But what could he do? Sending her to one of the many expensive private schools in the area was impossible, way out of his pocket. Move? Where? Closer to the city, in range of better facilities so the girls wouldn't be disadvantaged?

Later, after he'd watched Fifi walk across the road to her newly appreciated school, and carefully avoided becoming embroiled in the knot of indignant parents gathered at the far entrance, Brad went back inside to make a call. A very difficult call. Gina must have known this was on the cards. How could she not say a word? And was there more?

She picked up immediately with a businesslike, "Georgina Tait."

"It's Brad," he said, equally sternly.

She drew in a deep breath, and he pictured her arming herself to repel boarders. She must have known he'd ring. Get in first.

"You knew, didn't you? About the school closures. Our school," he said.

"About Birrigai Primary being under enrolled and over funded? Yes. But I don't make these decisions, Brad, I just present statistics as required by the client."

"Overfunded? That's a joke," he yelled. "Education is so neglected it's ridiculous, and the country areas fare worse than anyone. Unless of course you have the money to send your kids to private schools as, no doubt, the new residents of all these newly developed school sites will be able to do."

"I'm sorry," she said crisply.

"Why didn't you tell me?" She didn't even care, her voice was chilly and hard as hailstones.

"I couldn't tell you anything!" She lowered her voice abruptly. "Our work is confidential, and anyway, all that stuff in the paper was leaked. No decisions have been made. That's raw data plus some reporter's imagination."

"Leaked? At least someone has a conscience."

"Someone who won't have a job if they're found out."

"Who? You?" He snorted derisively.

"No," she snapped. "Look, Brad, if you don't have anything more to say I really don't need any extra flak." She stopped, breathing hard. "I certainly don't let slip confidential information deliberately, or otherwise, and I can't believe you would expect me to."

Brad bit his lip and grimaced. She must be under tremendous pressure. "I'm sorry. I know you wouldn't do that. You've always been open about your priorities and opinions." That sounded snide, but she appeared to take it at face value.

Her tone altered when she said, "My boss doesn't particularly agree with you. We're all under suspicion here at the moment, and he knows I've been to Birrigai a few times so he thinks that connection has dubious qualities. Plus we're pretty much besieged by TV and radio reporters wanting in on it all. I think it was someone from the education department."

"Won't they take your word?" he asked indignantly.

"More or less, yes, but tempers are frayed. The firm's reputation is under threat. Everyone wants a scapegoat."

"What sort of people are they? Do you want me to tell them you didn't say anything to me or anyone else in town? Unless you divulged your secret information to Stan while he helped with your car."

Gina laughed softly. "Thanks, but no. There's no indication a third person was involved. They're just spraying accusations about because they have no idea who leaked. They think I might be inclined to make this public because of my link with Birrigai. They think I might be sympathetic, opposed to any cuts, and want to stir up the media and the public in protest."

"And you don't, of course."

"What I want or don't want has nothing to do with this," she said coldly, reminding him of her integrity. The very devotion to her job that had grated so much on him when they first met. It was that integrity he'd rung up to abuse her for. If he hadn't been so shocked and infuriated by the article he would have thought it through.

"Fifi's terribly upset," he said suddenly.

"Oh! Poor little lamb." The concern in her voice was

completely genuine and disarming, and when she spoke next her tone had lost the ice. "That list in the paper wasn't official, Brad. It was simply the least viable schools financially, and the current commercial value of the sites. All sorts of other factors are taken into account before any decisions are made, and we both know how politically sensitive school closures are."

"Unfortunately, five-year-olds don't understand any of that. They just think their world is about to collapse."

"But it isn't. She has you and Claire. And the cat."

"Yes." Silence. He should hang up, but his hand wouldn't release the phone from his ear. "How are you?" His voice emerged softer than he expected. Impossible to maintain his rage when she was so evidently under extreme pressure. She needed support not attack.

"Fine." Her voice was tense. She didn't sound fine. She sounded tired and stressed. Under suspicion by some freaked-out boss who thought his own position was in jeopardy. What sort of job was that? What sort of life?

"You should quit," he said.

"I am."

"Really! Because of this?"

"No, because of various things, but I'm glad to be leaving now. The atmosphere here is pretty torrid at the moment."

"Where are you going?" He almost held his breath waiting for her answer. Not overseas, please. He closed his eyes.

"I haven't given notice yet, but I've decided to take a job with a group called Phoenix Enterprises. They're based in Switzerland."

"More money makers?" he asked with a hollow stomach. He sat down abruptly at the table. Switzerland? The far side of the world. For one exhilarating, fantastic, unlikely moment he'd imagined she might say she was having a rethink and winding back—trying a more simple life. In, say, Birrigai.

"In a way. They give financial advice to companies in developing countries. It means I'll get to travel a fair bit."

"Sounds interesting." Sounded terrible. She was going. Leaving him and his love. He'd told her to think about what he'd said, his declaration, and she must have given it at most a second. Maybe two. Then discarded it.

"Yes."

"So you'll be moving to Switzerland." He could barely articulate the words.

"No. They have an office here, but I may have to go there sometimes." A small relief. Not much but it left open a tiny window of hope.

"Well, I should hang up," he said reluctantly. "I have work to do."

"So do I," she said.

He stood up, end of daydreaming. She was a busy woman with pressures he could only half imagine. "Sorry. I've interrupted you."

"It's all right," she said quickly. "I . . . I'm glad you rang . . . it was nice to . . . talk."

"Yes. Well. Good luck, Gina."

He took the phone from his ear slowly and only just caught her voice as she said, "Brad?"

He whipped the receiver back into place. "Yes?"

"I . . . are you all right?"

The question startled him into blurting, "Apart from loving someone who doesn't love me, you mean? Fine." He grimaced, eyes closed. Hadn't meant to say that, it made him sound weak and pathetic. "Sorry," he muttered. "I'm all right."

"I didn't say I didn't love you," she whispered after a moment of breathless silence.

He said gently, "You didn't say you did, either."

Her voice changed abruptly. "Good-bye. Thanks for calling."

Brad frowned as the dial tone sounded in his ear. He hung up slowly. Someone must have entered her office unexpectedly. He wandered out to the workshop and picked up the chair leg he'd been sanding yesterday. Ten minutes later he realized he was still holding it in one hand with the sandpaper in the other, and neither had been employed.

Gina had changed. She'd softened. Undoubtedly he was partly to blame, and so were the girls. Could it be she was trying to tell him something but was incapable of expressing herself? Did she need help in telling him she loved him? She was a brittle, insular woman on the surface, and in her world that superficial armor was crucial. But in his world it was a hindrance. Maybe she didn't know how to divest herself of it.

Brad set to work on the chair, his mind a seething mass of possibilities. When Claire came home he'd sound her out. She was very close to Gina. And Fifi's input was important, too. They'd have a family confab because if what he proposed to do was successful, they would all be affected.

Gina typed up her letter of resignation that afternoon and took it to Fred. He wasn't happy. "You realize this could be construed as an admission of guilt, Gina," he said.

"It could be, but it isn't," she said sharply. "I've been thinking of moving on for a while now, and you know perfectly well my loyalty can't be questioned."

He exhaled noisily. "It's very inconvenient."

When she finally left his office she had one month to work. On November 25, she'd be temporarily unemployed. Phoenix had given her a late January start date. She'd have a vacation.

Gina arrived home exhausted shortly after six, having avoided the reporters at the front of the building by escaping out the back fire exit with the rest of the staff. The media was still buzzing despite the radio and TV news stating that, as she'd suspected, someone in the education department was now the target. She kicked off her shoes and let the heavy apartment door slam behind her with relief. Big Al strolled across and rubbed against her legs.

"Hiya," she said. He was her family, self-centered ingrate that he was, sitting by the fridge waiting for his dinner. No comforting words, no hug, no sympathy. How was little Fifi? Had Brad managed to calm her fears? Of course he would, he was her dad. And Claire was there to help. They were all very close, supporting each other. And no matter what happened with Birrigai Primary, Fifi would be all right. She was loved and secure in that knowledge.

Brad had offered her a part in that when he offered his love.

Love. Brad had said he loved her. Such a treasure he'd given her, and she'd been too reserved to accept it, too analytical, too scared of the full meaning to tell him the same. But she did love him. She knew that now, she'd known all along but just hadn't said it, to herself or to him. Too late. He wasn't in a position to be messed about by some city woman who played fast and loose with his heart. He had too much at stake to put himself in the same position again. And they'd been over and over the same ground. Round and round in circles.

Gina stripped off her dress and headed for the shower. So hot today. Her skin was grimy and sticky from the fumes and dust blowing about in the wind. The storms had gone although more were predicted this coming weekend. Where could she go on holiday? Alone. Spend summer in the city by herself? Catch up with friends, visit Cathy? Go overseas somewhere? Not much fun sightseeing alone, and she wasn't a tour group type. The mountains would be cooler and the southern high-lands always were. Birrigai. Grandma wanted to meet Brad at Christmas. No chance of that now.

Always Brad. Every thought led back to Brad. She'd never be free of him. His voice caressed her when he rang today. So unexpected. Not the attack, she knew they'd all be upset about the stupid, premature list. No, not that, she was totally unprepared for the emotion that welled when she heard his voice. The love that burst out from deep inside and caused that last desperate wail when he was in the act of discon-necting from her. He still loved her and was resigned to the fact he couldn't have her. Why? Because she was too scared to take that massive step and commit herself to him. Launch herself into the unknown with Brad and the girls and all the trials and tribulations that went with parenting and loving. The lack of control terrified her. She understood that about herself now. Brad had shown her. But he'd also shown her he'd be there as a safety net.

Gina stood under the shower and let the torrent pour over her head so the tears were mixed up with the water and she couldn't tell the difference. Finally she stretched out a hand and turned off the taps.

Big Al sat on her bed as she pulled on a singlet top and shorts. He meowed encouragingly, but she ignored him and rubbed her hair with the towel. She combed it, cool against her scalp, allowing it to dry in the warm evening air.

She scraped Big Al's dinner into his bowl and left him to it while she sat nursing a chilled glass of sparkling apple juice on the balcony, feet on the railing staring blankly at the changing, glowing colors as the sun set slowly behind her building. Was this how her life would be? Solitary, with only regrets and memories?

Good grief, she was getting maudlin. Red and purple bands stretched across the horizon. A cooler breeze danced across the roof tops and lifted the damp hair on her neck.

The intercom buzzer sounded. Gina placed her glass carefully on the floor by her chair and went to press the button. No idea who would be visiting. Claire? She giggled sadly. More likely someone visiting a neighbor and hit the wrong number.

"Yes."

"Hello. I was hoping you'd be home."

"Brad?" Unmistakably him despite the crackly sound.

"Yes. Can I come in?"

She pressed the downstairs door release. Would he remember her apartment number? Yes, of course he would. Hair? Still damp. Makeup? None, but he liked her natural skin. Clothes? Sundress better than shorts. She raced into her bedroom pulling off the singlet.

Her dark blue cotton wraparound. Good. He knocked on the door as she knotted the ties at the front. Deep breath as she strode to open the door. Heart pounding, legs shaking so much she could barely stand.

Brad took in the reddened eyes and pale, miserable face despite the smile. He held out his arms, and she walked into his embrace without a word. A sob sounded, muffled against his shoulder, and he knew his spontaneous trip wasn't in vain.

He shuffled her inside and the door closed behind them with a solid thunk. She pulled herself away enough to ask, "Why are you here? Where are the girls?"

"They wanted to come, but they're with Mel."

"They wanted to come? Why?"

"They want you to be their mother. I think you passed their test." He laughed at her startled expression. "*I'm* here to finish our conversation. But I don't think I need to now."

"I do. I don't understand." But she was beginning to have an inkling. The love shining from his eyes, and the tenderness of his expression was enough.

"You said you didn't say you didn't love me. I wanted to know what exactly you *did* say."

"I didn't say anything." She gazed directly into his eyes. There was no need for courage. What she wanted to say came naturally, easily. The dragon had gone with barely a whimper. "But I should have. I should have said I love you. Completely and totally."

"Yes, you should have." He smiled and kissed her so softly and with so much love she had to cling tightly to remain standing. He drew away, laughing, then kissed her again quickly, hard, and let her go. "You taste like apples."

"I was on the balcony drowning my sorrows. Like some?" She took his hand and led him into the living room.

"Apple juice not sorrows, you mean?"

She turned and looked up into his face. "Yes. No more sorrows, I promise."

She poured more cider and they took the bottle to the evening cool of the balcony to sit side by side, hands interlaced, watching the sunset with Big Al washing himself at their feet.

"Can we figure something out, Brad?" Gina asked. "So this will work?"

"Yes. We're two intelligent adults. We'll make it work."

"I might be away a fair bit with my new job." She glanced sideways to see his reaction. He turned his head and smiled, leaned closer to kiss her.

"As long as you come home to me, I don't care."

"From November 25 I have two months off before I start with Phoenix. Maybe . . ." Would it be too presumptuous if she asked to spend that time in Birrigai?

"Do we have to wait a whole month before you can come and stay?" he grumbled. "I want us together as much as possible. I want to marry you. Will you marry me?"

"Yes." The answer came easily with no hesitation and no doubt.

"In January?"

She laughed as he kissed her again. "That soon?"

"Why not? We can do it at home in the garden."

Why not indeed? Why wait when she was more sure of this than anything in her life? "All right. Mum and Grandma will be thrilled when they recover from being amazed."

"So will the girls although they can't understand why it's taken us so long." He stroked her fingers and raised her hand to kiss. When he spoke his voice was low and concerned. "Will you be able to organize your work around us? I don't want you exhausted and stressed trying to fit everything in."

"Until the end of November I'll only manage weekends, but some of my new work can be done from home." A pause. "If I have a good computer set up with Internet access."

Brad drew his hand from hers and rubbed his face. He sighed. "I've been thinking I may have to move closer to the city for the girls' schooling. And if you need to be closer too . . ."

Leave that lovely old house? The garden. His workshop? "Oh! But you're all so happy there."

"Except Claire," he said with a grin. "As you pointed out recently, correctly I might add . . ." He grinned and nuzzled her neck and cheek, which turned into a long kiss.

"What did I point out?" she asked eventually.

"The girls' schooling is important. Claire is already missing out, and if they go ahead with these closures, Fifi will be in trouble too. I don't want her bussing for nearly two hours every day at her age."

"But there are some very good private schools in your area!"

"Very expensive schools."

Gina said slowly, "I make very good money." She picked up her glass and drank to avoid seeing his reaction. She knew exactly what it would be.

"You don't have to spend your money on my girls."

"If we're married wouldn't they be my girls too?" she asked tentatively, unable to hide the hurt. That was what she had most feared from an arrangement like this, being the outsider in the family group. Never really truly belonging.

He clasped her hand tightly again. "Of course they would. It'll just take me a while to get used to having someone else to share the responsibility. But, even so, it doesn't seem right somehow. The money. It's yours." He frowned.

Gina put her glass down and swiveled to face him. "Don't do that macho thing, Brad! If we go into this I want us to be equals. And that means sharing everything. You share your beautiful children with me, I share my filthy money with you. And I think I get the better deal."

Brad held both her hands in his. "Do you? I think we all get a pretty good deal." He leaned forward to kiss her again.

"How long can you stay?" she asked into his mouth.

"The rest of our lives."

"Suits me."